"Give me a reason, one good reason," Carson said.

"Make me see how you can make love with me and then pull away the minute I start talking about anything beyond the moment. Make me understand why you walked out on me two years ago, why you walked away from our relationship."

Not now, Jill wanted to scream. *Not now, when nothing makes any sense*. But she didn't. Instead, she looked into the intense blueness of his eyes, and it shocked her when the words came. "We never had a relationship, Carson. It was a convenience for you."

It was so clear to her now, so simple to put into words. "You wanted me. You needed me, but on your terms, at your times, when it was right for you. You never shared with me, not your pain, not your doubt, not your fears. You never even told me about your nightmares, about you being in prison here. You wanted me there for you, but you were never there for me."

Dear Reader,

When two people fall in love, the world is suddenly new and exciting, and it's that same excitement we bring to you in Silhouette Intimate Moments. These are stories with scope and grandeur. The characters lead lives we all dream of, and everything they do reflects the wonder of being in love.

Longer and more sensuous than most romances, Silhouette Intimate Moments novels take you away from everyday life and let you share the magic of love. Adventure, glamour, drama, even suspense—these are the passwords that let you into a world where love has a power beyond the ordinary, where the best authors in the field today create stories of love and commitment that will stay with you always.

In coming months look for novels by your favorite authors: Linda Howard, Heather Graham Pozzessere, Emilie Richards and Kathleen Korbel, to name just a few. And whenever you buy books, look for all the Silhouette Intimate Moments, love stories *for* today's woman *by* today's woman.

Leslie J. Wainger
Senior Editor and Editorial Coordinator

Dream
Chasers

MARY ANNE WILSON

Silhouette Intimate Moments

Published by Silhouette Books New York

America's Publisher of Contemporary Romance

Books by Mary Anne Wilson

Silhouette Intimate Moments

Hot-Blooded #230
Home Fires #267
Liar's Moon #292
Straight from the Heart #304
Dream Chasers #336

MARY ANNE WILSON

fell in love with reading at ten years of age when she discovered *Pride and Prejudice*. A year later she knew she had to be a writer when she found herself writing a new ending for *A Tale of Two Cities*. A true romantic, she had Sydney Carton rescued, and he lived happily ever after.

Though she's a native of Canada, she now lives in California with her husband, children, a six-toed black cat who believes he's Hungarian, and five timid Dobermans, who welcome any and all strangers. And she's writing happy endings for her own books.

Julie and Amy...
for dreams found
and dreams yet to be.
All my love

Prologue

Five years ago

Carson Davies never knew how much he hated darkness until his third day in the crude prison in San Arman and his second day without light of any sort.

Gradually, insidiously, he could feel himself disappearing. He was losing a sense of who he was, who he had been before the soldiers had come to his hotel door and taken him to this place. He could feel himself blurring and fading.

He had stopped being the news director for a Chicago television station, a free man who could come and go as he pleased, even to a small South American country on the Caribbean. He had become a prisoner.

He wondered if becoming a prisoner in spirit as well as fact could be fatal to a human being.

"Talk to me, Martine," he said in Spanish through the blackness as he sat Indian-style on the cold cement floor. "Talk to me."

"What do you want me to say?" the man asked in the same tongue.

Carson had seen Arturo Martine, the only other person in the seven-by-ten-foot cell, just once when the soldiers had opened the solid metal door and pushed Martine inside. For a split second in the weak light from the corridor, Carson had caught a glimpse of the man—medium build, age about forty, ebony hair worn long, bronzed skin stretched across a high-cheekboned face that seemed faintly reminiscent of Indian heritage. He'd been dressed in white clothes—loose pants and a shirt knotted at his middle—that had seemed oddly immaculate for the life-and-death situation.

"Say anything, Martine. Just talk to me."

Before the man could respond, a muffled scream of terror came from a great distance, then stopped as suddenly as it had begun. It had happened so often Carson had thought he would get used to the cries, yet he hadn't. He closed his eyes tightly and clenched his hands into fists on his knees. "What do they want? Why are they doing this?"

"They want power. They perceive their actions as necessary to get that power." Martine's voice sounded matter-of-fact, almost bored. "You were just in the wrong place at the wrong time, my friend. If you had been a doctor or a car mechanic, instead of an American television newsperson, they would have been more than glad to let you go. They would have pushed you onto a plane and out of the country."

"What about you, why are you here?"

"Wrong place, wrong time. They will realize their mistake and release me soon. Until then..." He sighed, and Carson could hear him shift in the darkness. When he spoke again, his voice sounded farther away. "...there is nothing to do but wait."

He didn't understand how Martine could be so cool about this. Didn't having his liberty snatched away by a petty little dictator mean anything to him? "And what if they don't release you? What then?"

"I will be released. It is just a matter of getting the right amount of money to the right person. That is being taken care of by my people."

"Money? Is that what this is all about?"

"For me it is. But I was born here. I know these people. There are no sides with me. I have friends, no matter who is in power. I make very sure of that. This I did not see coming, so I did not have time to secure my place before the power shifted."

Carson couldn't help jabbing. "So, some of your friends put you here?"

"No, just a few zealous Estrada sympathizers, not my friends. But as I told you, I will not be here too much longer."

"And then what will you do?" Carson asked to keep the man talking. "What happens when you get out of here?"

"I will go back to my home north of this city. It is secure and a good place to stay until this madness is settled into some sense of order."

"Is it your family home?"

That made Martine laugh, a soft, bitter sound. "No. My *family home* does not exist anymore. It was destroyed years ago. It was torched when I was fifteen. A mud-and-cardboard hut burns very quickly. The home I will go to is mine, one I got for myself."

"And who's getting the money for you?"

"A friend."

"How about your wife and children?"

There was silence for a very long time before Martine answered in a flat tone. "I have no wife and children now. There is only me and my friends. How about you? Who will be there for you when you get out of this mess? Who is working to get you out?"

The first question stopped Carson, so he answered the second question. "My station and the network are probably doing what they need to do to get me out. I suppose the American government will also get involved.''

"And when that is all done and you are on a plane to America, who will be waiting for you when you step down on your home soil?''

Carson rested his head back against the rough brick wall and closed his eyes. ''Friends.''

"No wife and children?''

Even though he had been divorced for only a year, he had never felt attached, as if he really had anyone. It had been that way all of his life. Maybe he made sure it was always that way. ''I was married once, but it's over. Now, I'm on my own. I have my work and that fills in the spaces of my life.''

Martine laughed again, but this soft sound had a real touch of humor in it. ''Oh, your work is there to hold you at night, to kiss you, to make love to you? You are a very different man from most men, Carson Davies.''

The emptiness in Carson at that moment seemed almost to engulf him. He had never experienced anything that intense in his entire life, not in foster homes, not in the tiny apartments he'd rented over the years, not even when his divorce had been final. He swallowed hard. ''It will do until the real thing comes along,'' he murmured, trying to sound unconcerned.

"We all have our substitutes for the real thing, I suppose,'' Martine murmured. ''I certainly do. Poor substitutes.''

Carson opened his eyes and strained to make out the man across from him. But the shadows were complete. Only darkness was there, yet he could feel his emptiness echoed in the other man. ''But do we have to have *the real thing* to make our lives complete?'' he asked.

"I know I do, my friend. I have gone too many years without having that in my life.''

Carson knew he had gone his whole life without having it. There had never been a real connection between himself and a lover. The closeness had always stopped short of actually being one with the other person. He wondered if that ever really happened between two people. "But you have experienced it?" he asked.

Martine spoke softly. "Yes. In my soul. Just once. I do not know if it will ever happen again. That is the true reality of life."

A scream tore through the blackness, a long wail that the walls couldn't keep out, a cry that made Carson stop breathing and clench his teeth. Then it was gone. He sank back against the wall with a shuddering sigh. This was all the reality he could handle. "I'll settle for just getting out of here."

"For now, you will. But there will be a time when you want more," Martine said.

"I don't think so," Carson said, and the rest of his thoughts were cut off by another scream.

Chapter 1

The Present: San Diego, California

Carson wished he could sweep the last day of March under the rug and never be forced to look at it again. Problems had multiplied all day, and by the time five o'clock was nearing he felt burned out. Being the station manager at Channel Three Television was difficult, but today the stress had left him feeling strangely empty. He hadn't felt this way in a long time, so long ago he had to concentrate on remembering. Then he stopped.

He held the telephone tightly to his ear and swiveled his chair around to face the bank of windows behind his desk in the beige-on-brown office and concentrated on the voice coming over the phone. He stared out at the ivy-covered fencing that circled the Channel Three grounds, at the failing sunlight and a heavy sky with battleship-gray clouds.

"Morning scheduling is hell," he muttered into the mouthpiece, controlling the urge to yell at Frank Elliot, the head of the Network Affiliates' Association in New York, anything to make the man listen to him. "The network's poor ratings are killing us then. I'm not buying the programs. We've got a fifty-fifty commercial split with the network now, and if their programs can't pull in the numbers..."

He closed his eyes tightly while Frank calmly cut in to tell him about demographics and upcoming scheduling changes that were supposed to produce "magic" in the ratings.

He listened until he'd had enough, then interrupted. "I promise to think about it. That's the best I can do now." When Frank would have continued arguing, Carson spoke up. "I have to go. When I see you in New York, we can talk more." And he hung up before the man could get in another word.

He sat back in his chair and took off his wire-rimmed glasses. Massaging the bridge of his nose between his thumb and forefinger in an effort to stop the beginnings of a headache from intensifying into real pain, he took a deep breath. He felt drained, and the upcoming week in New York suddenly seemed appealing. He'd be spending his time there meeting with the managers of other network affiliates, but it would be a change of scenery, and he could stop in Houston on the way back to visit friends. It would be a break, of sorts, and he admitted he needed one right now.

When a knock sounded on his office door, he glanced at his watch. Five-ten. When it neared five-thirty and the news was getting ready to go on the air, he'd be surrounded by pressure, but not just yet. He didn't feel like talking to anyone or making any more decisions. So he stayed quiet, hoping whoever was there would go away and leave him alone for a few precious minutes of peace. Maybe his secretary, Bernice, would send them on their way.

The knocking came again, soft insistent tapping on the wooden barrier, then it finally stopped. Carson slipped his glasses back on, rested his hands on the wooden arms of his chair and stared outside. Daylight was fading fast and the world was looking cold and bleak. He'd come here the previous March to take over this job, but he could have sworn it had been warm and sunny then. This year there hadn't been two sunny, dry days to string together, and it looked as if the sky was getting ready to deposit more rain on San Diego.

"Carson?"

He spun around in his chair, surprised to see Jillian Segar standing in the doorway. Petite and delicate, with her dark hair feathered back from a face he had always considered strikingly beautiful, she was dressed in a vibrant red dress that enhanced her ivory-tone skin. He hadn't heard the door open, and it stunned him that he literally felt pain at seeing this woman with no warning.

He'd been prepared to see her when he'd first come to the station a year ago. The first thing he'd asked for when the network had requested his help in bringing Channel Three up in the ratings, was a list of employees, their shows and the ratings. Jillian's had been the top local show then, just as it was now. *Dream Chasers*. She did it well. He'd give her that much.

What he didn't understand was his sudden reaction to her today. He'd had a lot of face-to-face meetings with her since he'd taken this job. It didn't make sense. A bad day all around, he reasoned as he stared at her without speaking.

"I knocked, but you didn't answer, and Bernice isn't out there," she said in that silky voice that translated so well over the airwaves, the same voice that used to wreak havoc with his nerves.

"I was ignoring the world," he muttered tightly as she came into the room. He suddenly saw her clearly, each line and curve where the softly draped dress clung to her figure. Tipping back in his chair, he ignored the annoying remnants of old feelings that came from nowhere to tighten his middle and increase his pulse rate. "And I could have sworn *you* had a few more days of vacation left."

"I came in because I need to talk to you," she said as she came across to the desk.

He shrugged and felt the tugging of tension in his shoulders. "I've got a few minutes. That's about all I can give you." Suddenly he was thankful the news was coming up. It gave him an excuse to keep this encounter short, since most of his "discussions" with Jill were less than pleasant. He knew it was an exaggeration to say if he suggested the world was round, she'd insist it had elongated into an oval while he hadn't been paying attention. But not much of an exaggeration.

Short of closing his eyes, he couldn't help focusing on her. Reluctantly, he admitted that even the worst that had happened between them hadn't quite killed memories unerringly stored in the deep recesses of his mind—the hot silkiness of her skin against his skin, the way her body could tremble with passion, the fullness of her breasts under his hands.

But those remembrances were usually few and far between, only coming out at night to taunt him when he was in bed alone and his mind wouldn't shut down. About the only uncomplicated part of their past relationship had been the lovemaking.

Annoyed when his body began to respond to the mental images, he sat forward in the chair and deliberately shut out details about the woman. When he looked up at her, he zeroed in on her darkly lashed eyes, lavender with a flaring of blue, nothing more.

He pressed his hands flat on the desk and took a breath, thankful for the easing he felt in his loins. "What do you need?" he asked with more abruptness than he intended.

"I received the final schedule for the next three trips for *Dream Chasers*." Her eyes narrowed with a sweep of feathery lashes. "I want to know why you cut it up like a butcher?"

He lifted one eyebrow. "A butcher?"

"It bears little, if any, resemblance to the tentative schedule I saw before I left on vacation."

He turned his hands over and exposed them palms up. "The one you saw was exactly that—tentative."

"Tentative, Carson, not pure fiction."

He didn't want to keep looking up at her and feeling he was at a disadvantage, so he motioned to one of the leather chairs that faced his desk. "Have a seat, and I'll explain."

She hesitated, then did as he asked, settling in the chair before looking back at him. He well remembered that upward tilt to her chin, an innate stubbornness that at one time had been so endearing. Now it was vaguely annoying.

"All right. Go ahead and explain why you changed it so much," she said. "I asked for a week in San Arman on this next trip, and you gave me a week in Jamaica instead."

He really didn't want to do battle with Jill. He'd fought enough battles today to last him for a very long time. "That's what the schedule says."

"Why?"

Determined not to let this disintegrate into an argument, he settled into the more comfortable role of boss. Objectivity was easy on a business basis, and he enumerated logical reasons for his decision. "The place is so tiny it barely shows on the map, and I can't think of very many viewers of *Dream Chasers* who even know about it, much less care to go there. And the government has never been what one would call stable."

"That's in the past," she said as she sat forward. "When I talked to the president's director of public relations, he was enthusiastic about our going there and doing some programs. They'll help us any way they can. 'Complete cooperation,' he said." She touched the edge of the desk with her slender fingers. "He sent still shots of the country to encourage us to come. The beaches look marvelous. The sky is so blue it hurts your eyes. Best of all, the exchange rate right now really favors the dollar."

He pushed his glasses higher on his nose, a bit surprised to feel an unsteadiness in his hands. "I know San Arman, Jillian," he said lowering his hands to spread them on his thighs and out of her sight.

"You *knew* it six or seven years ago."

"Five," he corrected automatically, not any more anxious to remember that time than he was to remember two years ago in Houston with Jill.

"And you were only there for a few days while you worked."

Three months, two days and fifteen hours. He knew the time sequence without even having to think about it. "I was there long enough," he muttered, then tried to change the subject. "A full week there would take a big chunk of the budget, but if you did Jamaica..."

"I don't want to *do* Jamaica. Everyone's been there, or they've seen at least one definitive program on it. Give that part of the budget to San Arman."

"Why is it so important to you to go there?"

She shrugged, and the red material slid fluidly over her full breasts. Carson deliberately kept his gaze on her eyes as she responded. "It hasn't been done to death. I wanted to do something unique, something different and new by introducing San Arman to the San Diego viewing public."

"I understand, but Sam agrees with me that it's not a good idea right now," he said.

"Sam?" she asked, telltale color beginning to rise in her delicate cheeks. Yet her voice stayed level. "Sam Rollins who has the IQ of a peanut, whose most pressing question is if his jacket is color-coordinated with his socks, or if there's going to be a glare in the camera from his unpowdered nose? You're taking his opinion over mine?''

Carson knew Sam hadn't been Jill's favorite person since he had hired the man from a sister station in Philadelphia just before the Christmas holidays. But Sam had charisma—that nebulous "something" that fascinated the viewers—and he brought in even better ratings points for *Dream Chasers*. The program made a strong lead-in for the prime-time evening programming.

"Sam's been good for the program and for Channel Three," he pointed out in an even voice. "He thinks you should stick with the itinerary the way it's been approved.''

Her color deepened, but he had to hand it to her that her composure didn't slip. She looked right at him, took a breath, and said in a low, firm voice, "And I want to change it. This was my program and doing very well before you came here, and before you brought in your pet.''

Carson couldn't help smiling at that. "My pet?''

She nodded, her expression growing tighter by the moment. "Sam. 'Mr. Charisma.'''

He couldn't quite stop a chuckle, but it died quickly under the strength of Jill's unblinking glare. "I'm sorry." He shrugged. "The name struck me funny.''

"It's not. Sam is.''

"Why?''

"He's not my type," she muttered.

Carson felt his humor dying as quickly as it came when the image of Sam was replaced by another man, Boyd Stevenson. Before he could stop himself, he asked, "Isn't he like your friend, Boyd what's-his-name?''

Jill wondered if Carson had brought up the subject of Boyd just to divert the conversation. If he did, she wasn't about to let it work. "His last name is Stevenson, and thank goodness Boyd is no Sam Rollins.''

Carson's sandy-blond hair was mussed, probably from repeatedly running his fingers through it while he thought. That was one nervous habit of his Jill remembered clearly.

"That's your opinion," he said as he leaned back in his chair and folded his arms across his chest, his tanned skin contrasting with his white, open-necked shirt. His blue eyes, behind gold wire-framed glasses, narrowed. "You're entitled to it," he said in his deep voice.

Jill crossed her arms on her breasts, echoing his body language, annoyed that anger was so close to the surface for her. She didn't want to get angry. But it seemed that with Carson she didn't have much of a choice. There was no middle ground. "It's my opinion that going to San Arman would be a good move for the program."

At first Carson didn't respond, he simply studied her silently, the blueness of his eyes behind the lenses more intense than she remembered, the gray almost nonexistent. She watched him stand, slowly rising to his full six feet two inches, and thought how much thinner he seemed suddenly. No, he probably hadn't changed much, she just hadn't taken a good look at the man for a long time.

Now that she faced him squarely, she could see that his features looked sharper, more defined, his high cheekbones etched under taut skin touched by a tan. And tension cut deep brackets at either side of his mouth.

As he leaned forward, he pressed the tips of his strong fingers on the desk top, and the muscles of his exposed forearms flexed. "That's your opinion," he said.

Jill had a flashback to a time in Houston when she and Carson had been having a discussion. She'd been so certain she'd been right about something—she couldn't remember what now—but Carson had calmly proceeded to show her why she'd been wrong. She could tell the same thing was coming now, but instead of finding it fascinating, as she used to, she found it monumentally irritating. "And?" she prodded, knowing more was sure to come and wanting to get it over.

"*And* as far as *Dream Chasers* is concerned, I'll state the obvious. It's a travel show, a show meant to display countries at their best. It's meant to tantalize and tease with natural beauty and life-styles that are bigger than life. San Arman isn't like that. Jamaica is. San Arman doesn't justify a week of your attention, or a week of the show's budget. Jamaica does. San Arman isn't a big draw to tourists. Jamaica is. Those are probably a few of the reasons why San Arman hasn't been done to death by other programs."

The same tone. The same logic. And it made Jill feel slightly sick. She drew back, clasping her hands tightly in her lap. "That's your opinion, and you're entitled to it," she said, echoing his own words of moments earlier.

"And I'm the boss."

"And you haven't changed."

One eyebrow rose. "Oh?"

"You still believe only you can do this job, only you can go into a failing station and make it successful. You need to be in control, to believe you're the only one who can do what's right. You can't let go of that control." Once she started, the words spilled out, one over the next.

"Believe it or not, Carson, other people have good ideas. And—" she stood to face him across the desk and bit out "—there's more to life than news, weather, sports, the ratings and demographics."

She could see his jaw tighten, yet his voice was deceptively soft when he spoke. "Are you finished?"

She was in this far; she didn't see any point in pulling back now. The worst thing he could do was cancel her contract, and that actually wouldn't be the worst that could happen right now. "Believe it or not, I know my own program. I'm good at what I do. You spread yourself so thin you don't know which end's up, but you still think you can step in and make the best decision for everyone and everything.

"*Dream Chasers* is *my* show. I started it. It's the one show that you didn't have to save from drowning, and it's done well for the station. It's not my life, but I take pride in it. I talked this over with Boyd and—"

She gulped to a stop when Carson abruptly moved around the desk. He had her five feet two inches bested by a foot, and despite his wiry build he seemed suddenly very large and intimidating. "Since when does your friend know anything about this business? He's an attorney, an upper-crust corporate lawyer who never had to fight for anything in his gold-plated life! What does *your friend* have to do with this?"

Jill put half a pace of space between them, but she tried not to back down. "*Boyd*, Carson, his name is *Boyd*. And he listens to me. He's got more common sense than ten Sams have."

She thought he'd yell or, even worse, get that superior attitude that let you know this was all beneath him. But he didn't do either. He stared at her for a long moment, each breath he took unnaturally loud in the sudden silence, then unexpectedly he retreated. He moved back, sat on the edge of the desk and crossed his arms on his chest again. "When did this start?" he asked softly.

"You know I've been seeing Boyd for three months, ever since Christmas."

"No, I mean this fighting between us. I can't say it's day without you saying it's night. If I say it's black, you say it's white. When did it all begin?"

"I don't know," she said, but recognized the lie as soon as it was said out loud. It had all begun when he'd shown up in San Diego as "the savior of the station" in the ratings game. She'd been shocked, then angry, and had tried to avoid being near him. When she couldn't avoid contact there had been these draining confrontations. She hated them with a passion.

"It wasn't like this in Houston, was it?" he asked in a low voice.

His words took her off guard and conjured up long-denied memories of what could have been, what she had thought would be. And what, she knew now, never had a chance of happening. "You were never around long enough for us to have a good fight," she countered.

His expression stiffened. "I admit I wasn't there when you left without a word."

"No, you weren't. I left at four a.m., and you still weren't there. You were still in the production meeting at the station." She swallowed hard. "So I left you a letter."

He abruptly threw both his hands in the air and made her flinch. "A letter. A damn piece of paper. 'Dear Carson: I'm sorry... I regret.' You just walked away, Jill. You left the apartment, you left me, and you left the city."

"I didn't think you'd even notice I was gone," she heard herself saying and wished she hadn't. The last thing she needed with this man was to expose her vulnerability.

He stood straight, and for a minute she was afraid he was going to touch her, something she'd studiously avoided for a very long time. She wasn't quite sure what she'd do if he made that contact. She only recognized her relief when he rocked forward on the balls of his feet but kept his arms crossed. "Oh, yes, I noticed. And I noticed I didn't get a real explanation. Didn't I deserve one?"

"You had one. For weeks I'd talked to you and tried to explain why things weren't right. But you were so filled with your work, your drive to be the best, to not fail and to control every aspect of the station, that you never realized you had no room for another person in your life. I don't think I ever really knew you. You closed me out."

He rolled his eyes ceilingward. "Oh, God, don't start psychoanalyzing me and dissecting my psyche."

"I'm just stating facts, because I lived through it with you."

He drilled her with a glare. "So, you ran here to San Diego and found your friend."

"That's not fair," she muttered.

"Life isn't fair," he said with ominous softness. "If it was, you never would have turned your back on the love I was offering you."

She swallowed hard, shocked at the pain that radiated through her at his words. Love? He didn't know the meaning of the word. She swallowed hard and managed, "I came in here to talk about my show and the present, not the past."

He moved back abruptly, putting the desk between them again as he sank down heavily in the chair. "You're right. What was in the past doesn't matter anymore." He tipped back in his chair, clasping his hands behind his head and his eyes narrowed behind his glasses. "You've got your friend...sorry, Boyd."

"And you have your work," she said, a bit surprised at the pity she suddenly felt for Carson. She sank back down in her chair as foolish tears pricked at her eyes. The image of the man on the far side of the desk blurred and shimmered.

For just an instant Jill was hurled back into the past, into the softness of the night, watching Carson sleep and aching at the aloneness she sensed in him, her heart breaking for the child who had never had anything or anyone to call his own, and for the man who never stopped trying to prove his worth through what he could do, what he could accomplish.

And the nightmares he'd had that he could never remember when he woke in a cold sweat. Or maybe just never wanted to tell her about. "The past is the past," he'd say to her as he turned to her in the night. "You're my present and my future." But she hadn't been his future, not any more than he had been hers.

"Yes, my work," he said, "and that brings me back to the fact that this is my job, my decision, my call. I don't want *Dream Chasers* going into some miserable South American country that nobody knows about, much less cares about."

She took a deep, painful breath and blinked rapidly. "You're wrong, Carson," she said softly, the words actually a comment on the life he'd chosen for himself as much as on his decision now. She tried to concentrate on the present. "We've been formally invited to San Arman. They're encouraging tourism, and it's a reasonable trip."

"It's a nervous little country that never quite figured out what it wanted to be," he muttered.

"Spoken like a real cynic."

"Cynicism isn't all wrong, Jill. I've been in San Arman, and I didn't come away singing its praises. Some petty little dictator, your wonderful President Estrada, decided he could do a better job than the regime that was in place. It was a slice of war down there, for heaven's sake."

"And that was five years ago."

He ran his fingers through his hair, leaving it vaguely spiked. "And there are persistent rumors off and on about problems with the Estrada government," he countered back.

"Everything's all right. We've been in countries where there are problems, and San Arman isn't anything like the others. It's pretty settled, and President Estrada seems to be good for the country. Besides, I'm not making a political statement, and I'm not about to get involved in the politics down there. That's not why I'm doing these shows."

She exhaled and felt the past receding back into some dark corner of forgetfulness where it belonged. She spoke before Carson could say anything else. "I want to give the viewers something different. Give me a week in San Arman with my crew, and I'll give you some great shows.''

He exhaled harshly. As he sat forward, he rested his elbows on the desk and took off his glasses. In some way his actions spoke of weariness, maybe vulnerability, and it tugged at Jill. But before her reaction to him had time to do more than just flit through her, Carson looked up at her, the blue gray of his eyes unprotected by the lenses. His gaze was so direct she barely kept from flinching. ''Are you going to give up?'' he asked.

She didn't hesitate. ''No.''

For a long moment the office was completely silent, then Jill heard a soft intake of air at the same time Carson ran a hand over his face. Then he looked back up at her. ''If you're going to insist on this, all I can give you is three days in San Arman.''

''What?''

He slipped his glasses back on and looked down at papers on his desk. He shuffled through them, then lifted a yellow sheet of paper and read, ''Between your last day in Panama and the beginning of your time in Colombia.''

''A week was barely long enough, but three days—''

He sat back and tossed the paper onto the desk. As it floated down on top of the other sheets, Carson cut off her words. ''Three days, and you'll be lucky to get anything usable for your show.''

''What about the rest of that week?''

''Expand your shows from Colombia. Do something on the resorts to the east. They're being developed more extensively all the time.''

She wouldn't ask how he knew about the new development in eastern Colombia. It was just an example of his finger in every pie, of his need to be on top of everything that happened at the station. But she did need to know one thing. ''Why are you giving us the three days?''

"I'm tired of arguments."

So was she, but she wouldn't admit that to him. "Do I need to go over the schedule for San Arman with you again before I leave next Wednesday for Panama?"

"No. I'll be busy. I'm getting things in order so I can leave for a while."

That took her off guard. "You're leaving here?"

"Taking time off."

"Why?"

"Is it a shock I need time away from here?"

"The way I remember it, your idea of taking time off was driving the long route to work," she said without thinking.

He actually laughed at that, softening his expression and putting light in his eyes. The seductiveness of shared humor brought memories precariously close to the surface for Jill. And the smile made the man himself seem younger than his forty years. "That's not quite accurate, Jill. And this isn't a real vacation. I'm going to New York for an affiliates' meeting, then I'm stopping over in Houston on the way back to see Tim Levin."

"Say hello to him for me," she said as she stood, realizing how strangely like a divorce her break with Carson had been. His friends, her friends, all of them taking sides whether they wanted to or not. Quickly she turned to head for the door.

"One more thing, Jill?"

Carson watched Jill hesitate, then turn with her hand on the doorknob. The soft material of the dress swirled around her slender legs and her lips were slightly parted, as if she'd been surprised—or interrupted in her attempt to make her escape. "Yes?" she asked.

"We'll still do Jamaica, but probably in June. We can discuss it when I get back from New York."

Color came to her cheeks in a rush, and he had no idea what he'd said to cause it. "No," she said. "I won't be able to do Jamaica in June."

He moved around the desk to go nearer, but stopped within five feet of her, not wanting to be any closer to her than he needed to be. "You *won't*?"

"I was going to talk to you about this later, but I may as well tell you now. I might need some time off in June."

"You're on a two-week vacation now. Why do you need more time in June?"

She took a breath, then said something he had never expected. "Boyd asked me to marry him, and June's a good month for him."

Carson stared at Jill, her image painfully clear in front of him. Quickly he took off his glasses. The blur of myopia was a welcome buffer right then, a barrier he suddenly needed between himself and the shock of reality. "You and Boyd are going to get married?"

He fingered the earpiece of his glasses as he watched the soft blur of dark and light with splashes of red that Jill had become. Then her voice drifted to him. "He asked me last night."

"And you're going to have the wedding in June?"

"Boyd can get time off then between cases, so it makes sense."

Perfect sense, he conceded to himself, but heard himself saying the proper words. "I guess congratulations are in order."

"Thanks," she said softly, then turned and left.

As the door clicked shut behind Jill, Carson went back to his desk but didn't go around it. He sank down in the chair Jill had just vacated and was shocked that he could still feel a trace of her body heat there. He could even catch a hint of the scent she wore, as he inhaled.

Married.

Why couldn't he seem to take hold of the idea? He tossed his glasses on top of the papers on his desk, then leaned his head back on the soft leather and closed his eyes. He exhaled harshly, the sound echoing in the silent office.

Why hadn't he even considered the idea of Jill marrying? When she'd introduced him to Boyd Stevenson just after Christmas, he'd felt unnerved. He could remember shaking the dark-haired man's hand, and being vaguely aware of how unalike he and the man here. Dark, solidly built, barely six-feet tall and wearing a neatly trimmed beard, Boyd Stevenson was the antithesis of Carson's own lanky tallness. Jill hadn't looked for the same type a second time, he thought with an undisguised trace of bitterness.

Then again, she'd made it clear enough that she was getting on with her life, that she was making changes, going into a new phase. Boyd had appeared to become a part of it all.

He felt a strange surge of feelings from the past; feelings he'd thought were gone for good. That aloneness, that sense of not belonging that he'd felt so often in the foster homes. The sense of disconnection when hc'd traveled as a correspondent. The same feeling he'd experienced with a savage intensity during his time in San Arman. *That's it*, he decided. *It's all this talk about San Arman. It's opening old wounds.*

"Damn, what a lousy day," he muttered to the empty room.

When a knock sounded on his door, he sat up abruptly and reached for his glasses. Slipping them on, he glanced at his watch and muttered an expletive. The news broadcast. He'd completely forgotten. "Come on in," he called as he stood and raked his fingers through his hair.

James Chapman, a lean man with gray-streaked hair swept back from an angular, mustached face dominated by sharp blue eyes, came into the office. Carson and James, who did segments on the six and eleven o'clock newscast called *The Heart of the Matter*, were as different as night from day. Carson had always thought that was the very reason they'd been good friends for over ten years.

"How's it going?" James asked as he crossed and flopped down in the chair by Carson. He tugged at the red-and-blue tie he wore with an off-white shirt and the deep blue Channel Three blazer. Jeans and sneakers were at odds with the rest of his outfit. Casually he crossed his legs, resting one ankle on his other knee and began to fiddle with the lace of his shoe.

"Just fine, James." Carson said as he sank back down in his chair and swiveled it to face his friend. "Make yourself at home. Have a seat. Use my shower if you like. My office is your office."

James looked at him, the suggestion of a smile twitching under the mustache. "You've had a bad day, eh?"

Bad didn't begin to define this day for Carson. "I haven't smoked for almost three years, and I've been craving one good drag on a cigarette since ten this morning. Nothing but problems today."

"You have my sympathy," James said, then his smile died. "I saw Jill leaving."

Carson sat forward, rested his elbows on his knees and buried his face in his hands for a long moment. "She's right up there with some of my worst problems," he muttered.

"Why?"

Carson looked up, letting his hands drop to hang loosely between his legs. "She's taking *Dream Chasers* to San Arman next week for three days."

"San Arman? Lord, why would she want to go there?"

He shrugged sharply. "I guess she believes the encyclopedia that calls it 'a fledgling democratic country on the Caribbean coast of South America.'"

"How could she believe that when...?" His voice trailed off, then after a long moment of silence, James shook his head. "She doesn't know, does she?"

Chapter 2

No, she doesn't," Carson said, sitting back in the chair but maintaining eye contact with James. "She was out of the country during that summer working for a travel magazine. And the network kept everything as low-key as possible. You know that. They figured it made negotiations less complicated and less expensive." He rotated his head slowly, trying to ease the tension in his shoulders and neck. "It was my choice to keep quiet about it when I got back. I wasn't about to go on the news and do interviews. Right now, it's my choice not to talk about it."

James studied him with narrowed eyes. "Have you *ever* talked about that time to anyone besides me?"

"No, I haven't." He could hear impatience to be done with this topic in his voice. "Do you have a problem with that?"

James shrugged. "No, I never said there was a problem. Actually, I can understand why you don't particularly want to relive your time in San Arman."

Carson felt gooseflesh prickle across his skin as flashing images from the past tried to dart into his mind. "Thanks for that," he muttered, trying to shut out the memories.

"And what would it accomplish for you to tell someone about your time there, about being in a smelly hole without lights for twenty-four hours a day for days on end?"

Those words dragged the past closer than it had been for a long time, and Carson sat forward abruptly, glaring at James. "Why are you doing this to me?"

One dark eyebrow rose slightly. "I'm not doing anything. I'm just agreeing with you."

Carson barely controlled a convulsive shiver. "It's the past, James. Over and done with."

"But doesn't the past shape the present?"

Carson stood abruptly and circled the desk to stand in front of the window and looked outside. "Who knows? Who cares? It's *now* I'm concerned about." He took a deep breath and stared out at the gathering shadows of the coming night. He exhaled harshly. "Hell, San Arman is probably paradise now, even with Estrada still in power. I'm overreacting. I admit it. But I can still see that miserable man in his uniform walking through the jail the last day. And the posters all over the walls when they drove me through the city to the airstrip." He cut off the words in an attempt to cut off the mental image that hadn't lost any clarity over the past years.

When James kept silent, Carson finally admitted a particularly annoying truth. "I'm probably overreacting because the whole thing is Jill's idea." He turned and looked right at James. "I know, don't say it. It's childish but, damn it, we just can't seem to settle into any sort of friendship."

He leaned back against the window frame and crossed his arms on his chest. "You know, I've always heard when two intelligent people who have been lovers break up, they can be friends." He shook his head. "Don't you believe it."

"I don't."

That simple statement took Carson aback and he stood straight. "Oh?"

"If Bree and I ever broke up, I wouldn't want to see her again. I couldn't begin to think of seeing her and not having her." His dark brows lowered, narrowing his blue eyes with an intent frown. "I actually never understood how you and Jill could work together. I expected one of you to leave the station long ago."

Carson pushed his hands into the pockets of his dark brown slacks and turned back to the windows to stare out at the parking area where safety lights were flashing to life. "She's gone so much for her show, that we don't have very much contact. If we had to work together on a day-to-day basis, I couldn't do it. There are too many bad feelings, too many raw edges. Goodness knows I've tried, and now she's..."

"She told you she might be getting married," James inserted, but it was a statement not a question.

Carson didn't even ask how James knew. "Yes."

"And?"

"And what?"

"What does it mean to you?"

As Carson turned to look at James. "Why did you come in here?"

"I could lie and say I was passing by on the way to Studio 2 for my 'Heart of the Matter' piece on the six o'clock broadcast." James shrugged. "But the truth is I talked to Jill outside, and she mentioned she'd told you about Boyd proposing. I thought you could use some company."

Carson felt his annoyance dissolving. He really appreciated the thought, but the last thing he wanted now was a long talk about the past. If anything, he wanted to ignore it. "I'm happy with my own company," he lied as he glanced at his watch. "And it's getting late. You've got a broadcast to do."

James ran a large hand over his jaw. "Makeup's done their worst, and I've got the script down."

"Then *I* need to get ready for the broadcast."

"Why? You've got a terrific news staff."

"I still have things I need to check on." He watched James and diverted the conversation. "How's Bree?"

"I'm meeting her downtown when I'm through here."

Carson hesitated, then found himself saying, "Can I ask you something?"

James nodded. "Anything."

"How do you do it? How can you be married, have this intense focus on another person, meet all her needs and your needs, and still do such a good job on your programs?"

James shrugged. "I wish I could be that effective with my life. I love what I do here, but it still doesn't change the fact that I work to live, not live to work. I learned that difference back in Chicago." He shook his head. "I've never come close to being a workaholic."

Carson felt the accusation in the words. "You're not very subtle, are you?"

"Do you want the truth or subtlety?" James asked as he lifted one dark eyebrow.

He exhaled roughly, then shrugged. "I'd hate for our relationship to change now. Be blunt."

"You're obsessed with work."

"Obsessions aren't all bad. I do a good job," he countered quickly.

"A damn good job. And I understand your need to do well, to make something of yourself. Your background wasn't any garden of roses," James agreed, then the qualifier came. "But you can't compensate for bad luck in your life, or what was lacking in your childhood, by hoarding approval and success now.

"This station, or some other station, has owned your life for years, whether you were in administration or the reporting end of the business. Now every waking hour you're looking forward to a 'sweeps month' when you get to spend twenty-four hours a day glued to your desk and trying to control the outcome of everything." He sat forward intently.

"That's what took you down to San Arman five years ago. You were certain you were the only one who could get that story out when McDonald got sick, and in the end, you lost over three months of your life. But even after all the trouble, you didn't learn you can never win at this. It never stops. And what do you have when this is over and done? Who do you go home to?" James paused, then aimed a direct blow. "You certainly won't have someone like Jill to fill the emptiness."

Sickness burned the back of his throat, and Carson felt real anger at James, not a first in their relationship, but something he didn't need or want right now. "I doubt that I ever had her. She never understood this is my job. It's what I do best. It's what pays the bills and lets me live the way I want to."

"And it makes you who you are," James murmured.

"What's that supposed to mean?"

"You understand yourself in work terms—'the boy wonder of broadcasting,' 'the savior of stations.' It defines you when you're referred to as the 'best in the business,' or when the network sends you out to save their collective hides. That's why you're here." He tipped back slightly in the chair, then added, "That's why you're alone."

The anger dissipated into a vague bitterness deep inside. "Believe it or not, I *am* someone away from here."

"Who?" James countered softly.

"What?"

"Who are you?"

"I'm Carson Davies. I'm forty years old, six foot two, a hundred and seventy-five pounds. I jog three miles every morning. I have a terrific house overlooking the bay. I date when I want to, as much as I want to, and as intensely as I want to. I'm—to use your words—the best in the business at what I do." He stopped, suddenly feeling foolish putting up such a radical defense. With an intake of air, he finished firmly, "And I don't need someone else in my life to define me."

"It isn't a need, Carson, it's a part of existing for most human beings." James stood and tugged at his tie to straighten it. "So, what are you going to do now?"

Carson knew *he* defined his own existence, that he alone made himself what he was and who he was. Not anyone else. Not even Jill. Yet . . . He could admit there had been a need for her in the past, a basic need that he still didn't quite understand, but passed off as "physical." Whatever it had been, he hadn't been trapped by it, cornered or controlled by it, even though she was the one to walk away from the relationship.

He absorbed that thought as another came to overlap it. For the first time since she'd walked out, he could admit she had probably done the best thing for both of them. They mixed about as well as oil and water, even though a single spark could definitely ignite them.

"Well?" James prodded, waiting. "What are you going to do?"

"I'll make sure the news gets on at six," he said.

"No, what are you doing to do about Jill getting married?"

Carson crossed his arms on his chest and shrugged. "Congratulate her." He slowly rotated his head in another attempt to lessen the tension. "When I came here last year, I can't say it was easy seeing her again, but she's my past.

Not my future. I hope she'll be happy." He exhaled softly and knew he meant it. "She deserves happiness."

"That sounds noble," James murmured.

"No, rational," he countered.

"She's done pretty well down here, hasn't she?"

He stared at James, yet he found himself literally looking back into the past, to the day Jill walked into this office and found he was the new station manager. The lavender eyes had widened with shock, her voice had been low but controlled saying that she hoped they could work together, that they could go on with their own lives and be professionals. He swallowed hard as he closed his eyes for a moment to banish the memory, then he looked back to James. "I guess she has. She's got her friend."

James did up a single button on his dark blue blazer as he cocked his head to one side. "So, she gets married to whatever-his-name-is, and she lives happily ever after. Is that it?"

"If that's what she wants."

"What do *you* want?"

To not remember making love with Jill, or to be able to feel the touch of her under my hands when I wake from those dreams at night. A real day for truth, he admitted to himself, unable to lie when an ache began again in his body. *Physical, that's it.* But he hedged with a partial truth for James. "To be able to get on with my life, and that means getting the six o'clock on the air."

"Do you want to come downtown and have dinner with Bree and me after I do my piece?"

The idea of witnessing a happy domestic scene right now made him vaguely sick. "No, I've got things to do."

"Make use of your subordinates. Delegate, for heaven's sake."

Carson waved that aside with the sweep of one hand. "I've got to get things set for when I'm away, to get the scheduling down so there won't be any hitches."

"Things won't fall apart just because you're gone for a while."

No, but I might. The idea materialized before he could stop it. And he had no idea where it had come from. As his tension increased, he stood straight. "I'll make sure they won't."

"I know you will," James said. "I'll see you before you take off for the conference, won't I?"

"I'm not leaving until next week."

Unexpectedly James came around the desk and rested a hand on Carson's shoulder. "Remember how you *suggested* that I was going through a mid-life crisis a bit back? You were wrong about me, but maybe it's your turn now."

"I don't have time for a new crisis," Carson muttered, but found himself beginning to smile. "There's enough of them around here already."

"There sure are," James said with an answering smile, then turned and strode to the door.

After James left, Carson stared at the closed door for a long moment, then he reached for the remote control on the desk. With a push of one button, all three monitors on the side wall came to life. He dropped down in the swivel chair and stared at the three networks' broadcasts, but kept the sound off.

As he watched first one monitor, then the next, he found his mind filled with Jill and her upcoming marriage. June. He rapidly drummed his fingers on the desk. Jill and Boyd. Married. Suddenly he reached for the phone, pushed three numbers and heard Bryan Lake, a researcher at the station, answer.

"What can I do for you?"

"Bryan, get me everything you can on San Arman."

"San Arman? Sure. What do you need?"

"Find out what's going on down there now."

"Nothing newsworthy, but it's rumored that all might not be well in paradise."

Carson sat forward, his elbows on the desk, his eyes closed tightly. "What?"

"Nothing big. Just some dissidents voicing their objections to Estrada's so-called reforms."

"Who are they—the dissidents?"

"Nobodies. Peons. Estrada apparently isn't ruffled by their opposition. From all I've heard, *el presidente* is handling it. Whatever that means."

"Is there any danger of real problems?"

"The country is open for travel and . . ."

"Any media down there?"

"The international press office is open and doing well. A few magazine journalists. Estrada is encouraging good publicity. He wants everyone to forget just how he got in power, I guess."

Carson sat back, opening his eyes to stare blindly at the ever-changing pictures on the monitors. He deliberately didn't touch his shoulder. The pain was there so seldom these days, he almost forget about it. Until now. "I heard he's done pretty well."

"Sure. He's actually brought in some reforms, some loosening up in the absolute control he used to wield. That's why he's wanting to build up the tourism, draw people down there."

"Anything else?"

"I don't think so. But let me look into it, and I'll get back to you."

"Good. I'll be in Studio 2."

Jill was thankful James didn't want to stop and talk for too long before he headed off in the direction of Carson's office. With a deep breath, she turned and hurried along the blue-carpeted corridor, heading toward the red-enameled door of her small office. The hall, with its station colors, seemed to assault her eyes—red and blue were everywhere she looked. She wanted nothing more than to get inside and close the door behind her.

The crew members who passed by, literally running toward the studios at the rear of the building, emphasized a raw intensity building toward producing the live six o'clock news. It played havoc with her frayed nerves. She nodded to a camera man who bumped her and muttered an apology, then reached for the knob on her door. Why had she told Carson about Boyd's proposal? James had asked her that question, and she hadn't had an answer for him beyond a prosaic "he needed to know, in case I might need time off." She actually hadn't meant to tell Carson, not yet, not until she knew what answer she was going to give Boyd.

She pushed back the door and stepped into her office, another space filled with the station colors—red, blue and white. Thank heavens it didn't have the logo in here, a red heart slashed with the words *Channel Three, the Station with a Heart*. They'd only had the logo since Carson came, and she was tired of it, as tired as she was of the effort it took to keep her professionalism intact when she was around the man himself.

"How did it go?"

Taken aback when she realized she'd totally forgotten Boyd was waiting for her here, Jill stopped in the doorway and looked across the red-and-blue space. Boyd sat behind her desk, a glossy magazine open in front of him. She tried to produce a smile, but the expression felt tight and fake.

She felt even worse when his dark gaze touched hers, and she could see the genuine concern there. Better than anyone, Boyd understood how hard it was for her to confront Carson about San Arman. Ever since Boyd had come into her life the day after Christmas, he'd understood just about everything that came up. An even-tempered man, dark, handsome in a traditional sense, and balanced. That was the one word that really endeared him to Jill. Balanced.

"Carson gave me three days for San Arman," she said as she closed the door behind her.

"Three days?" Boyd stood as she came across the room. "Why not a week?"

"I don't know. It's his idea of a compromise, I guess," she murmured. She sank down in the straight-backed chair by the desk. "And three days are better than none at all."

Boyd came around, circled behind Jill and began kneading her bunching muscles. "You're as tight as a coiled spring," he said as his fingers gently prodded at the tension in her shoulders.

She closed her eyes. "He makes me crazy," she muttered without thinking.

The massage stopped for a fraction of a second, then started again. "My ex-wife used to drive me up a wall."

Jill tilted her head back until she could look up at Boyd. "You? Driven up a wall?" She'd never seen Boyd come close to losing his temper. "You're kidding."

"Maybe that's an exaggeration, but she used to get under my skin." He bent over her, dropped a fleeting kiss on her forehead, then came around to crouch beside the chair. His dark eyes, level with Jill's, were intense and unblinking. "Is this tension because you told Carson about my proposal?"

The tension had started the moment she went into Carson's office. "Not really. But I did tell him I might need time off in June if we get married."

"What did he say?"

"Congratulations," she said, and wondered why she had thought he would say more than that.

Boyd reached for her hands and pulled Jill up with him as he stood. "So, do I finally get an answer to my question?" he asked softly, holding both her hands.

She almost said, "Yes," rationalizing that if she committed herself to him, her life would settle and even out. She could be balanced. Something she hadn't felt since she'd met Carson. But she didn't say the word. Instead, she simply went into Boyd's arms and rested her head on his chest. She exhaled and concentrated on the solid strength of the arms around her and the steady thudding of the heart against her cheek. "After I come back from the trip, I promise I'll give you my answer."

"You're being awfully cautious," Boyd said, his voice a deep rumble in her ears.

"I've come too close to making some devastating mistakes in my life." She didn't want to think about something she couldn't deny—if Carson had asked her to marry him when they'd first been together, she would have jumped at it. She knew how lucky she'd been that he hadn't been able to totally commit himself to anything but his work. "I don't want to rush into anything," she whispered.

His hands traced slow, soothing circles on her back. "I understand, love, I really do."

Jill let herself lean on Boyd, but as she closed her eyes, reality shifted and the past began to overlap with the present. It was definitely Boyd's voice she was hearing, but it seemed like old times with Carson holding her, touching her, gentle yet demanding. Then it was his whispers drifting around her like a velvet cloak in the softness of the night.

The nights. She trembled as old, familiar feelings snuck back to life, growing until a heat flared in their path and a desire that should have died long ago found life again. Her breathing quickened and the heat created a heaviness deep inside her. Oh, no, she almost groaned and reached for sanity by letting her head fall back so she could look up at Boyd and focus on his face.

But even as she managed to utter, "Thank you for understanding," the treacherous memories of a blue-eyed man who had set her world spinning with a simple touch bombarded her.

Her tongue touched her parted lips, and for a second she wondered if she just held tightly enough to Boyd, if she let herself get lost in his essence, could she banish past ghosts? Surely she would feel real passion for the present, not a need for what she had never really possessed in the past.

Boyd lowered his head toward her, and she didn't try to avoid his lips. Yet she knew she didn't dare close her eyes again, so she tried to focus on the blurred face so close to hers, the soft tickling of his beard against her skin, and she willed herself to respond. She wanted to feel a reckless abandonment that would blot out all thoughts and all memories. But when she heard his low groan, felt his tongue demanding entrance to her mouth, she knew how fruitless her efforts were.

Awkwardly she drew back, then reached up to kiss Boyd on his cheek. "I . . . I'm sorry. I wouldn't want someone to walk in."

It was as if Carson stood between then, separating them, making the comparisons in the two relationships crystal-clear. But she didn't want what Carson had offered her, she reasoned; that was why she had left, why she had walked away. And it wasn't fair to any man, especially not to Boyd, to compare him to Carson. He wasn't Carson, he never could be, and she was thankful for that.

He looked at her, a fire deep in his eyes that she knew wasn't echoed in hers and without a word, he drew back. "I understand, love," he murmured.

She knew she cared for Boyd. She felt good with him, calm and rational. She'd had enough unreasoning passion to last a lifetime. She wanted a calm relationship and she had that with Boyd. *That's what a future can be built on*, she told herself as she reached for her purse on the desk.

The unsteadiness in her hands as she clutched the soft leather annoyed her, and she pointedly focused that annoyance on the real source—Carson. "Let's get out of here before Carson comes in and tells me I can't go to San Arman after all," she muttered as she started for the door.

As Carson approached the open doors to the ballroom of the hotel in New York where the Network Affiliates' Conference was being held, he stopped. Stepping off to one side to let the others pass into the room, he leaned one shoulder against a tapestry-covered wall and took off his glasses.

For a minute, he closed his eyes and massaged the bridge of his nose between his forefinger and thumb in an effort to ease a headache he'd had since flying into the city two days before. It throbbed vaguely behind the artificial barrier of three aspirins he had taken earlier, letting him know it wasn't completely gone and would probably be back soon. A lot like his past, he thought grimly. No, not his past, just Jill. Never quite gone, never quite out of his life, and always with the potential for causing problems.

"Hey, Carson."

He opened his eyes and turned to his left as he slipped on his glasses again. Joe DeLeora, a reporter with a Los Angeles station, was standing there looking at him. A middle-aged, balding man with a decided sunburn across his nose, cheeks and the top of his head, Joe looked uncomfortable in an ill-fitting tuxedo. "Joe. I've seen you in some of the meetings, but I haven't had a chance to get over and talk to you."

"I know. These things are crazy. I heard you were in San Diego now."

"With Channel Three," Carson said, not surprised that the news of his new position had preceded him.

"Taking on another sinking ship?"

"It's not a 'sinking ship,' just in need of new ideas. And it's picking up in the ratings."

"I think you should have come up to L.A. and tested the job market there."

"San Diego's fine for now."

"To each his own," Joe said, then nodded to the ballroom doors. "You coming inside?"

Carson nodded. With a tug at the cuffs of his dark tuxedo, he took a breath, then followed Joe into the main ballroom where the final dinner of the conference was being held. On the other side of the crowded room, they found the table reserved for the Southern California delegation with glossy folders laid out alongside china and silverware on the crisp linen table cloth.

Without a glance at the folder, Carson settled in a chair across the table from Joe. As his headache nudged at him, he narrowed his eyes and pressed the tips of his fingers to his temples. He knew the folder had a summary of the last "sweeps" ratings, a breakdown of advertising costs, available advertisers, even charts on age demographics for each program with the network. But he couldn't look at any more figures.

"...and a damned beautiful place, but I think I left just in time," Joe was saying to another man who had just sat down by him.

Carson glanced at the newcomer, a thin, dark-skinned man he didn't know, then back at Joe. "Maybe I've got the jumps," Joe continued, "but I didn't relax until that plane was twenty thousand feet in the air and well on its way back here."

"Damn shame, if you ask me," the man by Joe's side said. "I don't know when everything changed, but being a journalist these days means sticking your neck out. If you want the story you have to go where the news happens, and that can be dangerous."

Joe looked across at Carson. "With you being in management, I'm not sure you can relate to that, Carson."

Carson splayed his hand flat on the folder, pressing his palm on the cool, sleek paper. "Management has its hazardous side," he said dryly.

"Yeah, but you don't travel three hundred days a year. I just got back from assignment. Damn glad to be back, too."

"A rough one?" Carson asked just for something to say.

"Actually, I thought I had a cushy assignment for a change, since it wasn't the Middle East or Pakistan." Joe took a cigarette out of a silver holder in the middle of the table and reached for a slim lighter laid by the centerpiece. "But it ended up being the kind of assignment where you feel nervous until you're on the plane heading home."

"Where were you?"

Joe sat back and took his time lighting the cigarette, then looked at Carson through a haze of exhaled smoke. "A little do-nothing country in South America. San Arman."

Chapter 3

Carson felt uneasiness tighten his chest. The last he'd heard from Bryan, the peace in San Arman was intact. The dissidents were thinning out and some of them were disappearing into the back country. He stared at Joe for a moment before managing to ask with a degree of casualness, "What's going on there?"

Joe sat forward, his elbows resting on the table. "Oh, nothing overt, not like some places. They routed some of the opposition, quietly but firmly, and everything seemed to be settled, but..." He paused to draw on the cigarette. "Damn it, I could feel something about to happen." He shook his head. "It's like feeling eyes boring into your back, but when you turn around no one's there. The hairs at the back of your neck prickle."

"Is that all you have to go on, feelings?"

"Afraid so, but I pretty much trust my instincts." He sat back in the chair and exhaled smoke toward the ceiling. "There's been small pockets of opposition, but Estrada swatted them down. I don't think he's at all worried, yet there's unrest there. And that can explode at any time."

Carson knew how unexpectedly it could all explode. "When did you leave San Arman?" he asked.

"Three days ago. I flew out of Puerto Luis and came directly here." Joe exhaled more smoke on a harsh hiss. "I've been waiting, but haven't heard anything on the wire services. Maybe I'm hypersensitive after too many years of looking for trouble." He raised one eyebrow in Carson's direction. "Have you been partying too much while you're here? You look a bit pale."

Carson had tried to push all thoughts of Jill and San Arman out of his mind, but now the possibilities of what could happen stood squarely in front of him. He stood and said, "No partying, but I've got a splitting headache so I'm going to call it a night. See you tomorrow." With that, he turned and made his way across the room to the doors.

He stepped out into the almost empty lobby and headed to a bank of pay phones by the elevators. With a glance at his watch to find it was just after eight o'clock, he put through a call to San Diego. He heard two rings before it was picked up on the other end by the switchboard.

"San Diego's Channel Three Television, the station with a heart. How may—?"

"This is Carson Davies. Is Bernice Rule still there?"

"Yes, sir," the woman said, and in a second his secretary came on the line.

"Carson? Are you back?"

"No, still in New York. Has anyone from the *Dream Chasers* crew called in recently?"

"Their last check-in was when they were at the airport in Panama City getting ready to fly to Puerto Luis, the capital city in San Arman."

"When was that?"

"Two days ago."

A day after Joe had left Puerto Luis. "Nothing today?"

"No, they said they'd check in when they were finished there and were heading to Colombia."

Carson twisted the cord of the telephone receiver around his hand then closed his fingers on it so tightly his skin tingled. "Who's manning the foreign desk for the news tonight?"

"Tom Sandler."

"Connect me with him."

"He's gone for dinner and won't be back for…an hour."

Frustration was making his jaw clench. "Then connect me with research and Bryan Lake."

"Okay, hang on."

A brief moment later, Bryan was on the line and Carson spoke without preamble. "Did anything come in over the wires about San Arman in the past couple of days?"

"Not that I saw. Is something wrong?"

Carson ignored Bryan's question and asked another of his own. "Can you get me the name of the hotel the crew is staying at in Puerto Luis and the phone number for it?"

"Sure. It might take me a few minutes. I'll have to run down the hall. Do you want to hang on?"

"No, call my room when you get the information. Ten-fifty-two. I'll be up there in five minutes," he said and gave Bryan the hotel's phone number.

Just as Carson walked into his room and turned on the overhead lights, the phone began to ring. After closing the door, he hurried across the thick beige carpet to the desk by the draped windows and picked up the receiver on the third ring. "Hello?"

"They're at the Coronado Heights Hotel," Bryan said, and read off a phone number Carson copied onto the hotel stationery. "Anything else?"

"Let Bernice and the switchboard operators know that if anyone from *Dream Chasers* calls the station, they're to get in touch with me here. I'll talk to you later," he said and hung up.

Immediately he dialed the number Bryan had given him and a clerk answered, but the information he got didn't help. Yes, the crew had checked in on time, but no one from the crew had been at the hotel all day. They had left early in the morning, and the man had no idea where they were or when they would be back. Carson left a message for the show's director, Harry Malone, to call him, then he waited.

By midnight he had stripped down to his jockey shorts, had a pack of cigarettes delivered to his room and had placed four more calls to the hotel in San Arman—getting the same answer each time. "No, they have not returned. Yes, they will get your message when they arrive."

Carson sank down on the bed, lit the first cigarette he'd had in years, then stretched out on top of the spread. Taking off his glasses and laying them on the side table, he closed his eyes and drew deeply on the cigarette. He felt the acrid burn of smoke seep into his lungs, and he felt vaguely sick. Exhaling on a cough, he felt even sicker when images he had no control over circled in his mind. "What if's." Vivid imaginings of what could be going on in San Arman.

He felt out of control, and he hated it. He took another deep drag on the cigarette, coughed harshly, then with a low oath, reached over to grind the cigarette out in the ashtray on the bedside table. Then he switched off the lights, laid back and forced himself to inhale and exhale in a regular pattern. Closing his eyes, he gradually felt his muscles beginning to relax. Cool air brushed across his bare skin and the low drone of the air conditioner helped lull him into a state somewhere between wakefulness and sleep.

The darkness felt unusually soft and comfortable, but before he could relish it, the darkness became his enemy. In a split second, it filled him with a terror he thought he'd left behind five years ago.

A dream, Carson told himself, yet he clearly felt the chill of the cracked concrete floor under him in the windowless cell. The taste of stale dankness touched his tongue. And the darkness—total, complete, devoid of anything but sensations and sounds.

Pain, both physical and emotional, engulfed him when screams ripped through the blackness, echoing from down the long, tunnel-like corridor to fill the thick-walled cell area.

"Talk to me, Martine," he whispered. "Talk to me."

And Martine did speak through blackness, his deep voice the only anchor in that void. A dream or reality? Carson wasn't sure, but he needed the voice, something to hold on to, and it came to him.

"My arrest is a mistake. As soon as the new government knows of my arrest, I will be out of here. How will you get out of here?"

Carson knew he knew the answer to that, but other words came—a question. "What is reality, Martine?"

"Belonging with someone. Having someone mean everything to you, more than life itself."

That wasn't what Carson wanted to hear. He shook his head back and forth. "No, that's not right. That's not right."

He had never had emotional connections like that, no anchor, and he hadn't worried about not having them—until now. Then a sound, a single scream, piercing and terrible, seemed to surround him and fill him with a horror he couldn't begin to define.

A woman's scream. Pain tore it out of her throat, and the past and present mingled precariously. He could feel the ache in his shoulder where it had been dislocated by the soldiers when they had been questioning him. But he couldn't make his hand touch it, not any more than he could make his hands cover his ears to close out the horrible cries.

He felt himself crouch back against the wall, lower, lower, until he was curled into a tight ball with his arms pulling his legs against his chest and his face pressed into his knees. If only the screams would end. Then they did, as abruptly as they had begun. But a dragging sound came closer and closer, then light came from nowhere to banish the darkness, a glare that pained his eyes, blurring everything in a yellow brilliance.

Don't look, he told himself. *Don't look.*

But, as if compelled, he did look. Through the now-open door, out into the corridor, and in that moment of complete horror, he saw a woman, bloodied and terrified, being dragged away by two soldiers. Jill!

The dream shattered, and suddenly, his heart pounding, Carson was back in the hotel room in total darkness. Jerking to his right, he fumbled for the side light. When the yellow glow cut through the shadows, he fell weakly back in the bed and took several shaky breaths.

Jill. Oh, God, he could taste fear, but not for himself. For her.

Abruptly he sat up and reached for his glasses. Slipping them on, he picked up the phone and had to try the number in San Arman twice before he dialed it properly. When the clerk gave him the same answers, he slammed down the receiver and knew in that instant what he was going to do.

He put in another call, this one to the airport. He ran a hand over his sweat-dampened face and stared into the shadowed corners while he waited for someone to answer. When they finally did, he asked, "When is your first non-stop flight out to Puerto Luis in San Arman?"

"And so we leave beautiful San Arman, a small country rushing toward the twenty-first century with a determination to be one of the brightest jewels of South America on the Caribbean coast.''

Despite the ocean just a hundred feet behind her, Jill felt no letup in the oppressive heat of the April sun that beat down on her unprotected head and bare shoulders. Rivulets of perspiration trickled down her back and caught between her skin and the packet of the remote microphone clipped to the waistband of her lavender shorts. The light material of her peasant-style blouse stuck to her damp skin. Jill just hoped she didn't look as flushed on camera as she felt. Only with great concentration, she kept from squinting when she turned to Sam Rollins.

''This is one of the oldest and smallest countries in South America, a country it's rumored took in spies and refugees during and after the Second World War much the same way other South American countries did. San Arman is filled with beauty from its beaches—'' She motioned to the rolling surf behind her ''—to the rain forests and lush jungle-covered mountains we saw on our last program. A place of peace and beauty.''

She ignored the way the presence of armed government soldiers seemed to contradict that statement. The ten uniformed men had shown up this morning at the village in the mountains where the crew had stayed the previous night and escorted them back to the city. ''There is road work, and we are here to show you another route back to the city,'' the leader had told them. The roads certainly needed repairs, she conceded, but she didn't understand why the guards were still hanging around.

They stood in a row behind the cameras, where emerald tufts of grass met the silver sands of the beach. ''Sun, clean air, romance, mystery, the secrets of the ages,'' she said, ad-libbing on the prepared script.

Tall, blond, and a perfect foil for Jill's dark beauty, Sam nodded. "As fascinating as a beautiful woman, and every bit as alluring."

He said the words in a tone that bordered on being suggestive, and it irritated Jill. But she managed to keep her smile intact, grateful for her professional training, which kept the annoyance from edging her voice. "I thought it was ships that were considered to be 'shes.'"

He smiled, an expression almost as brilliant as the sun, and got in one last barb. "Any woman would be glad to be compared to a country as stunning as San Arman," he returned without missing a beat and went smoothly into the closing script. "On our next program, we'll take you dream-chasing to the beautiful city of Cartagena, Colombia. But until then, this is Sam Rollins . . ."

He looked to Jill who picked up her cue. " . . . and Jillian Segar saying, 'Thanks for coming dream-chasing with us.'"

"And cut!" Harry Malone called, as he got slowly out of his canvas folding chair to the left of the cameraman. "Perfect, perfect," he said and waved at the van parked on the gravel switchback road that led to the top of the cliffs. Its back doors were open to face the shooting site. "Let's get everything put away."

Sam walked away from Jill without a word and headed toward more canvas chairs set up in the shade of a clump of tall, slender palms that grew in the grassy area.

Jill turned to Harry, a pale-skinned man who was sweating profusely. "Anything else?" she asked.

"No. We have plenty for the show." He swiped at his face with his free hand. "I thought the villages were like saunas. But even near the water, the heat's miserable. I can't wait to go back up to the hotel and the bliss of air-conditioning."

Jill narrowed her eyes against the persistent glare. "Amen to that," she sighed.

Harry motioned toward the shade, where Sam was sitting low in one of the chairs with his eyes closed. "Why don't you sit there while we get things loaded in the van, then you can drive back to the hotel instead of taking the climb?" He glanced at stairs that went up the side of the cliff at an improbable angle. "You don't want to tackle those stairs in this heat. Take it easy. Do what Sam does so well," he said with a roll of his eyes.

"I was thinking of heading west down the beach for a while. The clerk said there are some small private coves that way," Jill said motioning down the beach.

"You wanted to do a shoot in one of the them?" Harry asked.

"No, I was..." She shrugged, seeing no point in explaining to Harry how much she wanted a little peace and quiet. She hadn't been alone since flying into San Arman. "I just wanted to see a bit more of the beach before we leave. But I'll go up to the hotel first and change. I'll wait for you and take you up on that ride."

Harry nodded, then headed for the van as Jill crossed to the shade of the palms. After a crew member helped Jill get her microphone off, Jill dropped down in a folding chair next to Sam. Tentatively she touched one shoulder and felt the heat still contained in her skin. Sunburn. Even with sunblock on, she knew by tomorrow she would begin to peel. So much for off-the-shoulder tops, she thought as she took a cold can of cola another crew member offered her.

Opening the can, she sat back and glanced at Sam. "You just had to say it, didn't you?"

He slouched lower in his chair and rolled his cool soda can slowly back and forth on his forehead without opening his eyes. "I couldn't resist," he murmured. "Just couldn't resist."

Jill grimaced at him as she took a sip and felt the delicious coolness trickle down her throat. Sam might be loved by the Channel Three viewers, and his smile might have most of San Diego's female population dropping to their knees, but not Jillian. She understood him completely. She'd known he was a jerk from the beginning, but a charismatic jerk. That made him bearable for now.

Jill reached for sunglasses from her tote bag, slipped them on, then took another sip of cola. Glancing over the raised can, she saw the ever-present soldiers who kept the growing crowds back on the grass. Lowering her can to touch it to her inner wrist, she looked past all the people to the rugged cliffs that soared into the heavens.

The handout the minister of tourism, Hector Gomez, had given her at the airport had been filled with postcard-type pictures and stated "Puerto Luis, the capital city, is built on bluffs that form a natural harbor of great and stunning beauty." A bit flowery, she'd thought, but definitely true. This area was spectacular. Even the Coronado Heights Hotel, one of the many splashes of white dotting the greenness far above the beach, was a study in old-world charm. With wicker, plants, brass touches and brilliant colors used in its decorating, along with lattice gazebos dotting the sea of grass that surrounded it, the hotel and grounds had not disappointed Jill.

Nothing had disappointed her in San Arman but the presence of the soldiers and the scattered pockets of poverty she had seen during the drive into the hills and the jungle. Yet she had expected the poverty. She'd been in enough of these countries to know the drastic separation of the classes. And anything for tourism was well away from the negative aspects of the country.

She looked back at the crowds, a different group than the people in the villages. Yesterday the locals had stayed inside, uneasy about coming out to watch the Americans, but not here. These people had stood in the broiling sun for an hour watching the taping. From what Jill could tell, there were very few tourists in the group. Dark-skinned, flat-featured people dressed in bright clothes and even some cutoff jeans, watched the procedure of taping the segments with unblinking interest.

There hadn't been very many tourists anywhere the crew had gone. Even the hotel was more than half vacant. And that was probably why Mr. Gomez was so intent on getting some exposure in America for his country.

"What a place, what a place," Sam muttered. "What they need is a real live casino and some legal gambling."

Jill glanced at him. "Why?"

Sam shrugged. "Something to liven things up a bit. You can only take peace and quiet for so long, then you want to party."

"I guess it's hard when a person gets bored so easily," she murmured.

Oblivious to her sarcasm, he stated, "Everyone needs some fun."

That was something Carson would never have said. He would be wondering just how he could hook up his computer and do his work while he sunned on the beach. The mental image almost made her laugh, then it stopped her dead. Since when had she thought of Carson and his traits without any bitterness? Maybe even with humor.

She prodded herself mentally, much the same way a person probed a sore tooth, but there was only a suggestion of the old hurt. Was it over? Had that glimpse of vulnerability in him when they'd talked in the office taken the edge off the memories? Had telling him about Boyd's proposal finally ended any lingering connection between them, despite her experience when Boyd had held her? She exhaled, more than a little relieved.

She barely acknowledged Sam as he stood and said, "I'm going back to the hotel with Harry," before he headed off. Nothing could be completely over as long as Carson was the station manager at Channel Three, she decided, but she could see things were actually better.

She'd passed that point of feeling a catch in her chest any time she saw a sandy-haired man with a lean, athletic build. Or a stranger in a Brooks Brothers suit. Or a lone jogger on the beach in the early morning. She didn't know quite when the change had taken place, but it had to have been sometime between the confrontation in his office and today.

She stood and looked down the beach to the west. Right now she wasn't about to question the drastic shift in her emotions. She simply let the surprise at ending that intense chapter in her life filter through her. Maybe it didn't feel exactly wonderful. Maybe she felt a bit empty, but she definitely felt relieved. More importantly, her decision about marrying Boyd might be easier to make now.

Before she could turn and go over to where Harry and Sam were deep in a heated discussion, someone called out to her.

"Señorita Segar. Señorita Segar!"

Jill looked up as the minister of tourism came toward her across the grass. Hector Gomez, a short, swarthy man dressed in a black suit worn with a white shirt buttoned up to the neck, looked unruffled by the heat. His dark eyes were narrowed against the glare. Jill watched him until he stopped in front of her.

"Mr. Gomez, hello."

"I am glad you and your people arrived back safely from the mountains," he said.

Safely? Jill faced him, his height only an inch or so above hers. "I didn't think the roads were that bad."

"The roads? Oh, no, no, just minor, annoying work," he said.

She glanced at the guards still hovering nearby. "Why are the guards still here?"

He waved that aside with a jerky notion of his hand slicing through the hot air. "Just a courtesy to make sure the people do not get too, how would you say it, pushy." He smiled at her. "It is a courtesy from our president, just as the schedule was that our people made out for your stay. We wanted to make sure you saw the best of our country."

She wasn't about to point out that two men could have handled the job that had been assigned to ten. Or that the best of the country couldn't quite hide the vast amount of the population that lived near or below the poverty level. "I do appreciate the thought."

"I came to the hotel to talk to you and they told me you were down here." He smiled faintly at the crowds nearby. "I am quite sure nothing else would draw such a group except American celebrities."

Jill glanced past the soldiers at the people who were still there, apparently fascinated watching the equipment being loaded into the van. "They've been here ever since we started filming." She looked back to Gomez. "What did you need to talk to me about?"

"The president's reception this evening. I came to check and be sure you had not forgotten about it."

She wasn't about to forget about the formal invitation delivered to them when they had arrived at the airport. Meeting President Estrada at his residence seemed a fitting way to end their stay in San Arman. "I'll be there. I'm looking forward to meeting him," he said, "and telling him how much we have enjoyed our stay. A few shots would be—"

Gomez shook his head abruptly. "No, that is not possible. *El presidente* does not allow filming inside the walls of his home."

"Is there a problem?"

The small man spread his hands as he shrugged. "No problem. No, no, not at all. But he values his privacy. After all, his life is dedicated to the people of San Arman. His time is taken up by their needs, so he tries to keep one spot where he can be himself."

Jill had met quite a few people in the public eye who were intensely protective of their private lives. "I understand."

"Good." He rubbed his hands together and rocked forward slightly on the balls of his feet. "President Estrada has been eager to find out how our country held up to your scrutiny." He lowered his voice a bit as he rocked closer. "He is also, as I told you before, a great fan of your American television and the stars on television."

She brushed at her face, damp from the heat, then ran a hand down the front of her neck to the top of her blouse. With one finger, she tugged at the neckline, trying to free the clinging material from her hot skin. "We aren't really stars—" she started to protest.

"Ah, but you are here. It is not every day a celebrity comes to our country. But maybe with your good publicity about what San Arman has to offer, that will change. And maybe you will come back some day just to enjoy our country. An invitation is always open for you here."

"Thank you," she said, thinking how appealing it would be to have the time to lay on the sand, listen to the soothing sounds of the ocean, sleep twelve hours a day and eat their delicious food.

Gomez smiled at her again, a strange expression that seemed a bit forced. "The president will send a car for you and your party at seven o'clock."

Carson stood partially hidden behind a grouping of palms on the far side of the van and watched Jill talking to a short man who seemed intent on every word she spoke. Carson watched Jill lift her hand to her face, then lightly brush at her hair. As she listened to the man, she touched one finger to her cheek, then slowly trailed that finger down to her chin. Lifting her head slightly, she moved her finger down her throat to the low neckline of her blouse.

As she hooked her finger at the neckline and tugged at it, the gauzy material lifted away from her skin, then fell back, clinging to the fullness of her breasts as if the pale lavender was a second skin. Carson felt a renewal of the sudden awareness he had had of Jill in the office, the day she had told him about her probable marriage to Boyd. And it was just as unwelcome now.

He closed his eyes for a moment, but not before he was aware of the sweep of her jaw and the vulnerability of her exposed throat. He shivered despite the oppressive heat and leaned to the right against the nearest palm tree.

There was nothing wrong here, at least not with the crew. Jill looked fine, better than he remembered, even, and he felt incredibly foolish—both for his reactions to her and the impulsive fear that he had experienced in New York.

From the time he woke from the dream early this morning at his hotel, he had felt fragmented and vaguely sick. Then he'd flown straight down here, walked into the hotel on the cliffs and learned that the crew had just come back from the mountains. They had gone directly down to film on the beach. His relief had come in a rush of light-headed giddiness.

He took off his glasses and rested his head back against the roughness of the palm's trunk. Why had he let his imagination get the best of him? Why had he left the convention early to fly into a country he had vowed never to enter again? Because of a dream, a woman screaming in his mind, a woman who had become confused with Jill?

He stood straight, slipped his glasses back on, then looked at Jill again. He watched her talking to the small man as she dug at the sand with the toe of her sandal, and he narrowed his eyes. She looked so delicate in pleated shorts and an off-the-shoulder top that exposed a lot of skin—slender arms

and the hint of cleavage at her full breasts. Her leather sandals wouldn't add enough height to bring her any higher
than his shoulder.

She looked well and safe, but in the dream she had been—
He cut off that thought and pushed the lingering remnants
of the dream as far from him as he could. They had no
reality in this tropical place. He watched Jill shake hands
with the small man and turn to walk toward the van.

In that split second, he knew he could walk away and no
one would ever have to know he had come down here. Then
he saw the soldiers. With a sharp intake of the warm air,
tinged with the scent of the nearby ocean, Carson left his
protected position near the palms and walked out onto the
sand into the full strength of the sun.

He could feel the silty beach under his shoes, and he
wished he'd taken time to change instead of paying the
bellhop to take his bags up to his room while he hurried
down here. Tie, slacks and a shirt, even with the sleeves
rolled up, weren't the right things to be wearing in this heat
on a beach. Thank goodness his glasses darkened in the sun
to take the edge off the glare. He swiped at the dampness on
his face, then braced himself and went toward Jill.

Chapter 4

Jill walked along the beach, her eyes averted from the glare to watch her feet pressing into the sand with each step she took. At the same time Jill sensed someone in front of her, she ran directly into a solid body. She stumbled backward from the impact, felt strong hands grip her upper arms to keep her from falling, and she looked up.

Her mouth was open to offer an apology, but any words died before they could be uttered. She found herself staring up at Carson, and even though she could feel him holding her arms, she had the fleeting idea he was a mirage. Maybe her thoughts moments ago had caused him to appear.

As he let her go, reality settled in all around her, and all she could manage was, "You."

"Yes, me," he murmured as he moved back half a pace.

Before she could say anything more, Harry called out from somewhere behind her. "Boss! What in the hell are you doing here?"

When Carson turned, as Harry huffed to a stop beside him, Jill moved back, needing to put more space between them. She didn't listen to what the two men were saying. She was too preoccupied with how foolish her thoughts had been. All Carson had to do was appear without warning and every nerve in her body came to life, leaving her feeling as if she had been punched in her middle.

Damn him, she screamed silently. Why did he have to turn up now? Why did she have to notice every little thing about him? The way the sun glinted off his glasses that had darkened in the bright light, the way his hair clung damply to his neck, and the incongruous clothes that had no place on the beach. But the slacks and shirt set off his lean build, defining his muscular thighs and the width of his shoulders.

She brought herself up short. He was here to control the program, to make sure everything was done his way. She didn't doubt that for an instant. Any sort of pleasant thoughts about Carson obviously only came when she thought he was half a world away from her.

She saw Sam hurrying over, smiling, pleased to see Carson. He didn't seem to find anything unusual about the station manager being here. "Good to see you," Sam said. "A touch of home."

As the men talked, Jill turned away from them and started across the sand. But not in the direction of the stairs. She went west, toward the outjut that she had to get past to find the hidden coves the hotel clerk had told her about. If she could get around the bend and out of sight, maybe she could find some peace.

But before she managed to get more than halfway to the point, she heard her name. "Jill?" She kept going, pretending she didn't hear Carson calling her. Just twenty more feet. She walked more quickly. Fifteen feet. Ten.

Then he spoke again, but from directly behind her this time. "Are you running away?"

She stopped, closed her eyes, but didn't turn. "What?"

When he didn't answer, she finally opened her eyes and found him by her side. Hesitantly she turned her head just enough to look up at him. Sun caught at the gold in his hair and emphasized fine lines that fanned at the corners of his narrowed eyes behind his glasses. A deep ridge cut between his eyes, and brackets framed his mouth.

"What's wrong with you?" he asked.

She shifted so her back was to the cliffs, and Carson had to stare into the sun. Pushing a clinging strand of damp hair off her face, she shrugged. "Nothing."

"You could have fooled me."

"What are you doing down here?" she asked, not up to any more hedging. "Did you come down to check on us? To see if we're doing what you wanted us to do? To see if you were right about San Arman?"

He pushed his hands in the pockets of his navy slacks. "Do I get a chance to explain?"

"You don't need to explain anything to me," she muttered. "You're the boss. You can do what you want and go anywhere you want."

"I was on my way back to San Diego and—"

"Oh, you were in the neighborhood, so you thought you'd just drop in?"

She could see his mouth tighten even more, but before he could say another thing, Sam hurried up to them and interrupted.

"Carson. When we get back to the hotel, let's get something cold to drink. I've got ideas for the program that I'd like to go over with you."

Carson stared hard at Jill, then glanced at Sam. "Maybe we can talk on the flight out tonight, Sam."

"Jill and I changed our flight. We have an invitation to the president's private residence this evening. I'm not expecting much, not after the quality of nightlife we've

Dream Chasers

found here. My only hope—'' he winked at Jill ''—is that some of the women there will be spectacular.''

Jill had never felt such dislike for *all* men as she did at that moment. Sam's remark was the last straw. "You don't need to stay. You could fly out with Harry and the crew and get into the wild nightlife in Cartagena," she said.

"Oh, I thought about it, but who knows what might happen tonight?''

"The crew's leaving tonight?" Carson asked.

"On an eight o'clock flight."

Carson looked back to Jill. "Why don't you fly out tonight with the others?"

"Sam told you. We were invited to the president's home for a reception of some sort."

"Are you going back to the hotel now?" Sam asked Carson.

Carson spoke to Sam without looking away from Jill. "I'll be up at the hotel in a few minutes, then we'll talk."

Jill watched Sam pat Carson on the shoulder, then head off across the sand toward the stairs. She finally looked back at Carson. "Now, are you going to tell me why you're here?"

Carson stared at Jill, at the flushed skin at her temples and forehead where tiny damp curls clung. He knew right then he wasn't about to tell anyone the truth. He felt incredibly foolish. "What's this reception all about?" he asked, buying time until he could figure out exactly what to tell her.

She shrugged. "I don't know. The minister of tourism met us at the hotel when we arrived and gave us the invitation. It seems that President Estrada is a big fan of American television, and he wants to meet us. It would be impolite to not send anyone. After all, he's been very cooperative with us, setting up locations for shoots and everything." She flicked a nervous glance behind Carson, then her eyes came back to his. "It's a good idea for me to go."

The idea of Jill or any of the crew being in Estrada's own home made him uneasy, no matter what the reason. "Why do you have the guards?"

"To keep the public from harassing us."

"Who told you that?"

She frowned up at him, a fine line cutting between her eyes. "Mr. Gomez. Why?"

The sight of the men in uniform prodded at his middle. Probably because the last time he'd seen the army out in a country like this, he had been their focus of attention. They had been driving him to the airstrip, saluting every picture of Estrada they passed on the way. "It seems like a bit of overkill. That's all."

She looked at him hard for a moment, then said, "You never answered me."

"About what?" he asked, but he knew.

"Why are you here?"

He couldn't hedge anymore, so he ad-libbed as he went along. "I was finished in New York, and I still had a few days left before I have to be back at the station." He smiled, hoping the expression didn't look as tight to her as it felt to him. "And I was jealous of the bunch of you down here having a good time."

"You've been to Houston to see your friends?"

The lie came with an ease that was mildly shocking to him. "Sure. Everyone's fine."

"Great," she murmured. "So you hopped a plane for Puerto Luis?"

He could tell she wasn't buying it, but he kept going. "A bit of sun sounded good to me."

"It's a pretty country," she said.

"That it is," he murmured. Pleasantries that meant nothing hung between them, and only underscored his mistake in coming here. "I left messages at the hotel for you or Harry, but—"

"We haven't been there since yesterday morning, but some of the crew went up earlier." Jill looked right at him and spoke bluntly. "When are you leaving?"

"Probably with the others." He hated the suggestion of relief that he could detect in her expression.

"Right now, I'm going for a walk..." Her voice trailed off, then she asked, "Did you need anything else?"

It shocked him when he knew what he needed was to touch her again, to make some physical contact as a way of reassuring himself that she was indeed all right. But he kept his hands in his pockets, shook his head and lied again. "No, nothing else."

At twilight Jill stepped into the elevator and headed down the two floors to the lobby. A shower, the cool air of the air-conditioned room and uninterrupted silence, had done little to soothe her nerves. She felt on edge, as if a shoe had dropped, and she was holding her breath waiting for the other one to fall. A silly reaction that originated from Carson's unexpected appearance. The man could go anywhere he wanted, but with a vengeance she wished he wasn't in her part of the world right now.

She looked at her reflection in the mirror-like surface of the closed elevator doors. She'd found her dress, a frothy piece of floor-length blue chiffon, in the boutique in the lobby of the hotel. A business expense, she reasoned, to help ease her conscience while she paid a prohibitive amount for it.

And a good investment, she thought now, looking at the way the soft neckline dropped to expose her slightly sun-burned shoulders, and the way the delicate material tucked in at her waist, then fell in a gathered drape to brush the floor. Expensive enough to choke a horse, she thought, but beautiful enough to make her feel better just having it next to her skin.

She adjusted the fine chain strap of the purse she'd bought at the same store, a scrap of glittery silver that matched silver heels she'd found there, too. As the elevator stopped and the doors slid open, she stepped out into the lobby. The space was light and airy, with mirrors everywhere, multiple ceiling fans, furnishings of wicker and brass on thick beige carpet, and the green lushness of potted palms that echoed the land outside.

She crossed to the glass entrance doors that were immediately opened by a formally dressed attendant, and she stepped outside into the gentle heat of the early evening. She took two steps on the cobbled walkway that led to the semicircular drive that swept past the entrance and stopped dead.

A black limousine was parked at the curb. It had a gold seal on the rear side door and small flags above the headlights at the front.

But Jill stared at the man standing by the open rear door. Carson. He was talking to a slender gentleman dressed in a military uniform who held the door open. But it was as if Carson was the only person there. The world narrowed and focused just on him.

When was the last time she'd seen him in a tuxedo, in tailored black-and-white, with a velvet tie at his throat, the stark whiteness of the French cuffs at his strong hands? She couldn't remember, yet she knew she'd experienced it before, knew that she had felt this total awareness of Carson. Yet her reaction now was even more intense because it was overlaid by real shock.

Carson was supposed to be on the flight out, not here looking larger than life. She had to take a deep breath before she could make herself continue down the walkway to the car.

As Carson turned, the intensity of his gaze on her was as potent as any touch could have been. She felt a deepening response to his presence, a reaction she apparently had no control over, yet she couldn't accept. She wouldn't accept it. Stopping three feet from him, she simply looked at him.

"Why...?" She touched her tongue to her lips and started again. "Why are you here?"

"The same reason you're here." He motioned her into the limousine. "The rest of the crew are at the airport, so it's just you and me."

She could literally feel her breath catch in her throat, and she had to make a real effort to speak again. "What about Sam?"

"Sam decided to leave with the crew, so I took his invitation."

"You what?"

"He gave it to me."

"Why would you want to go to the reception?"

"I'm the station manager. And Sam decided not to stay. I didn't want to offend the president." The lenses in his glasses annoyingly reflected back the lights of the hotel and hid the expression in his eyes. She remembered how frustrating that had been for her before. It was even worse now. "I think we should honor that invitation. I know you feel that way, don't you?"

She felt neatly trapped and knew she had no choice but to go ahead with the evening. Abruptly she brushed past Carson to get into the car, and as she settled on the plush seat as far to the left as she could get, she stared straight ahead. She was aware of Carson getting inside after her, the door closing, and the seat shifting with his weight.

She swallowed hard, held tightly to her small purse, and stared at the epaulets on the driver's shoulders as the car drove down the hotel driveway and onto the wide street. The silence went unbroken and Jill kept her eyes to her left and out the tinted window as the car proceeded slowly through the streets of the capital city. They went along thorough-fares lined with palms and businesses that were closed. Then they went into a more residential area, where old-fashioned street lamps were the only lights and multistory houses were done in myriad pastel shades.

As the shadows got longer, evening gentled the sur-roundings, but nothing could ease the sight of scattered pockets of poverty along the way near the eastern edge of the city. None of that would be on the film going back to San Diego, not the conglomerations of cardboard houses, and mud huts with animals tied to trees in the front, or these children—skimpily dressed in shorts and T-shirts, dark-skinned, dark-eyed, moving slowly in the shadows and ob-viously wallowing in poverty.

Jill found herself closing her eyes. This evening wasn't starting off in an auspicious manner, at all. Then she felt Carson stir by her side, and she looked back out at the night. The darkness was complete now, so nothing was visible ex-cept a fleeting glow of lights from homes now and then. Her own image reflected back at her in the window, haloed by the soft interior light behind her.

"Jill?"

Carson's voice seemed to blend with the shadows, soft and seductive. "What?" she asked, as she stared at her re-flection and saw the tightening in her own expression dis-torted in the glass.

"We're here."

She turned to look ahead, felt the car slow and saw a glow in the sky beyond the arch of the headlights. Then the lim-ousine swung to the right, through brick pillars that sup-ported open metal gates, and into an expansive courtyard. Palms and tropical plants, interspersed with lamps, lined a cobbled drive that swept up to an imposing three-story building of brick and stone. *A palace,* Jill thought, as the car approached the front and stopped by a sweep of stone steps that led up to a portico-covered entry.

Twenty-foot-high double doors were open, and the brilliance from crystal chandeliers inside spilled out into the night and tumbled down the stairs.

Jill looked at Carson who was staring out at the building, too. She could see the way his jaw tightened. "This is a *residence*?" she asked.

"The president's version, obviously," he muttered. The driver came around to open the door for them. Carson hesitated, then abruptly moved and got out. Jill slid across the seat, stepped out into the softness of the night, and heard music drifting toward them from the brightly lit lower windows and the open doors. She inhaled the sweetness of citrus blossoms drifting on the warm air, then her breath caught when she turned to the entry and saw a line of soldiers standing at attention, lining the steps going up to the doors. Soldiers, not footmen, standing stiffly, their gaze straight ahead and rifles on their shoulders.

A man dressed in a formal tuxedo appeared at the top of the stairs and hurried down to Carson and Jill. He spoke in Spanish, but Jill understood what he must be saying when he stopped two steps above them and Carson reached into his inside pocket to take out the embossed invitation.

Jill took hers out of her purse and handed it to the man. He glanced at them, then spoke in English. "Please, follow me." He led the way up the stairs, but didn't offer to give the invitations back to them.

Jill started after him, hating the way Carson casually cupped her elbow and stayed by her side. But she fell in step beside him, and as they went up past the soldiers to the open doors and stopped on the top expanse of marble stairs, Jill found that Carson's touch wasn't entirely unwelcome.

They walked through the doors, into a vast reception hall. The drone of voices grew louder and mingled with an old-fashioned waltz played by violins. Underfoot was inlaid parquet flooring trimmed with marble, and the walls were covered by intricate murals, soaring over twenty feet to a domed ceiling with gold inlaid sprays that fanned out from the base of massive chandeliers.

More soldiers stood near the walls in the thirty-foot-long room, and at the far end a series of marble stairs swept in half circles up to a massive arched entry framed in garlands, with gold-leaf cherubs set in bas-relief.

As they approached the marble stairs, Carson let go of Jill's elbow. For a flashing second, she felt abandoned, then caught herself and moved a fraction of an inch farther from Carson. The man in the tuxedo motioned toward the archway with a flourish. "This way." And led them up the stairs.

Jill sensed Carson by her side as she went up the steps as clearly as if he still held her. And when she stopped at the entrance to a room that dwarfed the first area, she felt the fine material of his jacket brush her bare arm. She concentrated intently on the room she was facing.

The ceiling in here was also domed, but it spanned fifty feet in either direction and took up almost all three stories of space. Walls were covered by rich, filigreed fabrics; the floor was done in patterned marble inlaid with gold flourishes at the sides; a multitude of round tables covered in white linen and decorated with gold urns filled with brilliant blossoms clustered around the sides of the room.

A long table laden with gold and silver dishes sat on a raised platform along the wall to the right. The cleared floor in the middle was being used by couples dancing to the strains of a five-piece string ensemble, and open French doors lined the back wall.

The contrast between the poverty Jill had glimpsed on the drive here and this sight almost made her physically sick. But the guests, maybe a hundred or a hundred and fifty, seemed oblivious to everything but having a good time.

White-coated waiters poured champagne freely, laughter drifted on the air, and a thin haze of cigarette smoke hung overhead.

The man by Jill pointed to a mirrored alcove at the left side of the room where a complete bar was set up for drinks. "The bar is there for your pleasure." Then he motioned to the head table and the series of high-backed chairs that were empty. "*El presidente* will be seated there."

"When will President Estrada be here?" Jill asked.

The man motioned to a group of men not more than ten feet from the foot of the stairs. "He is here already."

Carson recognized Estrada instantly. Even though he had never been in a position to face the man head on, the sight of him in the prison, and the memory of his face plastered all over Puerto Luis years ago on posters, made him very recognizable. He'd never forget the snow-white hair, sharp features, dark skin, dark eyes and rigidly straight posture. Even the uniform was the same—full-dress with the chest almost covered with impressive-looking medals.

Only his height surprised Carson. He'd always remembered the man as a towering presence, but reality was different. Estrada was little more than five foot six or seven. Only his ambitions and desires had been large.

Carson felt a clutching in his middle when Estrada inclined his head to the man by his side, Hector Gomez. The action brought back the memory of a nod of his head signaling death for an "enemy." An enemy, then, had been anyone who wasn't part of Estrada's revolution. That included American journalists, even his own countrymen who didn't fall into line, whose only flaw had been to love their country as it was, not as Estrada envisioned it.

"President Javier Estrada," the man said formally.

Three men stood behind Estrada, men in plain suits—bodyguards. That knowledge gave Carson a fleeting sense of justice being served. In some way it pleased him that Estrada couldn't roam freely, not even in his own home.

Just then Hector Gomez looked up, spotted Jill, and nodded. He leaned toward Estrada to say something, then came toward the entry. Carson killed the urge to grab Jill's hand and run as far and as fast as they could before the contact with Estrada was made. But he kept his ground by clenching his hands behind his back and breathing evenly.

As Gomez approached Jill, he held out his hand. "Señorita Segar. You look lovely. I am so pleased you could come tonight." He bent and brushed his lips across the back of her hand, then turned to Carson. His genial expression changed to a frown when he realized he didn't know Carson. "Excuse me?"

Carson deliberated. He didn't know Gomez, but then he'd never seen most of the soldiers who had kept him imprisoned, or any of Estrada's enforcers. "Davies," he said and held out his hand. "Mr. Rollins couldn't make it, so I came as an escort for Miss Segar." When he saw Gomez hesitate, he added, "I'm the manager of Channel Three Television."

"Ah," Gomez said, taking Carson's hand in a brisk handshake. "The boss, as you say?"

"Yes, the boss," Carson murmured.

"Good. Good. I am glad you are here." He motioned toward the president. "President Estrada will be anxious to meet you both."

Jill stepped down to follow Gomez, but Carson stayed where he was. How could he face the man? How could he look at him and act civilized, after knowing what he had done? Then he saw Jill going closer and closer to Estrada. Wasn't that why he'd ordered Sam to go on with the crew and taken his invitation? Wasn't protecting Jill right now as much a passion in his life as anything had ever been?

Without giving himself any more time to think, he stepped down into the room and went after Jill. By the time he got to her side, she was less than three feet away from Estrada. The guests parted and Gomez spoke up. "*El Presidente*?"

Javier Estrada turned to Gomez, his eyes black as night and narrowed under gray brows. His thin face held a tight expression that tugged at dark skin that seemed strangely touched by paleness. "*Si*, Hector?"

Gomez swept a hand in the direction of Jill and Carson and spoke in English. "The American television celebrities. Señor Davies and Señorita Segar."

Everything was vibrantly clear for Carson. Jill, Estrada reaching for her hand, clicking his heels, bowing formally from the waist, then lifting Jill's tiny hand to his lips. "Señorita Segar," he said in heavily accented English. "A pleasure."

Then he let her go and turned to Carson. "And Señor Davies. We are pleased you too have come this evening."

There was nothing there, no spark of recognition. Just dark eyes and an intense expression. Before Carson had to say or do anything, the music stopped and the president turned toward the room.

"Hector, it is time," he murmured, then with the men in business suits flanking him, he walked to the raised table. The string ensemble began to play music that bore a striking resemblance to "Pomp and Circumstance."

Estrada walked slowly toward the center chair, then he turned to the room and the music stopped. In the dead hush that filled the room, Jill could hear him clear his throat, then in a strong voice he began to speak rapidly in Spanish.

Carson barely listened to a thunderous oration about Estrada's love for San Arman, about his devotion to its people. Instead he moved closer to Jill, until he felt her shoulder against his arm. He needed the connection and knew he wouldn't break it until they were out of here.

Jill stared at Estrada as he spoke, not understanding a word he said but fascinated by the way he held the entire room in his grip. When he finished the guests broke into spontaneous applause and cheers, then the man slowly sat in the chair. With a sharp nod, he sank back and the violins began to play a waltz. One by one, the couples began to dance again.

Mr. Gomez exhaled as he turned to Jill and Carson. His words were polite, yet his face seemed grim. "Please enjoy yourselves. Later, when dinner is over, the president wishes to talk to the two of you privately." Then he was gone in the direction of the president.

Jill watched until Gomez was by the president talking to him, then turned to Carson, almost bumping against him. But Carson wasn't looking at her. His gaze was intense and focused on the two men as they spoke at the table. The grimness of his expression matched Hector Gomez's expression moments ago.

"Did you understand all of that?" she asked him.

Carson blinked, as if he had just realized she was there with him, then he looked at her and the lines in his face eased a bit. "Some. It was mostly propaganda." He exhaled, and motioned with his head to the dancers behind him. "Dance with me?"

She looked at him, the brilliance of the room dancing back at her in the reflection from his glasses. "No, I . . . I'm not much of a dancer, Carson."

"I know that," he murmured. "But this is a waltz. It's simple. One, two, three, four. And I'll lead."

When she held out her hand to object, he caught her hand with his. He laced his fingers through hers and when she would have drawn back, his grip tightened. "Carson, no—"

"Yes," he said simply, then still holding her hand, he turned and started toward the dance floor. Short of making him drag her through the tables, she had no choice but to go with him. When they stepped onto the dance floor, Carson turned her toward him, circled her waist with his other hand and drew her to him.

With a sinking feeling, Jill felt the memories there, the knowledge of how his hand would feel holding hers, how his body seemed to dwarf hers. Then he was gathering her closer until her hips were against his, and the past came treacherously close to the present.

"Slowly," he breathed against her hair. "One, two, three, four."

As Jill began to move with Carson, more memories, so real they could have been made yesterday, sprang to life. And the strength of the past caused her to close her eyes for a fleeting moment. She tried to concentrate on keeping time with the music, tried not to feel every nuance of his body where it touched hers, and she tried not stumble over her own feet.

She had told him the truth, that she wasn't much of a dancer, but when she used to dance with him, when she had been in his arms, the truth had always been altered—on the dance floor or anywhere else.

She stared at the tie at his throat, but remembered how she had always been able to feel his rhythm, to move easily with him. When she had turned to him, gone into his arms, felt him against her, his heat, his strength, their rhythm had been perfect. So perfect— She brought herself up short, sensing the heat in her face, which matched the growing heat at every point her body touched his.

Just get through tonight, she told herself. *Get through it, then never let it happen again.* She was a bit surprised when she realized, despite her overly sensitive nerves, that her feet seemed to move on their own, smoothly, effortlessly. It was her thoughts that were out of balance. Dangerously out of balance, she conceded and tried to make a bit of space between herself and Carson.

All her effort got for her was a tightening of his hold, and even more contact. Her breasts were crushed against the pleated front of his shirt, the stiffly starched fabric scratchy against the exposed skin above her neckline.

"Relax," he whispered against her hair. "I'm not going to bite you."

She took a deep breath, annoyed that it almost caught in her chest. "I'm no good at this," she whispered.

"You're doing fine. Just fine."

She didn't want to have compliments from Carson, not now. "This place, it's like a palace, isn't it?" she asked, looking past Carson's arm at the vast space around them. "It's almost obscene after what we passed on the way here."

That brought a chuckle and a deep, rumbling sensation against her breasts. She wished she could move back enough to stop the sensation, but knew better than to try that again. His hand rested proprietorially at the small of her back.

"Obscene? A perfect choice of words," he murmured, then without warning swept Jill into a flourishing swirl in the middle of the floor.

For a few moments she felt lost in the sensation of almost floating effortlessly, the music flowing around her. For a few precious moments she was free of the feelings of Carson against her, then she was back in his arms, and she gave up. It was no use fighting his hold on her, so she let her body do what it wanted to. She pressed against him and rested her cheek in the hollow of his shoulder.

She closed her eyes again, shutting out the glittering light all around. His jacket felt soft against her cheek as she shifted her head slightly, and his hold was gentle despite the size of his hands. With each breath she inhaled the fragrance of after-shave, something tinged with heat and the freshness of soap.

Then she realized the focal point of her sensations was lower. Her hips against his hips, moving seductively to the beat. *It's an old-fashioned waltz, for Pete's sake,* she wanted to scream at her body, yet that insidious heat grew in her. Her mind understood the danger of what was happening yet her body didn't seem to.

Chapter 5

Jill kept her eyes closed, willing the dance to be just a dance, Carson's touch to be as any other touch from any other man.

Another man. Boyd. She deliberately thought of him. She made herself remember *his* touch—solid, dependable, always there. The way he held her. His kisses, the way he touched her. But that wasn't enough to keep the memories away. The past, when there had been heat, passion, and a oneness that she had experienced only once in her life. With Carson.

It would never be that way again. Never. And the bare truth of that thought shook her to the core.

Never? Was that why she had gone so slowly with Boyd? Had she been trying to be cautious, or had she known she would never have with him what she had had with Carson. Those memories of the past had been blocking her future and edging out what could be with Boyd.

The past is gone! she wanted to scream at the top of her lungs. Gone, finished, nevermore! *The present is all I have.* As she bit her lip hard, needing the diversion of sharp pain to try and clear her thoughts, she turned her head just a bit, so her forehead was pressed against Carson's shoulder.

But her thoughts became more jumbled when his hand began to move up her back, inching precariously close to the skin exposed above her low neckline. *It's over. I made the right decision. And if I didn't let him touch me or hold me like this, and get this close, none of this would be happening. If only...*

Suddenly she realized Carson had stopped dancing, even though the music was still playing. And he still held her. Tentatively she tried to move back from him, and the taste of victory when his hold eased on her was short-lived when she opened her eyes. At first all she was aware of was Carson, his face so close she could feel each breath he took caressing her skin. Her own reflection showed in his glasses.

Then she realized the backdrop wasn't the ballroom but the night sky, with a heavy sprinkling of stars across the moonless expanse of the heavens. The music was softer, more distant, and the air smelled sweet without the tinge of cigarette smoke. She glanced to her left and saw the ballroom through the open French doors. She hadn't been aware of dancing out onto the stone terrace. She hadn't felt the roughness under her feet or the slightly cool breeze that skittered in from the distant water until now.

And Carson still held her, the fingers of one hand laced with hers, his other hand resting lightly at her waist. She had been lost in the war raging inside herself, a war she felt precariously close to losing.

Even so, she could walk away. His hold on her was light, yet she found she couldn't move. She stared up at Carson, vaguely aware of the surf pounding somewhere below the cliffs to her right. All she really knew was the closeness of

Carson, shadowed by the softness of the light from lanterns strung along the stone walls of the building. His eyes were hidden by his lenses, and her own reflection was still there, looking up, her lips parted, her eyes wide.

She looked as if she was waiting for something. In that split second she knew that was exactly what she was doing. Waiting. And she understood what she had been waiting for when Carson lowered his head toward her. And she understood that she had been waiting for this kiss since the moment she walked out of the apartment in Houston.

When his lips touched hers, the familiarity of the fire that exploded in her took her breath away. The sense of being gone on a long journey, then finally coming home, stunned her. And the way she moved closer, opening her mouth to him, wanting to draw him inside her, horrified her.

She felt as if she were standing back watching herself make the biggest mistake of her life, yet plunging headlong into an excitement that gave her life, real life. Her body tingled, flared with sensations, and she was alive. Yet she could taste the saltiness of tears deep inside. Oh, God, it hadn't died. It hadn't stopped. Her desire for this man, her need for his touch, was a living, vital thing that a million Boyds couldn't blot out.

Boyd. Cold reality came with that single name. And Jill caught a hold on reality the way a drowning man clutched at a life preserver. This magic, this fire that could come with a single touch wasn't enough. It never had been. It never would be. And with sorrow for what might have been, she pressed her hands flat on his chest and pushed free.

Carson let her go as easily as a petal floats down from a rose. A foot of space separated them, and the balmy night air felt like ice on her exposed skin. She could hear his ragged breathing over the music that drifted through the open doors, an echo of her own attempts to take air into her lungs.

"So, it's not dead," he said, in a rough whisper edged with the same shock she felt.

It hasn't even weakened. She bit her lip hard before she managed to speak a lie. "It's over."

"Is it?"

"Yes," she whispered, hoping it would become the truth if she said it often enough. "Yes."

He turned from her and pressed both hands on a waist-high half wall of stone that framed the back of the terrace as well as protected from the plunge over the cliffs. "Oh, I don't think so."

She clutched the chain of the all-but-forgotten purse still on her shoulder, and she admitted a painful truth. "There...there was never anything wrong with us. Not with..."

"Our making love?" he asked, his gaze on the distant night.

Not love. Never that. "Physically being close," she said.

Slowly Carson took off his glasses. He let them dangle from his thumb and forefinger by the earpiece as he stared out at the night. Just when Jill was beginning to think of running, he turned to her with narrowed eyes and watched her for a long moment before he spoke. "I like you like this."

She didn't understand, or maybe she didn't want to. "Like what?"

"Without my glasses on. You're blurred, soft, gentled. The way you used to be after we had—" he paused and she could see the slight curling of his lips with humor that grated on her frayed nerves "—been physically close. It makes me think that anything can be possible, that life's hard edges and disappointments are temporary. Being myopic has its rewards, Jill."

She shook her head. "Not looking at things clearly is a delusion."

"Reality is that you responded to me just like you used to."

She exhaled harshly, one hand clenched on the purse shoulder chain so tightly that the silver metal was pressing into her palm. "I didn't mean to." That sounded so foolish when the words were said out loud. "I just . . ."

He twirled his glasses by the earpiece between his thumb and forefinger. The lights from the palace caught crazily on the frames and lenses as they went silently round and round. "You wanted what just happened as much as I did."

He couldn't have. She prayed he hadn't. "You arrogant . . . ," she started, but stopped the words, as angry at herself for her lack of control as she was at him for saying the words.

He straightened and took one step, coming within inches of her again. "No, I'm just stating a fact." His voice was low and vibrant in the night. "What I'd like to know, is how you can even consider marrying Boyd when you respond to me like that?"

The intention of slapping his face barely materialized before her free hand shot out, as if by its own accord. But she didn't have the satisfaction of making contact. She didn't even see Carson move before he had her by her wrist, not tightly, but effectively stopping her motion.

For what seemed an eternity, he looked down at her, his fingers an imprisoning bracelet on her arm. Then she found the ability to move and jerked hard on the hold. Freed so abruptly that she almost stumbled backward, she caught her balance and hissed, "There's a big difference between lust and love, Carson."

In the lantern light, she could have sworn a flash of pain crossed his face for one brief moment, but it was gone so quickly she wondered if she'd only imagined it. Maybe she only *wanted* Carson to feel pain, too.

"I don't need you to define words for me, and don't ever try to hit me again," he said ominously as he slowly put his glasses back in place.

She looked up at him, and the damned lenses were hiding his eyes again. "Let's make a deal," she said in a slightly breathless voice. "I won't hit you, if you won't touch me."

"No deal," he said without hesitating.

"What?"

"No deal."

"Why?"

"I never make promises I have no intention of keeping," he said softly.

"Ah, here you are."

Jill jumped at the sound of a man's voice and turned to her left. When she saw Hector Gomez coming toward them she deliberately took a step back from Carson, but that didn't minimize the intensity of his gaze on her.

"I have been looking for you," Gomez said as he got closer. "I am afraid I have some bad news. President Estrada has been taken ill and will not be able to visit with you this evening."

When Carson didn't say a word, Jill spoke up. "I hope it's nothing serious?"

"No. He is just under a great deal of pressure right now. He has great love for this country, and it is very draining to do all he wishes to do for his people."

"I understand, but I'm sorry we won't get to talk with him," Jill said, very aware of Carson coming closer to her.

"President Estrada also regrets that." Gomez motioned behind him to the open doors. "Dinner is ready to be served. Will you come in with me and be seated?"

When Carson finally broke his silence, the words stunned Jill. "Actually, Miss Segar isn't feeling very well, either. That's why we came out here. I think it would be best if we go back to the hotel."

Jill looked at Carson, shocked by the blatant lie, for she had never known him to lie even for expediency. Before she could deny what he said, Gomez moved a step closer and spoke with concern. "You are not well, *señorita*?"

She shook her head. "I don't—" she began, but Carson cut in.

"Maybe it's the water. That can be upsetting." Then he touched her, circling her shoulders as if she were an invalid, and hugged her tightly to his side. Stiffening, Jill stood very still and glared up at him. "I do apologize," he said, "but I think we should leave."

"Of course. Of course," Gomez said quickly. "Is there anything I can do?"

"No," Jill managed as she looked back to Gomez. She thought of claiming a miraculous healing, but kept with Carson's lie. This evening had been ruined from the moment she saw him at the limousine. Going back to the hotel was probably the best thing to do. "Thank you for inviting me, and do thank President Estrada for his kindness."

"I do hope you will come to our country again. You must come back here and visit with President Estrada."

"We should be on our way," Carson murmured and looked down at Jill, his expression one that could have been concern. "I want to get you back where you can lie down."

"I'm feeling *much* better," she said, her jaw tightening until she could feel the muscles aching.

"We don't want to take any chances. We have to fly out in the morning and be ready to work." His fingers tightened on her shoulder, hovering just this side of pain. "Now, you don't want to completely ruin the shooting schedule, do you?"

He had ruined everything, ever since the moment she had run into him on the beach. Him and his control, but she didn't understand why he was doing this. He was talking nonsense, yet seemed intent on making it work. "Thank you for everything, and give our best to President Estrada," she said to Gomez.

"I shall. Now, I shall see that your car is brought around to the entrance." With that he clicked his heels together faintly and bowed low. "A good evening, friends."

Carson didn't let the man get inside before he spoke in a tight voice. "*Now* is the time to leave."

"What's going on? Why did you lie to that man? I'm not sick."

He looked at her long and hard, then released his hold on her shoulders only to capture her hand with his. "Come with me and I'll explain in the car."

Jerking out of his grip before he had a firm hold on her, she walked away from him without a word. By the time she stepped into the room, Carson was beside her, silently going with her through the crowds who were being seated at the tables. They went toward the entry, and Carson was never more than inches from her.

When they went through the long hall and out the entrance, she saw their car idling at the bottom of the steps with a uniformed soldier at the side door. With a silent nod, he opened the door to let Jill and Carson inside, then swung the door shut while they settled in the interior.

Jill moved closer to the far door, making sure there was at least a foot of space between herself and Carson. She waited until the car was on the road back to the city before she turned to the man by her side. She cursed the darkness for hiding his expression.

"All right," she said, "what's going on?"

"You're not feeling well," Carson said in an even voice.

"I'm not feeling well?" she countered.

"That's what I said."

"How in the—"

Unexpectedly he reached across the space that separated them and touched her, his finger shockingly cold on her lips.

"Shh. Take it easy," he said, not reacting when she twisted her head to avoid the touch.

She pressed against the door until she could feel the cool metal trim through the fine material of her dress. But it did little good since Carson moved closer, and leaned toward her until his face was just inches from hers. In a low whisper, as the heat of his breath brushed her skin, he said, "We'll talk at the hotel." He motioned with his head to the driver. "When we are alone."

"Yes, we'll talk," she muttered, and turned to the window in an attempt to distance herself from Carson. Gripping her purse in a death lock, she bit her lip hard and kept silent. At the hotel, she was going to say a lot of things to Carson she should have said a long time ago. Walking out on him in Houston without waiting for him to come back had been a mistake. She wasn't going to walk away again without letting him know exactly how she felt.

After what felt like an eternity of tense silence in the car, the hotel came into view. There was a faint grinding of brakes as the car stopped at the entrance. As Jill got out and went through the glass doors into the lobby with Carson beside her, she didn't say a thing. But when he firmly steered her away from the elevator with a gentle nudge at the small of her back, she stopped and looked at him. "What are you—?"

"My room," he said softly. "It's just down the hall, and we need to talk, now."

It didn't make any difference to her where they spoke, as long as she could put her thoughts into words, so she silently turned to follow him. Carson led the way down a broad side hall to the last door on the right. She watched him slip his room key in the lock, then as he stood back, she brushed past him into heavy shadows.

For a fleeting moment she caught the scent of the man clinging to the room, then she deliberately ignored it and looked at Carson as he went past her into the shadows. He stopped, turned to face her with just a few feet of space separating them, but he made no attempt to turn on a light.

"Finally we can talk without our conversation being a public event," he said.

"That wouldn't bother me," she countered. "You're the one who lied back there, the one who had to control the situation. I don't have a problem with anyone listening to the truth."

"Well, I do," he muttered and reached in her direction. But instead of touching her as she feared he intended, he reached past her and swung the door shut with a muffled thud.

Jill backed up slowly, until she felt the solid coolness of the wood against her back, then slipped her purse off her shoulder and let it dangle, by its chain, from her fingers. "Okay. You have your privacy, now tell me what's going on?"

"The president wasn't sick."

"How do you know that?"

"Did he look sick to you?"

"No, but—"

"But he wasn't sick. And there was no point in us staying there to find out what was happening."

She cocked her head to one side, thankful for the shadows that refused to let her get a clear look at Carson. "So because of your suspicions, you decided we should have come back here. You did what you thought was best."

He exhaled softly. "Exactly."

"Exactly," she repeated in a voice heavy with sarcasm, and she let her purse fall to the floor. Crossing her arms on her breasts, she hugged herself tightly. "That's the way it's always been, hasn't it? You do what you want, how you want, when you want, and you expect everyone else to be pulled along in your wake, because you think you know what's best for everyone.''

''Just a minute. I—''

''No, you wait just a minute.'' She stood straight and the words tumbled out, words that had been inside her for so long she felt branded by them. ''It's always been you, your way, your work, your needs.''

''My needs?'' he demanded.

''Yes, always. You went to a production meeting at seven in the evening, and you stayed plotting strategies with Bob Randall and the others until dawn. You never once thought about what it was costing me. You never called. You never wondered why I wanted you back early. There was never 'us.' Just you. You never could let go of business, of work, of proving yourself, of being what you thought you needed to be. You're filled with it. You're obsessed with it.''

He was ominously silent, so she kept going. ''You never had any room for me, for us, but it took me a while to realize it. And tonight, it's still the same.''

''Why did you want me back at the apartment that night? You never told me, never.''

She bit her lip hard, hysterical laughter painful in her throat. She could still see the champagne, the candles. ''It was my birthday. You knew...'' Knowing it and having it be important to him, were two different things. ''Never mind. That's not important. It was just the final straw.''

''That's why you left.'' A statement, not a question, as if he had finally realized the truth.

''Not just that. Everything. I had to leave. I couldn't stay. I wanted more. Damn it, I deserved more, Carson.''

''I'm sorry about your birthday. I really didn't remember.''

''My birthday isn't the issue. And I know you're sorry.'' Her eyes burned, but no tears came. ''The issue was and still is, I wanted a real life, with a real person, someone who would make a full commitment to that life."

"Someone like Boyd?"

"Yes, someone like him. A man who isn't afraid to give his heart away. A man who doesn't see himself diminished if a business deal doesn't gel or if another station gets one point higher in the ratings. A man who has room for someone else in his life, and a man who wants that person there."

She heard him exhale, the sound a low hiss in the shadows. "You think I'm that self-centered and shallow?"

"I don't know." She'd seen depths to the man that still tore at her when she remembered them. The nightmares, God, they had come from his soul, but were never explained. He'd just reached for her, and she'd been there. "I think you're confused about . . . about priorities."

He didn't move, but she could hear his breathing through the stillness. "I wanted you. I needed you," he whispered.

"You wanted someone to fill a niche. Someone who wouldn't complicate your life. Someone who would be there when you wanted her there, and someone who would disappear without a protest when you didn't want her there."

"That's what you believed?"

"That's what I knew. What I know."

"You don't *know* anything, Jill. You *think* you do, but you're wrong."

"Then tell me why you forced me to leave the president's dinner. Explain that to me. Make me believe it wasn't a whim of yours, some selfish means to an end, or some idea that you know what is best for everyone."

He turned from her, walking across the room to the drape-covered terrace doors, and with one motion he tugged the heavy fabric open. Moonlight sliced into the darkness, making a stark silhouette of Carson in front of the doors. Jill stared at him, at the square shoulders and lean build, the way the moonlight lightened his hair in a halo. She could see him take a deep breath, then he spoke without turning to her.

"This place, that man, Estrada . . ." His voice trailed off. He clicked open the terrace doors, then pushed them back and the sweetness of the night spilled into the room. But it didn't take the edge off the emotions that crackled in the air. Abruptly he turned, the silvery light at his back. "Can't you just trust me that I—?"

"Trust you? We were at a dinner, at a formal gathering, and you chose to lie to Hector Gomez. What does that have to do with trusting you?"

He shrugged, the movement a sharp gesture that shouted impatience, but his voice never got louder. "Sam did what I asked without questions, why can't you?"

"Sam? What did Sam do?" she asked, but before the words were out, she knew. "You made him leave, didn't you? You told him to go with the others and let you use his invitation?"

"He wasn't anxious to attend and I—"

"You what? You said, 'Sam, get on the plane and give me your ticket. I know what's best for you.' Is that what you said?"

Silently, he came back and stopped within a foot of her. "Actually you're right . . . more or less," he said softly.

She felt choked by anger and frustration. This was Carson at his best, wielding power and manipulating people for his own ends. "More or less," she echoed.

"I wanted to be there tonight, and Sam was just as happy to take a hike."

She leaned back against the door and closed her eyes. "Great. And you don't see anything wrong with that, do you? You just snap your fingers, have your way and get what you want."

"What I want?"

She opened her eyes, but stared up at the dark ceiling. "That's the bottom line, isn't it? What *you* want, what *you* need?"

"No, it's never been that cut and dried."

She looked at him. "How can you say that?"

"If I had what I need, what I want . . ." He was very still, then he slipped off his glasses and set them on a table by the door. Unexpectedly, he reached out and cupped her face in the coolness of both his hands.

Jill froze, aware of every spot his skin touched hers. The coolness, yet the heat it caused in her. The gentleness of the contact, yet the complete control Carson had. "Don't," she whispered.

"Yes," he said simply as he lowered his head to hers. His kiss was swift and fierce, an overwhelming onslaught of demand and impatience. It was as if he was taking the breath out of her, denying it to her. He had grasped control firmly, making the world spin, reality slip.

Yet strangely, the anger she felt began to drift just beyond her reach. Frantically she tried to hold to that anger. She needed it to keep her safe, to keep her from plunging back into a world that was populated by only her and Carson. Clamping her teeth tightly shut, she concentrated on staying very still, on not responding outwardly to the internal turmoil this man was causing in her.

But the memory of the kiss on the terrace was still there, haunting her, teasing her with the passion it had ignited. That passion was still there, but Jill had to have control. She wouldn't let herself go like that again.

"Oh, yes," Carson whispered against her lips. "Yes." She trembled as his tongue traced the tight line of her lips. The contact, soft and as light as a feather, made her lips tingle, prodding at her control, edging her toward the point of no return.

Remember the past, she told herself frantically. Her hands balled into fists and she pressed them on Carson's chest. She twisted, trying to get free, but Carson still held her, his hands cupping her face even when he drew back. Opening her eyes, she found Carson so close his image was vaguely blurred.

"You want me," he whispered roughly. "Don't you?"

Wanting was making her heavy and uncomfortable, and she didn't know what to do about it. She couldn't bring anything to mind that would separate them. She couldn't think of why she should run and keep running. So she closed her eyes again, hoping that shutting out the sight of the man would give her much-needed strength.

Then she felt his kiss at the hollow of her cheek, trailing to her closed eyelids. His breath was warm on her skin. His thumbs moving sensuously on her jawline, reality narrowing to every point where Carson made contact with her.

Don't let his taste get inside, her mind screamed, yet perversely her tongue tentatively touched her lips and memories flooded back with the lingering flavor of the man there. She swallowed hard. *Don't move,* she ordered herself, but before the thought was fully formed her body began to sway toward his as if drawn by a powerful magnet. It eased into every well-remembered curve. Each beat of his heart vibrated against her breasts, his hips pressed against hers, and she felt the evidence of his desire.

In one shattering moment of truth, Jill knew she was lost. Even worse, she didn't care. Not anymore. This moment had been inevitable, she just hadn't understood that until now. Being here was all that counted, no matter what the terms. Terms? There were none, no commitments, no promises, no future, just complete surrender.

Tentatively she opened her mouth to his, inviting him to enter, and her arms slowly lifted to circle his neck. With those admissions of surrender, the damn burst. Passion burned white-hot through her, singeing her soul, and she was frantic with her need for the man. She pressed closer, trying to melt into him, to become a part of his being and to never be shut out again.

Chapter 6

When his hands circled her waist, then slid up her back to push under the material of her dress, the contact was like fire to Jill. Then Carson brushed the dress off her shoulders, tugging the soft material until it was down to her waist. Never breaking the contact of the kiss, he found her lace-covered breasts and in an instant the flimsy material was gone and skin touched skin.

Jill hated Carson in that moment—because she couldn't resist him and because she wanted more. Much more.

A whimper changed to a low groan in her throat as his hands cupped her breasts, and the sound vibrated in the stillness. She arched toward his touch, her hatred being edged out by the erotic sensations surging through her that left no room for anything else. She felt the past mingling with the present, and every nerve in her being was alive... again... finally.

His thumbs teased her sensitive nipples, peaking them and sending shock waves down into her belly, starting a throbbing, deep, deep inside her. Her breasts swelled, and the intensity of the experience almost brought tears to her eyes. Then Carson bent low, his lips replacing his hand in the sweet torture, and he drew her into his mouth, his tongue making silky circles around a tingling nipple.

"Yes," she gasped, her head back, her eyes closed, stunned that the feelings could grow to this intensity, yet she didn't explode. Every atom of her existence was centered on this man's touch, on what he could do to her, the feelings he could make her experience.

Then she had to touch him, too. She needed to feel him under her hands, to give pleasure as she was receiving it. She pushed her hands under the heavy material of his tuxedo jacket, then skimmed her hands to his shoulders, pushing the jacket back and down until it fell to the carpet. With unsteady fingers she unfurled the soft velvet tie, then found the buttons on the stiffness of his shirt. With one tug, she popped them, then pushed aside the starched cotton and finally found the heat of his skin under her palms.

She raked her nails across his chest, felt him shudder and his nipples pucker, and she knew she too had power. It wasn't all Carson. She could pleasure him, too. And his moan as her hands circled under the shirt and found the hollow at the small of his back, made her heady with that power.

"Yes," Carson groaned, and in that instant swept her up into his arms.

Through the shadows he carried her to the bed, tumbling onto the bedspread with her, their bodies tangled up with clothes and each other.

Their urgency was almost painful, their patience completely exhausted. Then the clothes were gone, tossed into the shadows until there was nothing between the two of them but silky heat. And tears came for Jill. Pain and joy were so close, truly kindred spirits, and she experienced each with equal intensity as she went to Carson, holding him, tasting him, remembering.

His hands roamed over her with a familiarity that tugged at her heart, finding secret places that only he knew would give her pleasure. And she responded in a way she never had with any other man. Her hands on him stilled and she held her breath as his touch trailed down her belly, closer, so close she ached for completeness.

His hand hesitated, then her legs parted and her whole body arched toward his touch. He gripped her there, released her, then found her again with his fingers.

His lips fastened on her nipple, the combination of invasion and possession overwhelming, and Jill arched frantically to the source. "Yes, yes," she gasped, holding nothing back, thrusting her hips up to his touch.

Then her hands found him, felt his desire for her, and she gasped, a sound of mingled awe and tears. Carson suddenly stopped, balanced over her on one elbow, his body so close, yet not close enough. "Did I hurt you?" he breathed through the shadows.

"No," she gasped, knowing she'd feel pain only if he stopped now.

"I never stopped wanting you," he breathed. "I swear, I never have."

And she knew she had never stopped wanting him. No other man had made her turn her back on everything and give herself freely. And she knew that no man ever could, except Carson. Maybe that was her burden for life, she didn't know. She didn't want to know—not now. All she wanted was to quench this thirst she had been enduring for the past two years.

"Please," she whispered. "Please, love me."

And he came to her. She felt his strength touch her, silky, hot, demanding, and she opened to him. She felt the pressure of him, then the slow, gradual filling of that aching emptiness. It was like coming home, to have been in a foreign land and finally be back where she belonged. In that moment, she felt complete. For one instant, she knew she had found a lost piece of herself.

Then Carson moved and all thoughts were blocked. The rhythmic sliding, slowly at first, then increasing to a frenzy that left them both trembling, made thoughts impossible. Pure sensation took over, driving her, hurtling her, higher, higher, until the world fragmented into shimmering brilliance that literally took her breath away.

Two voices cried out at the same time, words that echoed in the stillness, then the sound was lost in the thundering of her heart and the ragged rhythm of her breathing. Sensations were dissipating, losing intensity, but gaining a mellow completeness. There was touching, reassuring stroking as the world settled, then Jill was next to Carson, curled into his side, his leg heavy and warm across her thighs.

She saturated herself in the blissful lethargy she felt, and she refused to think about anything but what had just happened. She closed her eyes, trailed her finger over the silky heat of his skin and sighed.

"It hasn't changed, has it?" Carson murmured softly.

She twisted to taste the salty heat of his shoulder with her tongue, letting his essence tingle there. She felt as if she were wrapped in a cocoon, his arms around her and his body at her side completing her protection. She began to trace lazy circles on the ridged muscles of his stomach, feeling the soft hair over the smoothness of skin. "Mmm," she breathed. "It's wonderful."

His fingers buried in her tumbled hair, and she felt his lips brush the top of her head. "This is right. You and me. Just the way it always was."

Her hand stilled, and she wished she could block out his words the way she had blocked out reality since he kissed her. "It's different," she managed. It had to be.

He hugged her tightly to him as he chuckled roughly, the sound vibrating against her face. "No, it's not. You finally see we should be like this. Together. You stopped running, and..." he shifted with a sigh, settling with his cheek rested on the top of her head "...you're where you belong. We had to come to this godforsaken country to realize the truth."

She froze, the rosy afterglow of what had happened gone with his words. She felt certain she had tumbled back through time to two years ago. *"You're where you belong. Don't be crazy. Stay with me."* The words echoed through her. *"Be here with me where you should be."* And it was just as devastating as it had been back then. Maybe more so. The magnitude of her mistake made her nauseous, and she had to swallow hard to keep sickness down.

She didn't say a thing as she closed her eyes tightly. Carson stroked her shoulder, then his hand stilled and his breathing became slow and shallow as he fell into a deep sleep.

No mistake in her life had been this clear-cut for her. How could she have done this? How could she have destroyed everything she had worked for? And Boyd...? More sickness rose in her. Boyd. Thankful Carson had fallen asleep, she carefully slid out of bed, paused just long enough to pick up her clothes, then she moved across the room.

By the door, she awkwardly put her clothes on, stopped and picked up her purse where it had fallen earlier. Finally she touched the doorknob. She hesitated, then silently she went back to the bed. She looked down at Carson, his hair tousled, the moonlight casting a gentle glow on the sharp angles of his face. Each breath he took rippled the muscles in his chest, and his hands lay at his sides, open, flat on the linen.

Her heart lurched. She knew why she had let herself be with him. She loved him. God help her, it hadn't stopped. But it was just as futile a love as it had always been. He wasn't different. But she was. And she knew it. That's what made it hurt so much. Ignorance was bliss, and she wasn't ignorant.

Brushing at her burning eyes, she clutched her purse to her aching stomach and silently left his room. Numbly she went up two floors to her room, stepped inside and had barely closed the door behind her when sickness came with a vengeance.

Drifting up out of a dreamless sleep Carson remembered immediately what had happened, and he reached out for Jill. The spot where she had lain with him in the tangle of sheets and bedspread was cold and empty. For a heart-stopping instant he wondered if he had only dreamed last night, if it had all been wishful thinking.

Then he inhaled and caught the clinging scent of her perfume in the pillows, and knew the satiation in his body hadn't come from a dream. He pushed himself up to his elbows, squinted at the grayish light, a foggy haziness that spilled in through the open doors, and called out, "Jill?"

When there was no answer he pushed up farther, then raked his fingers through his hair. Just the memory of last night made his body tighten, and he looked at the bathroom door. It was partially open, but he couldn't hear anything inside. Getting out of bed, he crossed the soft carpet and pushed back the door. The bathroom was empty. One look and he knew Jill had never been in there.

Suddenly he remembered the apartment in Houston, walking in at dawn, calling out to her and finding emptiness. It made his heart skip painfully in his chest. He couldn't endure that loss again. He had barely survived the first time. Quickly he crossed to get his glasses, put them on, and hurried to the dresser to get fresh clothes.

She had gone to check on reservations. Or she'd gone down to get some breakfast. Or she had gone to her room to pack. Easy answers. Logical explanations.

He stepped into slacks, then pulled on a white shirt and rolled up the sleeves over his forearms. He bent to reach for his loafers, but a knock on the door stopped him.

Jill. Relief made him slightly giddy. She had come back, and he knew in that instant how afraid he'd been she would never come back. The foolishness he had felt for his impulsive flight down here returned as he hurried over and reached for the doorknob. He took a steadying breath and pulled the door open.

"I was beginning to..." he started, but his voice trailed off when he saw two men standing in front of him. The men, one short and heavy, the other taller and no more than a teenager, were dressed oddly. Jeans were worn with dark brown shirts, peaked hats and heavy boots. Arm bands fashioned from what looked like scraps of white material showed a single red circle. For a second, Carson thought they were playing a game, some sort of costume thing, until he saw the guns strapped to their sides. The guns looked very real.

"Carson Davies?" the shorter one asked in heavily accented English as he glanced at a rumpled piece of paper he held.

Carson nodded. "Yes."

"We regret that there is a slight problem."

All he thought of was Jill. That something had happened to her. "What is it?"

"There has been a..." In heavily accented English, he stumbled over the words, then read them directly from the paper he held. "There has been an internal readjustment in the government." He looked up at Carson, his eyes wide and unblinking. "At four o'clock this morning, the people of San Arman reclaimed their country from the hands of a traitor.''

An older fear, an all-encompassing fear that had been relegated to his dreams, until these past few days, surged through Carson.

"There is a problem," the soldier had said five years ago. *"Javier Estrada, has claimed the land of San Arman for the People's Republic Army."*

Carson closed his eyes for a fleeting moment, trying to banish the past and concentrate on the present. "What are you talking about?" he asked, holding to the knob so tightly it was becoming painful.

"There is no reason for worry. The Brothers of Liberty are in charge, and we are contacting all visitors to explain what is happening."

"We need to contact all visitors, to make sure everyone understands what is happening."

Carson touched his tongue to his cold lips. "President Estrada . . . ?"

"Both the traitor Estrada and the People's Republic are no more. The real people of San Arman, the Brothers of Liberty, have their land back. A military panel is taking over until there is time to form a full government."

"Our new president, Javier Estrada, has taken control and he will make this a better country."

The speech last night, the sudden illness, the rumors. Sourness touched his tongue, as the staggering horror of reliving the past engulfed him. He had the fleeting idea of slamming the door and barricading it, but reason told him that would do no good. So he tried to maintain some semblance of calm, at least outwardly. "What . . . what do you want from me?"

The short man held out his hand. "Your papers. We need to verify them, then make arrangements for you to leave on the first available flight to your country."

*"We will take care of you, of all the visitors who are here.
We will make sure you get back to your country, but first
you have to come with us—so we can get all the information we need."*

He braced himself, knowing he could never walk into the
lion's den like that again. He wouldn't innocently go with
them, be taken into a room, then transferred to the prison.
He'd rather die than do that again. He took a step back.
"My papers?"

"Si. Your passport, so the panel can verify it. Then you
will be free to leave."

*"Tell us what you are here for, Señor Davies. Tell us who
you work for, how you are involved with the CIA. Everyone knows you American journalists are a front for the
CIA, but if you are truthful with us we will be lenient."*

Carson turned from the men, going to his case on the
dresser to take out his passport. He held the stiff folder for
a moment, staring at the American emblem on the front,
then he closed his eyes tightly. When he opened them, he
made himself turn back to the soldiers. He was unnerved to
see they had followed him into the room and weren't more
than five feet from him.

"Is this what you want?" he asked, holding out the book,
immeasurably relieved to see his hand was reasonably
steady.

The man took it, glanced at it, then nodded. *"Si,* this will
do for now." He handed the passport to the man behind
him, then looked at the piece of paper in his other hand.
Carson glanced at it. Reading quickly upside down, he saw
the sentence the man had read to him, then a list of names
in block printing. Near the top he saw Carson Davies—
American. Just a little farther down the page he saw Jillian
Segar—American.

"Gracias, señor," the man said, then turned to walk to
the door. There were no guns, no threats, and no "re-

quest" for him to accompany them. But the soldier stopped at the door and turned, pinning Carson with his unblinking stare. "Señor Davies. For your own protection, it would be best for you to stay in your room until we come back again. A few hours. That is all, then this will be all over. The Brothers of Liberty will have everything under control."

Carson nodded without speaking, willing them to go out into the hall. And when they did leave and the door closed behind them, Carson finally drew some air into his tight lungs.

Not again. Not again. He ran a hand roughly over his face, trying to think. Jill. He spun around and in one stride was at the bed reaching for the telephone. He held the cold receiver to his ear and dialed the number for her room. After one ring, a woman came on and spoke in heavily accented English.

"Operator."

"Connect me with room 315, please."

"I am sorry, but our hotel telephone lines are not working right now. Perhaps you wish to try later?"

He took off his glasses and tossed them on the bed, then pressed an unsteady hand to his eyes. "Connect me with the long-distance operator."

"I am sorry, sir, but all overseas lines are full right now. Perhaps you can try later?"

Without another word, Carson hung up. Sinking down on the bed, he rested his head in his hands. He tried to think, to figure out what to do. But all he knew was that he had to get to Jill, then get the two of them out of San Arman. Waiting for the soldiers to come back wasn't even an option.

He knew without a shadow of a doubt that when the two men returned, when they knew that both he and Jill were with the press, there wouldn't be any trip out of the country.

Grabbing his glasses, he slipped them on, then stood and crossed to his case again. Get out. Get out. The two words ran through his mind like a protective chant. Quickly he took out his traveler's checks and all the cash he had with him. Then he grabbed his large suitcase, put it on the bed and opened it.

Slacks, dress shirts and suits. Not a thing that would go unnoticed in a crowd around here. He reached into a small nylon case in a side pocket and took out his well-used running shoes. Scuffed and worn-looking, they didn't look like they had cost much money. Those would do, he thought, and tossed them on the bed.

Finally he picked up a blue dress shirt, looked at it long and hard, then knew what he needed to do. In less than two minutes, he had both sleeves torn out of the shirt and he'd changed clothes. He wore the shirt untucked with the navy slacks and the running shoes without socks. Carson looked in the mirror, then frowned. He had "American" written all over him.

It was the best he could do for now, he decided, and reached for his money, pushing it into the pocket of his slacks. With one last look around he hurried to the door, knowing there was nothing here of importance to take with him. Then he opened the door and looked out into the hall.

A scruffy-looking man with a rifle resting against the wall by his side had been stationed where the hall entered the lobby. Another man stood by the elevators, his rifle hanging from a strap on his shoulder.

As quietly as possible Carson moved back inside and closed the door, then leaned his forehead against the wood. He had to get to Jill, but how? Then he turned and saw the open doors to the terrace. Jill was only two floors up, but near the other end of the hotel. If he was lucky, this was one of the buildings that had outside stairs that went to the upper floors.

He crossed to the doors and stepped out onto the stone terrace. His attention was drawn to the east. What he had thought was fog earlier, appeared to be clouds from smoke, gray at the top and almost black where they touched the coastline.

Five years ago there had been no warning, but this time he'd known. He really had, yet he'd ignored all of his instincts. He went to the railing and looked down the cliffs the hotel was built on, to the beach below. Not a soul was on the sand. He hurried to the corner of the terrace and in one easy movement he jumped over the rail and landed with a soft thud on the thick grass that grew along the side of the hotel. Not more than ten feet from the corner he spotted the outside stairs, wooden, solid and servicing each of the six floors with accesses through arched doors at each landing.

He could see people near the front of the hotel grounds and jeeps driving down the streets with soldiers standing on the seats, guns in their hands. Voices were raised over the sound of motors, shouting orders. In the distance he heard a vibrating rumble he couldn't place, and the billowing clouds of smoke were drifting toward the hotel.

He moved along the wall, staying close, making his way behind clumps of banana trees and bird-of-paradise plants, scraping his back on the rough stucco. As he neared the stairs, voices sounded closer—along with muffled pops that could have been motors backfiring, but he knew they weren't. The skin at the back of his neck tingled. He knew they were gunshots. This wasn't any more a peaceful takeover than Estrada's had been five years ago.

He reached out, gripped the smooth wooden handrail, made sure no one was looking, then ran up the flight of stairs, taking them two at a time. Praying that they were not organized enough to think of stationing soldiers on each floor, he eased open the arched door to the third floor and looked inside.

At least one thing was going right today. The hallway was completely empty. Quickly, he stepped inside and ran silently on the carpet runner down to room 315. He rapped softly, once, twice, but when Jill didn't answer he tried the doorknob. It turned easily, clicking open, and the door swung back.

As he looked inside, he felt his heart lurch into his throat. No one was in the room, but he could tell the soldiers had already stopped there. The bed was torn apart, with the sheets and bedspread in a tumble on the beige carpet. Three pieces of luggage were sitting open on the bed with the contents piled in the middle.

Breathing became so painful for Carson that he had to press a hand to his breastbone. ''Jill?'' he called softly, in hope she was there somewhere. ''Jill?'' But only silence came back to him.

Why would they have taken her and not him? Had they recognized her from the location shooting, or had someone pointed her out? Then he thought rationally. They wouldn't have had to look for her papers if Jill had been here. No, she hadn't been here when they came.

Moving quickly, he crossed to the bed and looked down at her suitcases. He inhaled and caught the scent of Jill clinging to the clothes. With an unsteady hand he touched a pale blue nightgown, and he remembered the night just past. It seemed like a hundred years ago. It had no part in this horror, except for intensifying his urgency to find her and protect her.

Drawing back, he hesitated, then pushed aside the gauzy material and felt in the side pockets of the suitcases just in case she had kept some money there. But they were empty. He stood up and looked around the room. He had to find her before she was found by some of the overzealous soldiers. But where would she be? Why wasn't she in her room?

Then he knew where Jill was. She had actually told him yesterday where she would have run to when she wanted to be completely alone and think. He looked back at her clothes, picked through them until he found what he needed, then headed for the door.

Jill dug her heels into the warm sands and leaned back against the rough granite of the sheer cliffs. She narrowed her eyes behind the dark glasses and stared blindly out at the ocean, the gentle sounds of the small cove soothing to her frayed nerves.

She had been here since just before dawn, sitting, watching, thinking and crying. Now the tears were all gone and an emptiness filled her. She knew what she had to do. There was no life for her with Carson, there never had been. But last night with him had ended any life she had thought she could have had with Boyd.

She couldn't go back to Boyd. She couldn't tell him what had happened and try to make their relationship work— even if he might still want to try. There was nothing there. There never had been more than a comfortable friendship. It had been so appealing after her emotional roller coaster with Carson. But it wasn't enough to fall in love and make a life together.

She couldn't go through a life with Boyd, always remembering the way it had been with Carson—remembering and comparing, and always finding her relationship with Boyd wanting.

She pressed her forehead to her bent knees. Carson had made it impossible for her to be with someone else, yet he made it equally impossible for her to be with him. She wished she could hate him. But she knew it was all her doing. All she had had to do was say no, to walk away, and she hadn't.

She chuckled without any humor. She had literally fallen into his arms and asked him to make love to her. *Pitiful,* she thought, trying to push away the surge of memories and the accompanying physical need for the man that came with them.

"Lust, damn it," she muttered through clenched teeth. "Lust, not love." But even as the words were uttered, she knew the magnitude of the lie. She really did love Carson, uniquely and passionately.

That admission brought a pain to her that almost made her double over. Why? Why him? Why couldn't the need and desire die as time went by? Why couldn't she look at another man and want him with a single-mindedness that blotted out reason? Why couldn't she—?

"Jill!"

She jerked at the sound of her name and looked to her left. Hallucinations were part and parcel of her delusion with the man. She could have sworn Carson was coming toward her down the beach, the sun catching at the gold in his hair, his long legs eating up the distance that separated them.

When he called out to her again, she knew this was no delusion, that he had found her. And she knew she wasn't ready for this confrontation. Swallowing hard, she got to her feet and brushed at the clinging sand on her bare legs and on the cotton of her blue shorts. Then as she heard Carson coming closer and closer, she made herself look up.

"Oh, God, I'm so glad I found you," he gasped as he came to her and pulled her into a suffocating hug.

She stood very still, fighting against the urge to stay in his hold forever and the equally intense need to be free, to never touch him again.

When his hold on her eased, she moved back and his arms fell from her. It was only then she became aware of his labored breathing and the flush to his skin. She stared at him not more than a foot away from her, at the way his hair clung damply to his temples, the beads of sweat on his upper lip.

The walk that had taken her an hour had taken him no more than minutes. Jogging was a passion with him, and she was vaguely surprised that he appeared to be out of breath. He reached out for the cliff on his right and pressed one hand flat on the rough surface. "I've been in every damned cove between here and the hotel looking for you."

"You should have given up," she managed.

The brilliance of the image of the man in front of her was physically painful for Jill. She didn't need to remember last night to feel the pain. The sight of Carson inflicted pain. Every angle, every plane was etched so clearly in her mind that she could almost feel his strength under her hands. She wrapped her arms around herself and held on tightly.

"I wasn't about to give up," he said, either not understanding or choosing not to understand.

Confrontations had never been her strong suit. That was why she had walked out of the apartment in Houston when Carson hadn't been there. But she knew this time she had to look him in the eye and explain. She took a deep breath, but instead of the considered words she had rehearsed alone in the cove she found herself blurting out, "Last night was a mistake."

He looked totally confused for a second, then she could see his face tighten. "What?"

"A mistake. Wrong. Stupid," she said, bracing herself for an attack.

But none came. Carson simply stared at her, his face touched by a bleakness that made her throat constrict. "Last night," he echoed, then leaned forward, bracing his hands on his knees, and his head hung down. "Whew. Back to square one. This *is* a morning for shocks." He exhaled harshly and shook his head from side to side. "No, I should have seen them both coming. My fault. My fault," he muttered as he straightened up.

Jill had expected anger, or maybe that cool, analytical approach that Carson had become famous for, but she didn't expect the deeply etched tension at his mouth. She almost looked away when he took off his dark glasses and covered his eyes with one hand.

When he looked up at her without the protection of the lenses between them, she had to swallow hard to try and ease the lump in her throat. She wished she could turn and run and never stop. But she couldn't, not this time.

"I'm sorry," she said, hating the unsteadiness in her voice. "I'm really sorry things got so out of hand."

He put on his glasses, then raked his fingers through his damp hair. "That's my department, being sorry. And it's up to me to tell you something, and I don't know where to begin."

"No, you don't have to." She moved back half a pace, hoping a bit more distance as a buffer between them would make this easier. "It's over. I—"

"No," he cut in abruptly. "It's just begun."

Chapter 7

Jill shook her head sharply. "No, it hasn't."

Carson effectively erased the buffer of space between them with one half stride. "Jill, listen to me. We'll talk about this later when I can make some sense of it, but now I need to—"

She wouldn't let him put it off. "This won't wait. This isn't something you can schedule a talk for." She hugged herself more tightly. "You . . . you're—"

"I'm scared spitless."

She stared up at him. *Don't be in pain, don't be vulnerable.* She couldn't handle that, at all. She turned from him and stared blindly out at the deep turquoise of the Caribbean. "This isn't easy, I know, but—"

"You were in your hotel room?" he asked abruptly.

"I went there, but left a while ago."

"How long ago?"

"I've been down here since just before the sun came up."

"You've been down here all that time?"

"Yes."

"Good."

She slanted him a sideways glance and found him staring at her intently. "Why?" she asked.

"You had visitors a while ago—soldiers."

"What are you talking about?"

He touched her on the shoulder, but the contact was too much for her and she jerked away. She turned to face him with her back to the cliffs. "*Don't*. Don't ever touch me again."

He stood his ground, but drew his hands back and held them up palms out. "All right, all right," he said, "just listen to what I'm saying and believe me."

"Listen to what?"

"There's been a coup, a takeover of the government."

He wasn't making any sense. "Where?"

"Here, damn it! San Arman. President Estrada is no more. He's gone. Out. The 'people,' whoever they are this time, have taken control of the government. It's martial law, pure and simple. And since we're with the media, we're going to pay." He motioned back over his shoulder. "Look at that sky. It's smoke. The whole damn city is probably burning to the ground."

She could see the haze, the spirals of gray. She had been so engrossed in her thoughts she hadn't noticed it until now. But the grayness was beginning to climb into the sky, inching closer to blotting out the sun. "It looks like fires, but—"

"It's a purge. I didn't know a thing until soldiers came to my room, took my passport and told me to stay there until they came back . . . to take me to the airport and out of the country."

She stared at the clouds beginning to make an eerie halo around the sun. "President Estrada . . . ?"

"Gone. Maybe dead, maybe in exile, or maybe he took off last night before it all happened. Maybe that was his illness at the dinner."

She slowly sank down until she was sitting on the warm sand with her back against the cliff. Carson stayed standing over her. "But I didn't hear anything, Carson, or see anything. How could they do all that?"

"As easily as the sun coming up," he muttered.

When she looked up at him the sky was taking on an eerie pink glow, as the sun filtered through the spreading smoke. She had to ask, "Are you sure?"

"That's why I'm here. We have to get out of San Arman any way we can."

She shook her head. "But you said the soldiers told you they would take you to the airport. We just have to go back, and—"

"No, we don't go back. We can't."

She scrambled to her feet, grasping at the only logical solution she could think of. "We have to. We go back, we talk to whoever is in charge and get on a flight out to Colombia or any place the planes are going. My passport's in my room. I can..." Her voice trailed off when Carson shook his head. "What?"

"They took your passport and your money. There wasn't a cent there when I looked."

"There was five hundred dollars," she murmured, "with my passport."

"If we go back, the soldiers will come to the hotel again. But they won't take us to the airport, because they'll know who we are. We'll be driven to whatever they call headquarters and we'll be interrogated. Then we'll be detained."

She couldn't believe this was happening, not here, not now, not to the two of them. "Carson, this sounds like the script of a bad movie."

"It's not a movie. It's life. It's real. It's what we have to face."

She saw the tension in his jaw, the harsh set of his mouth. What shocked her was the unsteadiness in his hand when he raked his fingers through his hair. He really was upset, or maybe he was just overreacting. She hated a growing need in her to reach out to him, to try and put the world right for both of them. No, what she needed to do was move, to do something constructive, like going to the American consulate. "I . . . I'm going back. There has to be some—"

As she went to walk around Carson, his hand shot out, and his fingers clamped painfully over her upper arm. "You're not going anywhere, except with me," he ground out.

Jill twisted, but she found no freedom this time. His hold never eased on her, at all. "Let me go, Carson."

"You'll stay with me until I figure out what to do," he bit out.

She looked up at him, and she knew better than to fight him. Instead she stood very still. "Why are you doing this? You don't know what's going to happen. We could walk back to the hotel and be escorted to the airport. Or we could call—"

His fingers tightened for an instant before letting her go. "I know what I'm talking about." He paused, then said, "I was here five years ago."

"I know. You told me you've been here. That was part of the reason you didn't want to bring the program down here."

"Prophetic, wasn't I?" he muttered.

"You were just flexing your muscles of power as station manager. You didn't know this could happen. No one could."

"Maybe I was emphasizing my control at the station," he admitted. "But I *knew* this could happen. Five years ago, when I was with the Chicago station, we had a correspondent down here. He was in the middle of a feature when he got really ill. Some fever he picked up in the higher jungle. To make a long story short, I came down for a few days to finish his assignment so we wouldn't lose the whole thing and be out the time and money.

"He flew back, I stayed, and the next day Estrada staged a coup, a bloody revolution, and took over the country."

"But, you . . . ?"

He looked away from her, staring down at his running shoes pressing into the sand. "In twelve hours the country was turned upside down." He looked up at her, his jaw working with tension. "They came for me, told me I just had to answer a few questions. All I had to do was tell them what I was doing for the CIA."

"The CIA?"

He smiled, but the expression did little more than curl the corners of his mouth. "That's me, a big-time spy."

"When you told them the truth, they let you go, didn't they?"

He shrugged sharply. "Sure. Over three months later."

She was at a loss. Carson had never hinted at anything like this when she had known him, and she felt as if she had never known the real Carson. "You were in jail here?"

"In the prison outside the city. A rat-infested hole in the ground." His hands clenched into fists at his sides. "I was literally kept in the dark for days on end, then taken out to be interrogated. I was in a seven-by-ten-foot cell with another man, at least for a while. The other man kept saying it was a mistake, that he just had to wait until his friends reached the right person with enough money.

"And he was right. One day they came for him and let him go. He said he'd try to see what he could do for me, but it took another two months before I was out. One of the guards told me Martine, the man with me, was a neutral and they had been too quick to pick him up." He took a deep breath. "But anyone with money was suspect, the way anyone with the news was suspect."

Jill sank back against the wall, suddenly understanding the nights when Carson would wake in a cold sweat and be unable to sleep again. The nights he would flip on the side light and not turn it off until dawn. "The nightmares you had, those—?"

"A residual effect," he muttered, waving them aside with a motion of his hand.

And he had never told her. Just one more way he had shut her out of his life. "You could have told me. You should have."

"That was all the past, until now. There wasn't any point in telling you."

"No, I guess there wasn't." She moved away from him, walking to the water's edge. "Carson?"

"Yes?" he said from somewhere behind her.

"How *did* you get out?"

"The network negotiated quietly and finally got me out after they promised no reprisals, no publicity. They kept their word, and Estrada's people put me on a plane to Chicago."

"Who knows all this?"

"James."

"And?"

"Only James and the people immediately involved in the negotiations and my release."

She bit her lip hard, then turned. "What now?"

"We can't go back. We can't let ourselves be taken in for questioning." He came closer. "I won't go through that again."

If the terror of that first time had been damaging to him, it would be deadly one more time. "No, you can't," she said.

Killing the urge to touch him, to try to reassure him somehow, she pushed her hands into the pockets of her shorts. "What can we do?"

"Without our passports we can't leave the country in the conventional ways, that's for sure."

She began to understand their position, and it seemed insurmountable. How could one get out of a foreign country without flying or leaving at a main port? "Then how?"

Carson motioned her back into the protection of the overhang of the cliff. "We can try to get to the American consulate."

She shrugged and tried to laugh, but the effort failed miserably. "That's what they do in the movies, isn't it?"

"They do, if they're smart enough." Carson shrugged. "If we can get there and get inside, we're on American soil."

"Then that's what we'll do." She frowned at him. "How do we find it?"

"I saw it on the way from the airport. It's on the corner of the main road, Via Camino, and Calle Medusa. A big pink stone building behind a brick wall."

"If we can get there..." She shivered despite the growing heat. "We're Americans. They can't just..."

He reached for her, gently putting his arms around her shoulders and drawing her to his side. The contact felt extremely reassuring, and she leaned against him, letting him support her for a moment.

"I'm afraid they can do anything they want to do, love. But it's up to us to make sure they don't get the chance. We sink or swim, but we do it together."

"It *is* like a bad 'B' movie, isn't it?"

"Yes, but I'm afraid it's real, very real."

"All right," she said, reluctantly moving back enough to look up at Carson. "Tell me what to do."

He smiled suddenly, an endearingly gentle expression. "Now that has possibilities," he murmured.

Her heart lurched, and in self-protection she moved farther from him. "I meant—"

"I know what you meant," he said, and when she looked back at him he was deadly serious. "We have to move right now. The more time we let go by, the more time they have to shut down the whole country."

"How can we go anywhere in the open?"

He looked at her. "With luck you could pass as a local, with your dark hair and tan . . . as long as you didn't look right at one of them or have to speak. But me, now that's another matter."

For the first time she really noticed what he was wearing. The blue shirt looked as if the sleeves had been ripped out of it, the slacks were crumpled and his running shoes well-worn. "Where did you—?"

"I improvised." He lifted the front of his shirt and took a small bundle from his waistband. He held it out to Jill. "Here. I looked through your things, and these were the closest I could get to ordinary clothes."

She took the rolled up clothes and shook them out—a pair of cutoff jeans that she had forgotten about bringing and a loose-fitting black blouse with short sleeves and a simple V neck. She looked at Carson. "You thought of everything, didn't you?"

"I didn't find any shoes that would do." He glanced down at her sandals. "They'll pass."

She held the clothes in her hands. It seemed silly that after what had happened between them she felt embarrassed to change in front of Carson. She didn't know if he sensed her uneasiness or not, but he surprised her by saying, "Get changed while I look around to find the best way to the top of the cliffs."

"Sure," she said, then he turned and jogged off farther to the west. When he disappeared around a curve, she quickly changed into the clothes he had brought. By the time he showed up again, she was ready to go.

He came up to her and stopped. "There are steps farther down the beach, a steep climb, but direct. There's some sort of parade of military equipment, with lots of people following it. Some look like celebrants, some look like refugees. With any luck we can blend in with the crowd."

He looked up at a sky that was getting more spooky with each passing minute. The rosy haze was deepening to a violet, blending to magenta. And the sun looked as if it was shining through a smeared filter. "If we can get into the city, there are lots of alleys and back streets, and with these fires the focus should be on the losses." He took a deep breath and held out his hand to Jill. "Let's go."

She looked at Carson, then willingly put her hand in his. "Let's," she whispered. "And God help us."

An hour later Carson realized that finding the rough granite stairs cut into the cliffs and getting to the top was the easy part. Blending in with the natives was something else again. When they stepped onto the sea-grass-covered ground, they found a world gone crazy.

San Arman five years ago and San Arman today blended with horrifying ease for Carson. The road at the top of the cliffs running parallel to the shoreline was full of tanks and trucks with insignias crudely blotted out by black paint on the olive-drab doors, and the new symbol—the red circle—was splashed on the front of the hoods and the side doors. Ragtag soldiers, oddly dressed in anything from jeans to dress slacks, rode in the vehicles or walked beside them on the blacktopped road. The two things they all had in common were the guns held at the ready and the arm bands with red circles on them.

San Armanians lined the roadside, some cheering, some raising their hands in fists into the air, some solemnly watching the procession, their faces unreadable. The sky was growing darker all the time, and the sun was blood-red as it shone through thick smoke that haloed overhead. The world looked as if it had been drenched in sepia and rose tones.

Surrealistic, muted, yet horrifying. And very real, Carson thought with a chill. Just like Estrada's march, only the symbols had changed from blue bands to red dots on white. Strangely, as he viewed the turmoil in front of him, he regretted the lack of cameras to record the scene, a record that the rest of the world could view.

He held to Jill and stayed by a group of standing palms not more than twenty feet from the road. "We'll have to mingle and get in with the crowds," he said in a low voice as he bent close to her. "Thank goodness some of the locals have light hair. But we have to look worn, more disheveled." He motioned with his head to the crowds. "Just like them."

Jill glanced at the milling crowds and the steady stream of trucks, then turned wide lavender eyes on him. "You're right. But how?" she asked simply, and he felt overwhelmed by his need to make sure she wasn't hurt in any way. No wonder his years as a foreign correspondent had been years he'd been alone, by choice. He had never had to worry about any other person, not even when he was in the prisons here.

Instead of doing what he craved, holding her to him, he stooped to the ground and dug at the damp grass until he came to dark soil. Picking up a handful of it, he rubbed his hands together, then skimmed them over his slacks as he stood. With just a glance at the nearby people, he lifted his hands to his face and felt the grit smear across his jaw.

"Sorry," he murmured to Jill, as he reached out and cupped her face in his filthy hands. Gently he stroked her cheeks, touched the end of her nose, then the tip of her chin, leaving a dirty smear with each contact.

She stood very still under his touch, her eyes never leaving his. When he drew back, she bent over, pressed her hands into the dirt where he had dug and stood straight. With a solemn expression, she touched her hands to his shirt and dragged them down the front of it to his stomach. "We're even," she whispered.

He glanced at the soiled front of the blue shirt, then back to Jill. "Good work." He reached for her hand, the grit still clinging there. "Let's mingle."

Without a word, he walked toward the road and into the middle of the crowds. Being surrounded by screaming, surging people made Carson feel claustrophobic, but he held his ground and began to move forward with them after the tanks and trucks. He only allowed himself a few glances at Jill as they walked, but he never let go of her hand. He needed that connection, as much to protect her as to reassure himself.

He was jostled sharply by two men who pressed past to be nearer the tanks, but he kept walking, adjusting his pace to the rest of the people. And Jill stayed close to his side. She never once tried to take her hand out of his. He was struck by how trusting she was right then. It was almost the way it had been last night, her giving herself to him freely.

That brought his thoughts up short. After what she had said on the beach, he had no idea what she felt—or what there was for them. And Boyd was a heavy shadow over everything. Old pains and new pains mingled, but Carson tried to ignore them. Later, when they survived, if they survived, he could deal with everything, even Boyd.

Gradually, Carson and Jill moved back in the crowds until they were on the tail end of the procession as they passed the hotel, then went farther into the city. Here the smoke was thicker, the sounds of gunfire nearer and the people more aggressively pushing for places on the street.

Carson watched, and as they came abreast of a small alley framed by houses on either side, he sidestepped toward it and tugged Jill with him. In three strides, he was in the narrow passage and out of the crowds. He looked ahead at garbage and boxes littering the way, then exhaled and turned to Jill. "All right. We made it."

"It's so hot, and it smells."

The mingled odors of garbage and the burning city were an assault to his senses. "Wood smoke is pleasant, but heaven knows what's being burned here. The whole city could go up in flames."

She glanced at the opening, as some people went past yelling and shouting. When they had gone off down the street, she turned to him and took her hand from his to brush at her hair. "How do we find the American consulate?"

He hated the loss of contact. "I know the general layout of the city and I know the consulate is facing the central park area. We're south of it, so we just have to go due north to hit the main street, then west a few blocks."

"How do you know all that?"

He wouldn't admit that he knew where every American consulate was in every foreign country he'd visited these past years. He automatically took in details, remembered streets and directions. "I remember the layout," he hedged.

Old habits never died for him, that need for reassurance he looked for when he was out of the States. He took in Jill's flushed face, with the dirt smears and the palpable fear in her eyes. She was one old habit he didn't want to ever go away. He just hoped he'd have the time later to convince her of that.

He turned from her, motioning for her to follow as he started walking down the alleyway. "Let's go."

Jill followed him, regretting the fact he didn't hold out his hand to her again. So she stayed close, never taking her eyes off his back. She had never felt alien in a foreign country, not until now, and she found herself praying that the American consulate would know exactly what to do to get them out of here.

When Carson stopped, Jill almost ran into him, then steadied herself with both hands flat on his back and looked around his shoulder. They were at the end of the alley, and the street beyond was filled with screaming and the sound of heavy motors rumbling past.

Carson bent down, picked up something, then turned to Jill. He held up a beat-up straw hat with a huge floppy brim. "A bit more disguise wouldn't hurt," he said as he put it on and tugged it low over his face.

It shielded his eyes and most of his face, and it had the instant effect of making Jill feel alienated, of being completely alone and cut off. But she shook off the notion and asked, "Is it safe for us to go out there?"

"As safe as any place in Puerto Luis is now, except the American consulate," Carson said. "Just stay right beside me, keep your eyes on the ground and don't stop moving unless I tell you to. I hope everyone is too involved in his own personal survival out there to look right at us. If we don't draw attention and stay out of the way of the over-zealous soldiers, we'll make it."

"What if someone talks to us? I was scared to death someone would in that walk here."

"I understand Spanish. If I squeeze your hand once, say '*Si*' and if I squeeze it twice, say '*No*.' If I keep up steady pressure, look at me and pretend to be faint. Trust me." He hesitated, then touched her face with the tips of his fingers, the contact riveting for her. "I promise. I'll get you out of this mess, love."

Jill knew, despite everything, she did trust Carson. He meant what he said, he always had. He just hadn't always meant what she thought he said. His definitions were vastly different from hers. But this time they both knew the stakes. Survival. She covered his hand with hers, curling her fingers around his familiar warmth. Instead of saying something foolish, like, "Don't ever leave me, not until we're out of this thing," she settled for, "We had better get going."

He nodded, drawing her hand down with his to his side. "Now," he whispered and started off.

Jill felt her heart lurch when they broke free of the alley and onto the street. But she knew Carson had been right. The sight in front of her here was one of destruction—rubble, small fires smoldering in the blackened shells of what had once been homes. Smoke haloed everything, dark and gritty, raising in plumes upward.

And people were totally involved in their own survival. These people were not cheering for the incoming soldiers of the Brothers of Liberty, or following a makeshift parade. These people were trying to hold together, to make it through until some semblance of peace was given to them.

Jill pressed close to Carson's side, taking an occasional double skip to keep up with his pace. They made their way down the narrow street without eliciting so much as a sideways glance from any of the locals. They sidestepped debris, gave loose animals a wide berth, kept their heads down and made eye contact with no one. At the end of the street, Carson tugged Jill to the right into another alley littered with garbage, but where the air was a bit clearer. The block-long alley was empty, but the sounds from the other areas came in and echoed off the broken brick walls and tilted roofs.

By the time they came to a broad boulevard, Jill was damp with perspiration and vaguely out of breath from hurrying. But Carson never broke stride. He turned left onto the street, keeping himself between Jill and the road, staying as close as possible to the buildings.

Fires had reduced some buildings to black skeletons that still smoldered, belching out incredibly dense smoke that spiraled up to darken the sky. Cars, jeeps and a scattering of tanks rumbled up and down the four-lane thoroughfare. Screams and shouts from the milling people on the sidewalk and in the street waving white scraps with the red circle filled the air, mingling unpleasantly with the sound of unmuffled engines and popping fireworks in the distance. No, not fireworks, but gunfire, Jill realized.

A siren cut through the commotion, then an ambulance careened through the traffic and people jumped out of the way to keep from being hit. With everything going on, no one paid any attention to Jill and Carson. They went down the street, jostled sharply by a huge group of people going the opposite direction chanting in unison, words Jill couldn't understand at all.

When rapid rounds of gunfire echoed off down the street, Jill held more tightly to Carson's hand, trying not to breathe too deeply of the acrid, smoky air. She looked sideways and saw that Carson was holding the brim of his hat with his other hand, keeping it low enough to hide his face. Jumping over a tangled mass of abandoned fire hose laying on the cracked cement, Jill hurried to keep up with him.

They crossed another street, dodging between parked cars to get to the far corner. "You *do* know where you're going, don't you?" she gasped in a low voice.

"I do now," Carson said, never stopping as he glanced at her.

The eye contact helped, giving her some link that she desperately needed right then. *"Now?"* she asked with a feeble attempt at a smile.

"Don't quibble with success," he countered softly, then looked ahead of them and kept going. "I've done this sort of thing before, when I was a correspondent."

"Like this?"

"Not under these circumstances, but I've had to blend in, to not stand out. People only see what they want to see, so give them what they want."

She knew he was nervous, probably more than a little afraid, but he seemed completely in control now. He walked quickly, without hesitating, and she could see him taking in everything around him. "What are you thinking?" she asked before she could stop the question.

He glanced at her for only a moment. "Actually I was wondering if this was getting good press coverage. It would be a shame if the rest of the world doesn't see what's going on here."

"I guess you hope Channel Three puts it on the evening news, don't you?" she asked, tasting bitterness in the back of her throat. Even now, here, during this, he was worried about news and broadcasting it.

"They'd damn well better be giving this the lead spot," he muttered, and tugged her to hurry her up.

Jill knew her decision just hours ago had been right. This was Carson's life. Getting a story and putting it on the air. Any story. Even his own.

She looked ahead, realizing the street seemed darker with smoke than the areas they had just left. She could hear a strange wind-like sound that seemed to whistle and whoosh at the same time. Carson looked down at her again.

"How are you holding up?" he asked.

"I'll be fine as soon as I get on American soil," she said, realizing she wanted to add, "and as soon as I can put some distance between the two of us."

"With any luck..." His voice trailed off; then he squeezed her hand so tightly she almost cried out. "Soldiers," he said in a low hiss, the single word bringing such fear to Jill that she felt almost faint for a moment.

Chapter 8

". . . and our lead story on Channel Three News at Noon, *is the violent overthrow of the Estrada government in San Arman and the disappearance in San Arman of Channel Three's station manager, Carson Davies, and the cohost of 'Dream Chasers,' Jillian Segar.*

"Less than twelve hours ago the government of President Javier Estrada was shattered when a faction group calling themselves the Brothers of Liberty, took control of the country by force. Davies and Segar, scheduled to fly out of the country on an early-morning flight, had stayed in San Arman an extra day to attend a reception at deposed President Estrada's home. The last contact from them was with the other cohost of 'Dream Chasers,' Sam Rollins. Rollins spoke to Davies just before the crew left, and . . ."

It took great courage for Jill to glance up, and when she did she saw five men coming down the street, guns on their shoulders, the familiar arm bands in place. "What do we do now?" she whispered.

"Keep going, and if they say anything, just remember, one squeeze, two squeezes, or faint."

Carson slowed his stride, making it easier for Jill to keep pace, and she looked down at the littered sidewalk. She found she had to concentrate to just keep putting one foot in front of the other as she got closer to the soldiers. She literally stopped breathing when she heard one of them call out, *"Alto!"*

She understood the word for "stop," but Carson kept going until another one of the soldiers shouted, too. *"Alto!"*

Carson stopped, his hand firmly holding Jill's as he turned and looked at the soldiers as they crossed to him. The Spanish from the men came so quickly Jill couldn't even pick out words, then Carson was speaking, his voice hoarse and low, his free hand pressed to his throat.

The man closest to them stared at Carson hard for a second, then turned to Jill. As Jill stared at the him, she realized he was little more than a teenager who looked as if he was playacting at being a soldier. But the gun was deadly real, and the intensity in his face as he began to speak to her in rapid-fire Spanish, made her chest tighten uncomfortably. When he finished talking, he stared at her, waiting, then Carson squeezed her hand once, hard. She nodded once, not trusting herself to say the word.

He narrowed his eyes, then said something else. She tried to keep eye contact with him, then Carson squeezed her hand twice. She shook her head no.

The man spoke again, coming a step closer, studying her intently, then his hand moved to the gun in his waistband. At the same moment, Carson squeezed Jill's hand in one long grip, and she didn't have to pretend to feel faint. She turned to Carson, saw his image begin to recede into a soft grayness, and the next thing she knew she was in his arms. Holding her to his chest, he spoke to the soldiers in a harsh, angry voice.

Jill stayed very still with her face turned into Carson's chest and felt immense relief when she heard one of the men mutter something that had the tone of an apology. Carson muttered one short sentence, his hold on Jill solid and sure, then he stood very still. After a long, tense moment he whispered, "They're gone."

Jill didn't bother looking. She exhaled, unaware she had been holding her breath. "Thank goodness."

"Damn them," Carson muttered as he started off down the street still holding Jill. "They're full of themselves and some perceived sense of power."

Now that the danger was past, Jill was intensely aware of Carson holding her as easily as he would a child. And she didn't want it. She couldn't cope with it. "Let me down, Carson. I can walk now."

He stopped and lowered her to her feet. "Good acting," he said as she stood in front of him.

"Who was acting?" she murmured, covering a spontaneous shudder by hugging her arms around herself. "They gave me the creeps. What did they want?"

"They just wanted to give us a hard time. It's the equivalent of joyriding," he said. "They're looking for trouble, but they aren't very smart."

"What did you tell them?"

"That we . . ." As he looked past her down the street, he inhaled sharply, then whispered, "More soldiers. Let's get moving and stay close to the wall."

Without another word, he took her hand and led the way. Her heart raced as a group of six or seven soldiers came abreast of them, then hurried past. But before she could breathe a sigh of relief, a mighty roaring accompanied by a violent jarring of the ground was everywhere. At the same time, winds grew to a thundering rush, whipping down the street, and a split-second brilliance turned everything pure white.

Jill had time to do little more than wonder if this was an earthquake before she felt Carson's body crash into hers. Then both she and he were flung through the air before they stopped with a jolt as they hit something hard and ungiving. Jill heard Carson's breath leave his body in a harsh rush at the same time hers did, then she fell down and onto the pavement, partly on top of Carson.

Everything seemed to stop—sound, movement, sensations. In the next second, the world was filled with a frenzy of noises and action. People were screaming, sirens blared, gunfire exploded, and acrid, heavy air was everywhere. Then Jill heard Carson moan and she shifted back off his legs and onto the pavement. She braced herself with her hands and looked at him slumped against the brick wall that had stopped them. Then he looked up, his hat and glasses gone, and his eyes slightly glazed.

"Carson?" she whispered, reaching out to touch his hand on his thigh. "Are . . . are you all right?"

He leaned back against the wall, closed his eyes for moment as people ran all around them, then he looked at Jill. "I'm in one piece. How about you?"

"I . . . I'm all right, I think." She scrambled to her feet, grabbing his hat and glasses off the pavement. "What happened?" she asked as she watched Carson ease himself up using the wall for support.

He stood, steadying himself for a moment, then took the hat from her and pushed it on his head. When she handed him his glasses, he put them on and looked at her. "You sure you're not hurt?"

She brushed at her shorts. "I'm fine. You broke my fall."

He rubbed at his right shoulder, flexed his arm, then looked past her and froze. "Oh, no. It's gone," he whispered hoarsely.

She turned and through the surging throng of shouting, screaming people she caught glimpses of what must have been a huge building, maybe brick, which had literally been torn apart. Partial walls still stood, but the roof had sunk to the bottom floor, its beams protruding like broken bones and everything was in flames. Crowds of San Armanians, with their hands raised into the air, shouted chants in front of the demolished building.

A section of wall close by swayed and fell, and an insignia that must have been over doors or on the front toppled into view. In that instant, before the people rushed to trample it, Jill clearly saw the seal of the United States.

"Oh, no," she whispered, then felt Carson drawing her away from the carnage.

He tugged her back into an alley, out of the way of the crazy mob, and far enough into the narrow passage to be out of sight of the street. Easing her back against the wall, he held her by the shoulders and looked down at her. The dirt on his face seemed very dark against the paleness that touched his complexion. "We'll have to come up with Plan B as fast as we can."

"That *was* the consulate, wasn't it?" she asked, foolishly hoping she had been wrong.

But he only reaffirmed what she actually knew. "Yes. What's left of it."

Closing her eyes, she leaned back against the wall. "What now? What can we do?" She couldn't get the image of the San Armanians with their silly arm bands looking overjoyed that the consulate had been totally devastated. "What's left to do?"

"I wish I knew," she heard him breathe, and wished she'd never asked. She had expected him to have an answer. After all, he'd been in situations like this before. If he didn't know, who would?

She opened her eyes and saw Carson staring at the opening to the street. His jaw worked, and his hands on her shoulders tightened perceptibly. "I'm sorry about all this," she said. "If I hadn't insisted on San Arman, you wouldn't be here in the first place."

He turned to her, his eyes bleak behind the darkened lenses. "It's not important why we're here, it's important how we're going to get out."

"You're right." She touched her tongue to her lips, actually able to taste a hint of the acrid smoke there. "I wish I knew someone here, someone who could tell us where to go and what to do."

"Yes, someone who isn't part of this madness," he said softly.

"What?"

"Arturo Martine."

"Who?"

"Arturo Martine. The man I told you about who was in prison with me."

She felt a flicker of hope for an instant before it took a nose dive. "If he was in prison with you, don't you think he . . . he might not be hanging around to see this happen?"

Carson shook his head. "He'll be here. He was adamant about not leaving, not leaving his business and his home. This is where he was born. And when they found out who he was, they let him out."

"Then he's allied with Estrada," she said glumly.

"No, he said he's apolitical, neutral. He hates politics. He goes along with whomever is in power. I suspect anyone who has enough money is left alone to do what he wants to do."

"If he's here, could you find him?"

"I know where he lives. He told me often enough and described it. The village, Santa Bella, the house, the layout, the grounds, the road that goes up to it.'' He frowned. "*Hacienda del Oro*. The Golden House. He used to laugh about that, saying how true it was.''

She swallowed hard. A chance? Maybe, maybe not. "What if he was lying to you? What if he was crazy?''

"But what if he wasn't?'' he said softly.

Gunfire sounded, nearer and more sharply than before. And the cries of the people began to surge into a thunderous roar that echoed all around. Jill looked at Carson. "Where is this Golden House?''

"It's west of the city, about ten kilometers, near the water, built on rock cliffs.''

"That's it? Do you have an address?''

"He never told me one. But the way he talked about Santa Bella, it's a tiny place. There probably isn't any need for addresses.''

She hoped Martine had told Carson the truth. "Our one hope is to go ten kilometers away from here, and try to find a place that's maybe there to find a man who's probably there?''

Carson smiled, a strained expression that nevertheless eased something in Jill. "That's a fair assessment.'' He flicked at her hair with one finger, brushing a stray strand off her flushed face. "Ten kilometers isn't as far as ten miles, but it's a long way.'' His face sobered completely and his hand stilled. "The bottom line is, we don't have time for other options, Jill. Not unless you have a better idea?''

She wished she did, but her idea had gone up in smoke minutes ago. "What if we go all that way, find the place, and he's not there?''

"Then we'll keep going to the west until we either find someone to help us, or we walk right out of this damned country.''

"We're going to walk all the way to Santa Bella?''

"I hope not,'' he murmured, drawing his hand back.

"We do have to walk right past all those soldiers out there."

He glanced at the end of the alley, then turned back to Jill. Without warning he picked her up in his arms again. She circled his neck with her arms and looked up at him over her. "What are you doing?"

"A little more acting, like we did with the first soldiers. I told them you were stunned by the destruction, that you had seen your family home destroyed. When I picked you up, I told them you had taken a blow to the head earlier and were dizzy, disoriented."

"You're going to carry me for ten kilometers?" she asked.

His hands shifted on her, easing into a familiar hold that she fit neatly into. He almost smiled as he murmured, "I'm not going to carry you any farther than I have to."

More gunshots sounded, close enough for Jill to hear an eerie whistling sound after each bullet fired. She trembled in Carson's hold. "I hope Arturo Martine can help us, that he's not dead or something."

Carson adjusted his hold on her. "So do I," he said softly, then really smiled at her, a genuine touch of humor that almost made her cry. "And I bet he hopes he's not dead, too."

Shouts of soldiers echoed in the alley, and Jill ducked her head into Carson's chest without another word.

"Here goes," he whispered and started walking.

For what seemed an eternity, Jill lay in his arms, the beating of his heart and his rapid breathing, the only sounds in her world. For a while she could pretend everything was fine, that this was no different than other times in the past.

Like the time Carson had carried her up from the beach when she had turned her ankle on the sand. He'd taken her across the beach spotted with tufted sea grass to the cottage they had rented for a week.

She could still remember the heavy scent of summer blossoms in the air, the soft whirring of the overhead fan in the whitewashed room. The touching, the exploring, the ultimate lovemaking. The ankle had been totally forgotten, lost in a world where pain had no place. And she had wished those days would never end, that they could have stayed at the cottage forever.

Right then Carson readjusted his hold on her, and her thoughts stopped in their tracks. Make-believe. Fairy tales. Wishful thinking. Foolish, she admitted and clenched her teeth. She didn't want to think about that, not now, not ever. It would be hard enough to forget about last night when San Arman was far behind them.

She spoke softly without looking up, "Where are we?"

"No idea, but I spotted something we might be able to use to get to Santa Bella," Carson said. "It looks like some sort of evacuation station. Just a few more yards, and I'll find out what's going on."

He took a few more strides, then stopped walking and Jill could hear many people talking in low, urgent voices, the sound milling all around her. Then Carson spoke in Spanish and someone spoke to him quickly, running one word over the other. Jill could feel his tension in his hold on her when he responded, then he took a few steps and spoke again.

Jill heard a motor, the grinding of metal on metal, then people jabbering excitedly. "Hold on," Carson muttered and moved abruptly. He stepped up and Jill could feel an unsteadiness in him that wasn't there before. Then she inhaled and caught the odor of musty age, heat and animals? "Where . . . ?" she whispered, but Carson cut her off.

"Later," he muttered and kept walking as if on a rolling ocean.

Finally she felt him stop, shift, then sit down. Adjusting his hold on her until she was sitting on his lap, he laced his fingers in her hair, holding her head to his chest. The other hand went around her waist and rested on her thigh.

Cautiously opening one eye just a slit, she could see they were inside a vehicle of some kind, with broken windows and walls written on with spray paint—white splotches with the red dots in the middle. She shifted her head a bit more and realized they were on an old bus. She could see down an aisle packed with frantic-looking people standing and more people crowded onto the hard bench seats.

Someone up front yelled orders and the people pressed back farther in the aisle. An elderly woman came abreast of Carson, glared down at him, then clutching a paper bag to her chest, she turned her back on him.

When the motor roared to life and the bus took off at a lumbering pace down the road, Carson lowered his head until his lips were near Jill's ear. "Stay very still. This is an evacuation bus of some sort. It's going west." He spoke more loudly in Spanish, and Jill could see the elderly lady turn, then Carson was moving over even more giving the lady a few inches of bench to sit on. She sat down, twisted to face forward and an elbow struck Jill in the knee. The lady muttered something in a thready voice.

"*Si*," Carson responded, then Jill felt him settle back, but his hold on her never wavered. He released a held breath, then shifted until she was resting at a better angle in his arms.

Jill closed her eyes completely and let herself rest against Carson. The rolling motion of the bus and the continuous buzz of voices that she didn't understand, acted like a drug on her. Despite the fear and need to flee, she found herself sinking into a sleep of exhaustion, sleep that she had been robbed of the night before. In Carson's arms she felt safe for now, and she nuzzled into him. For now, she thought. Just for now.

"Jill?"

She shifted, as she was pulled out of a sleep that was deep and dreamless. For a minute she couldn't figure out why she was being held, or why she was laying like a baby in someone's arms. Then she inhaled, caught the scent of Carson, unique and compelling, and everything came back to her.

She opened her eyes and saw the old lady had left. Her spot on the bench was empty.

"Jill?" he whispered again.

"Mmm?"

"We're getting off. I've heard about roadblocks farther down and before the old lady got off back there, she said Santa Bella is really close."

She could feel the bus slow, then stop with a hiss of brakes. She heard someone shouting in Spanish. Then Carson awkwardly got to his feet, lurching out into the aisle. "*Si*," he called. "*Si*."

Someone spoke rapidly to him, Jill caught the word *muerte*, and wondered if Carson was telling them she was dead. Maybe that she might die. She wished that wasn't so close to the truth.

She trembled, covering it with a whimper that she hoped sounded as if it had been produced by pain. Carson said something to her in Spanish, and she just hoped he was telling her to be still. She did that, letting herself go completely limp, then she felt him start to walk, that odd rolling sensation on the bus, then down and onto firm ground and into hot air and brilliant sun she felt through her eyelids.

"*Gracias*," Carson called out, then turned and began to walk. "Another ten steps, then you're walking on your own two feet," he muttered for Jill's ears only.

Finally he stopped. "Here we are."

Jill opened her eyes as Carson carried her into a small building done with rough board walls that sagged inward slightly and a roof that was missing sections. The air inside was still and hot, smelling of the musty earth and dampness. As Carson lowered her down, she stood on shaky legs, and reached to steady herself with one hand flat on the only furnishing, a wooden table.

"Where is *here*?" she asked.

"Close to Santa Bella, I hope," Carson said as he swung the door shut on the sunlight. "The driver said it was, but I think he just didn't want us on the bus any longer."

"Why?"

"I told him I thought you were dying." He ran a hand roughly over his face and tugged off the large hat. His hair was molded to his head by the band of the hat, and perspiration ran in rivulets from his temples down his jaw. "They don't want to think about others dying. They just want to keep from dying themselves."

He flexed his right shoulder, then began kneading it with one hand. "I think we're about a kilometer from Santa Bella. We can rest for a few minutes, then find the turnoff and start walking."

The door to the shack swung back, struck the sagging wall with a resounding crack, and bright light glared into the darkness.

"What the hell do we have here?" a rough voice demanded.

Chapter 9

Carson spun around, his bad shoulder twisting painfully as he shot his arms out to protect Jill behind him. But instead of finding some ragtag San Armanian soldier with the arm band facing him, he saw a tall, bulky man, so blond his lashes and eyebrows were white. Dressed in green fatigues, the man stood in the doorway, pointing an automatic rifle into the shed.

A mercenary. Carson had done a feature on a man like this years ago when he had been in Miami. If enough money was offered, the man would be loyal to any side and any ideals. He didn't know what could be worse, a San Armanian who felt he was protecting the new government or someone who did anything for anyone who had money.

"I asked what I found here?" the man said in English touched by a rough southern drawl. He took a step into the hut, his rifle leveled at Carson's middle. "I want answers."

Maybe the man wasn't very smart, a macho type who used a gun because he couldn't do anything else. Gambling on that, Carson started to speak in Spanish, hoping to bluff, but he got no more than two words out before the man jerked the rifle in his direction. "Cut the bull. You ain't one of the natives. The lady ain't, neither. Who are you?"

Carson felt Jill move closer to him and her hand touch his back. "What do you want with us?" he countered, meeting the question with his own question.

"I ain't going to kill you—not yet." He lowered the gun until it was hanging by its strap from his shoulder. "My guess is you're Americans, and I don't get paid for doing in Americans."

Carson kept silent, hoping Jill would stay behind him and not draw any more attention to herself.

"That hair of yours is a dead giveaway." He motioned to the hat on the table. "I wouldn't go out without that, if I was you." He took a pack of cigarettes out of his pocket, lit one, then exhaled and looked at them through the haze of smoke. He tossed the spent match on the dirt floor. "So who are you and who's the broad?"

"We're Americans," Carson said quickly.

"And?"

"What?"

"If you was just Americans, you would have been on one of the first flights out of here. They don't want no problems with America. So why ain't you on a flight out?" He raised one pale brow. "What are you two up to?"

Carson stared straight at the man, but he was intently aware of Jill's hand pressed to his back. "We work for a television station in San Diego, California."

The man came closer, getting within two feet of Carson. "Celebrities?"

"No, just working in television. But I knew how it would look to the group taking over from Estrada."

"You two got names?"

"Carson and Jill."

"All right, *Carson*. I'm Sergeant Rexel. What are you up to? Why are you out here? I saw you getting off the bus. Looked like she was half dead, but—" he cocked his head sideways to get a better look at Jill "—now you look as if you're just fit as a fiddle."

"We're trying to get out of the city and find a friend. He used to live near here in Santa Bella."

Rexel took another drag on the cigarette, then dropped the butt on the dirt and ground it out with the heel of his boot. "Santa Bella? We've just come from there. Who are you looking for?"

Carson knew what absolute truth could do in a situation like this, so he lied and made up a name. "Roberto Juarez."

Rexel shook his head. "Some Juarezes there, but no Robertos. Just what's Juarez going to do for you?"

"Help me. Maybe let me stay at his place until this settles down a bit."

"I wouldn't count on it. Everyone around Santa Bella's spooked. They're watching out for their own backs, not worrying about protecting anyone else's. War's ugly." He took out another cigarette and offered the pack to Carson. "Smoke?"

Even though the idea of a cigarette seemed amazingly appealing to Carson, he shook his head. "No, thanks."

"My best advice to you is to head east, mister," Rexel said around the cigarette he was lighting. "Go back to the American consulate in Puerto Luis. Let them take care of you, and not this guy Juarez."

"Good idea," Carson said, hoping Jill wouldn't offer any explanation about the explosion. He didn't mind Rexel thinking they were going to head back to Puerto Luis. "After we rest, I think we'll do that."

Rexel tugged his cap lower on his head. "I'm heading out now. You can come with us, if you want."

"No, I don't think so."

"I understand." He took a long drag on the cigarette. "Santa Bella wouldn't be a good idea anyway," he said through exhaled smoke. "The whole damned town is owned by some guy who no one touches. Some big honcho. The guys I work for want the man 'unmolested' by the war. How's that for a cushy setup?"

"He must be important."

"I seen enough of these 'conflicts' to know he's just rich enough or smart enough to stay on everyone's good side. The way I hear it, Martine's got it made."

Carson felt Jill's touch on him jerk slightly at the mention of the name. "Who?"

"Some local guy named Martine, Arturo Martine. He's sure sitting in the catbird seat, living through all of this in a big house on the cliff." Rexel touched the peak of his cap. "I got to go. Good luck to you," he said, then stepped out into the brilliant sunlight and closed the door after him.

Carson looked down at Jill as she came up even with him and stared at the door. "He's still here. Martine didn't leave," she breathed.

He touched her shoulder, almost as relieved that Rexel had left without bothering Jill as he was that Martine was close by and in some position of power. "Now we have to get to him," he said, drawing his hand back as she evaded his touch by moving closer to the door.

The simple act of her moving away from him seemed monumental to Carson, as if she was deliberately distancing herself now that she knew they were close to getting help. "Let's not question it," she said pushing back the door. "Let's go and find your friend."

Carson looked at Jill, her tiny form silhouetted by the brilliant sun outside. He realized he liked it better when he was carrying her, even though it had caused horrible pain in his bad shoulder. Now she stood alone by choice, sure that rescue was imminent. Being careful not to make contact

with her again, he went past her and through the door out
into the heat and sun.

The road was deserted now, the stillness almost painful
after all the confusion and noises earlier on the bus. He
looked right and left, saw some movement down the road,
but whatever it was appeared to be going away from them.
He looked down the road in the other direction. "Come on.
Santa Bella is that way, then toward the water," he said
starting for the road.

Jill fell in step beside him, but didn't offer him her hand.
And Carson stared straight ahead. Later, he could think
later, he reasoned as he got to the road and turned west.

Without the smoke to block its rays, the afternoon sun
beat down in full strength on the land. After half an hour on
the road, they came to a Y where the paved road swung left
and a dirt road went right. A crude wooden sign fastened to
a huge tree at the intersection read *Santa Bella* and had an
arrow pointing to the right.

Carson stopped and took the watch he had always worn
out of his pocket. "An hour past noon," he said, squinting
up at the high sun, then back at the sign. "I wish it gave a
distance."

"I'd kill for a cold drink," Jill said.

He shook his head. "Let's hope we don't have to be that
extreme," he said as he pushed the watch back in his pocket.
"And let's hope Santa Bella is really close."

They started off down the dirt road and had only gone
over the first rise when they saw Santa Bella. They walked
slowly toward the village, which appeared to be little more
than a cluster of adobe-walled houses clustered around a
central plaza. A few shops edged the street and seemed to be
doing good business.

This place held little resemblance to the craziness in
Puerto Luis, except for two army jeeps that sat on either side
of the dusty street midway. The four soldiers in each of the

two jeeps were smoking and talking, saying things to villagers as they passed. They were laughing, joking with the people, their guns laying discarded on the seats.

As Carson and Jill approached the first of the shops, he pulled her to one side and into the shade of a canvas awning. He drew her nearer the wall of what looked like a rug shop and leaned against the thick adobe. "Santa Bella," he murmured.

"Now what do we do?" Jill asked.

"Well, we don't go up to the soldiers and ask if they know where Martine lives, that's for sure."

"Then what?"

"We try to blend in with the locals, get past those soldiers, then keep our eyes open. I'll recognize the road to his place when I see it, and if he's as important as Rexel said, he can't be hiding."

She closed her eyes for a minute. "So near, yet so far."

"Just like other things in life," Carson murmured cryptically, then nudged her on her shoulder to urge her back out onto the street.

They got to the far end of the street and past the soldiers without drawing any attention. At the far side of the village, the road forked again, one section continuing northwest, the other going northeast. "This way," Carson said, going up the right-hand fork.

When Jill got close to his side, she asked, "Why this way?"

"It's in better condition. If Martine is as well-off as he sounds, he would keep his road passable."

That made sense, and even more sense when Jill first heard the sound of the water. Breakers crashing against cliffs. The jungle on either side of the road thinned and the air held the tang of the ocean. The road wound to the right, under a canopy of palms and broad-leafed trees, then at the crest of the hill, Jill felt her heart sink.

Not more than twenty feet farther down the road, stood broad metal gates at least eight-feet tall. They were anchored in a fence of stone that disappeared into the jungle on either side. She couldn't see what was beyond the gates. But she did know this wasn't a road, but a driveway. Martine's house was probably behind the gates, but no barrier had looked so insurmountable to Jill in her life.

"How do we find out if this is Martine's place?" Jill asked in a whisper.

"I'll ask."

"Carson, what are you talking about? You can't just walk up to the gate and ask who lives here!"

"Do you have any better ideas? I'm open to suggestions. We just don't have the luxury of time. I speak Spanish. I can look reasonably foreign if I keep my hat on and they don't look too close. We'll know—one way or the other."

"And what about me?"

"You stay out of sight. If anything happens, go back to the fork in the road and take the other route. Martine has to be down that way if he's not here."

Jill didn't know what to say. She had no alternative plan, no sensible suggestion, so she clasped her hands tightly in front of her. "If it's not Martine's...?"

"I'll try to get away without causing problems."

"And if you don't?"

"I'll worry about that when it comes up." He touched her fleetingly, a brief caress on her cheek. "We don't have time for 'what if's.' We need to do something now."

She nodded and his hand fell to his side. Without another word, Carson motioned her into the trees, then turned and headed for the gates. She moved behind a clump of bushes and pulled back the branches until she had an opening to see the gates.

She saw Carson approach the barrier, look around, then touch something in the pillar to the right. Nothing happened at first, then one side of the gates slowly swung back and a man dressed all in black, looked out.

When he saw Carson, he raised a rifle by his side, then spoke quickly. She could see Carson nodding, taking a step back, then the man was out through the gate, followed by four others. Carson held both hands in the air, and shook his head from side to side as he tried to move back slowly.

The gates were too far away for her to hear the voices clearly, but what she did hear clearly was the clicking of rifles being cocked. The man in front closed the distance between himself and Carson so quickly Jill didn't understand what was happening until he jerked his rifle up and drove the butt into Carson's stomach.

Jill stared in horror, frozen to the spot. Nothing had prepared her for this, and she had to press a hand to her mouth to keep from crying out as Carson doubled over, almost dropping to his knees. The man crouched down to look Carson in the eye, then pressed the barrel of the rifle under Carson's chin.

"No!"

A voice cried out and Jill saw another man come out through the gates. Medium height, slender, with ebony hair that brushed his collar and a shoulder holster worn over a loose white top, the man moved quickly and grabbed the man with the rifle by the shoulder. He jerked him back, then took his own pistol from the shoulder holster and aimed the gun at the top of Carson's bent head.

Slowly Carson looked up, both men stared at each other, then the man in white lowered his gun. He pushed it back in the holster and reached for Carson, grabbing him by one arm to help him stand. Carson straightened up still clutching his middle, and the man yelled orders at the other men and one of them ran to push the gate farther open.

Carson straightened more, rubbing at his middle with one hand as he held out his other hand. Martine. The man in white had to be Martine. Relief coursed through Jill, making her legs weak. When Carson turned in her direction, motioning her to come to him, she couldn't move for a minute.

When she finally had the strength to go to him, she found herself running up the road until she was at his side. She clutched his arm tightly and looked at the man in front of them.

"Jill," Carson said in a voice still breathless from the blow to the middle. "Arturo Martine."

She stared at the man she hoped would be able to help them get out of San Arman. He was older than she had expected, maybe forty-five or so, with deeply tanned skin and dark eyes. He smiled at her, a genuine expression that deepened the lines at his eyes and mouth, and she could feel relief growing inside her as if it were a living thing.

He acknowledged her with a brief nod of his head, then spoke in lightly accented English, "Come inside. Both of you, quickly." He turned and motioned to one of the men by the gates and spoke in Spanish.

The man ran out, grabbed Carson's hat, which had fallen off, and offered his arm to Carson for support. But Carson brushed it aside and headed for the gates. When Jill and Carson were inside with the others, one of the men closed the gates.

She watched the man put up a crosspiece of metal to secure them, then she glanced around at Martine's home. She realized Rexel had been right about the man's wealth. A curving driveway of inset stones and bricks led up to a massive three-story house done in whitewashed rocks and perched against the blueness of the heavens on a massive outcropping on the cliff.

Martine spoke quickly in Spanish to the men and they scattered in all directions with the man in black taking off at a trot on a side drive that led into thick trees. Then Martine looked back to Carson and Jill. "I must find how you got this close without being seen."

"We walked up the road," Jill said without blinking.

That brought a chuckle from Martine. "A direct attack, eh?"

Carson rubbed his middle again, the color in his face almost normal now. "I was the one attacked."

"I am sorry, my friend, but with the state of things, one cannot be too careful." He motioned toward the house. "Come. We need to get inside and out of this heat, then you can tell me how you happen to show up at my doorstep after you told me you would never again be in my country." He looked at Jill. "And you can tell me who this lovely lady is with you."

Carson glanced at Jill, then back to Martine. "Yes, we have to talk as soon as possible." He reached out to Jill, touching her arm, but he continued speaking to Martine. "One thing, do you have a phone?"

"Of course."

"Can I get a call out to San Diego?"

Jill held her breath, wondering why she had thought Carson would be more concerned with their escape than with making contact with the station.

"A call anywhere is out of the question. The lines have been blocked since late last night," Martine said.

Carson seemed to sag slightly. "Damn."

Jill echoed the word mentally and let go of Carson to head up the driveway to the house.

Jill sat in a wicker chair near a bank of high, arched windows in a garden room on the ground floor of Martine's home. She sipped a delicious fruit drink and stared out at the distant ocean while Carson explained why they were here. When he finished, Jill heard a chair scrape on the quarry-tile floor, then Martine came across to the windows near her. When she looked up at him, his dark face was sober, his eyes intent on the horizon. He was silent for a few minutes, then turned back to the room.

He looked across at Carson, who was still sitting at the table. "I regret it is not possible for you and Jill to stay here. One of my agreements with the new government is total access to these grounds at any time. It was the only way I could convince them I was not plotting against them." He chuckled, a harsh sound with no humor in it. "That and a great deal of money has kept me out of prison this time." He sobered. "Keeping you here is out of the question."

Carson sank back in his chair, his drink resting on the wicker arm. "That was only one option. What we really need is to get out of the country as quickly as possible."

"If you can get to the border you will be safe. There is no extradition agreement between Colombia and San Arman."

"That's what I was hoping," Carson said, sitting forward. "And the sooner we get there the better. The longer it takes, the more organized the new government will be. The question is, how can we get across the border?"

Martine glanced at Jill, then went back to drop down in his chair at the table again. He sat forward, his elbows resting on the tabletop. "That I do not know. I cannot send you with one of my people. They are known, and it could come back on me and on those I care for." He shrugged sharply. "There is no logic to this thing, no overruling honor with these people. You, of all people, should know that."

Carson nodded. "I understand. But I still have to get out."

"Of course."

"I'll do anything," Carson said, sitting forward in the same way Martine was. "Anything. I can get money—"

Martine brushed that aside with a sweep of his hand. "I can give you money, but sometimes that isn't enough.

Whoever helps you must not care about anything but that money. And I do not know..." He sat up straight. "Maybe..."

"What?" Carson asked intently.

Jill watched the two men, one eager for anything, the other unsure for some reason of saying what he was thinking.

"Damn it, Martine, give me anything! I need out of here!" Carson bit out.

Martine sat back and stared at Carson. "All right. I know of a man whom I can contact. He will do anything for the right amount of money, but he is..." He frowned. "I know he is crazy. He will risk anything to do what he wants to do, but I fear he cannot be trusted."

"Why?"

"Rumors. Things I have heard from others. Deals gone sour."

Carson didn't hesitate. "I'm willing to take a chance."

"But, what if—?"

"What if the army comes in here and finds us? What if we are locked up, or shot? I'm willing to take my chances."

Martine glanced at Jill, who had silently watched the conversation. "What about you, Jill? Do you feel the same way?"

She stood and came across to the two men. She didn't have to think for more than a second before she answered. "Yes, I do. I want to go home."

Martine stood. "Very well, but we must figure out a way to give you better odds of making it." He exhaled. "I will send one of my men into the village to find out where the man is. It might take a few hours. And this is just between the three of us, and the man I will trust to be a messenger."

"Of course."

"Good. I will show you to a room where you can rest and clean up. I will send up some food, then I will come for you when everything is set."

Carson stood. "I will never forget this."

"That is exactly what I want you to do, my friend. Forget this ever happened," he murmured, then crossed to the door, opened it and looked out into the hall. He glanced back at Carson and Jill. "Come," he said and motioned them to follow him.

They went down a long, stone-floored corridor, its twelve-foot ceilings fashioned in an arch, up a sweep of carpeted stairs and down another corridor on the second floor to the back of the house. He opened a door, stepped in, and Jill and Carson followed him into a room that was shaped like an octagon. Its angled walls were made of stone and painted a pale blue. With accent pieces of pastel green and violet tones, the room seemed light and airy, despite the heavy dark wood of a massive poster bed and an armoire that almost touched the ceiling.

Martine pointed to a door on the right, to one side of the armoire. "The bath is in there. The food will be up soon, but it may take a few hours for me to make my contact. Please, do not come out of the room until I come for you. If you hear a bell ringing, there is trouble." He looked at Carson. "I am trusting you to do whatever is needed so you are not seen by anyone who shows up here."

Carson nodded, then put out his hand to Martine. "Thank you."

Martine looked at the outstretched hand, then took it, but instead of shaking it, he pulled Carson against him in a hug. "We will not go through what we did five years ago, my friend," Martine said as he stood back. "I promise you that." And he left, closing the door behind him.

Jill crossed the floor, which was carpeted in the softest blue looped carpeting, then turned in the center of the room, one hand on the heavily carved post of the massive bed. "He's a good friend," she said to Carson.

He looked at her, then leaned back against the door. "Yes, he is."

She looked around the room. "Do you know what he does to support all of this luxury in the middle of a country that is basically below the poverty level?"

He frowned, then stood straight and began undoing the buttons of his dirty shirt. "No, I don't."

"And we shouldn't ask?"

He shrugged out of the shirt and tossed it on a side table. "I don't think we should bite the hand that's feeding us, do you?"

She shrugged, whatever Martine did to make money was of little concern to her right now. All she knew was that she didn't want to look at Carson, at his bare chest, and remember. "No, we shouldn't." She glanced at the telephone by the bed. "Too bad the telephone lines are out."

"A damn shame," Carson muttered. "Do you want to use the bathroom first?"

"No, you go ahead," she said and turned to the windows.

"Jill?"

"What?"

"When I found you on the beach this morning, what was that all about?"

She shrugged sharply, pressing her hands on the stone window ledge and staring out the thick leaded-glass windows at the distorted image of the day outside. The blue of the ocean and the sky seemed as distorted as her feelings. Could she love this intensely, yet have the strength to walk away? She didn't know, all she did know was that she wasn't up to any sort of confrontation now. "We'll talk about it later."

His touch on her was unexpected, and she spun around, breaking the contact. "Don't," she whispered.

Carson was less than a foot from her. "I think we're past this stage, aren't we?"

"What stage?" she asked, hating the breathless quality in her voice.

"The 'don't touch me' stage, Jill. After last night—"

She moved around him, thankful he didn't try to stop her. She wasn't up to this, at all. Not when she could feel herself literally craving his touch, wanting to go to him, to let him hold her and... She headed for the bathroom door. "I'll take you up on your offer of using the bathroom first," she muttered and went inside without looking back.

The room was round, done in marble, and all the fixtures were fashioned in gold. The floor underfoot was covered by thick white carpet. Jill closed the door, and leaned back against it. The tub, directly across from the door, was sunken to floor-level, round like the room, and looked as if it had been carved out of solid marble.

She didn't have to ask what Martine did for his money, she was pretty sure she knew. Just the way she knew she couldn't trust her feelings about Carson. Feelings were subjective, not objective, and she had to keep some objectivity. Either that, or she was lost in more ways than one.

A knock on the door startled her, and she called out without opening the barrier, "Yes?"

"Martine sent up some food and a change of clothes for us," Carson said through the thick wood.

She took a deep breath, then opened the door. She knew Carson had some clothes in his hands and he was offering them to her. But that was only peripheral. Carson filled her whole realm of awareness. Each line, each plane of his face, the breadth of his chest, the soft matting of hair. And he had taken his glasses off. She wished he'd never take them off. That was the only time she really saw vulnerability in the man.

"Martine said I can use a bathroom two doors down the hall," he was saying. "If I'm not in the room when you come out, I'll be there getting cleaned up."

She nodded, then quickly grabbed the clothes, muttered a thank you and closed the door again. She stood very still, letting her breathing come back to a regular rhythm, then looked at the clothes in her arms. They were black and white, funeral-like, she thought, then looked more closely at them.

Dark jeans and a black pullover top that looked a bit large and a folded robe of white velour. After she put them on the vanity to her right, she stripped off her dirty clothes, stepped out of her sandals and crossed to the tub.

In a jar on the edge of the marble were some bath-oil beads, and when she started the water she dropped two pale green beads under the stream of water. Fine bubbles grew and the scent of jasmine filled the air. For a few minutes she was going to forget everything and luxuriate in the bath.

Then the idea that it might be her last bath came from nowhere and chilled her. But as soon as it came, she pushed it back, ignoring it, and stepped down into the warm water.

Carson showered quickly in the small bath off the hall, scrubbing at his skin to take the stickiness off. His shoulder throbbed painfully, but the hot water began to ease the tension in the muscles. He tried not to think about Jill, and tried to concentrate on what was ahead of them.

Thank God Martine was here. He let the water run over his face, and he didn't allow himself to wonder *why* the man had what he had in a country like San Arman. He wouldn't ask questions. Whatever the man did was his own business. Moralizing didn't have any place here and now. What counted was the fact that Martine was doing all he could to get them out of the country and to safety.

He turned to let the water beat down on the back of his neck and realized how thankful he was that Jill hadn't pressed for answers about Martine's business. That simple thought brought Jill's image to him full force, and he felt sick remembering the look in her eyes when he mentioned last night. He didn't have to ask her about it. He knew she regretted it, that her impulse in making love had cost her a great deal. Boyd was a reality in her life. And Carson knew he wasn't any closer to having her than he had been when she'd walked out of the apartment in Houston. But this time there was someone waiting for her, worrying about her, being scared for her.

He stepped out of the shower in the narrow room and grabbed a white towel by the vanity. With vigorous strokes he began to dry off his skin. He wished he could wipe Boyd off the face of the earth. The idea of him holding Jill and loving her made Carson physically sick. As sick as the idea of a life without her.

Years without her. Years of not having her, of not being able to hold her, not being able to reach out in the night and feel her heat under his hands. He closed his eyes tightly. Was it possible to live like that? To be alone, to be lonely and not die from it?

He opened his eyes. People didn't die of loneliness, or of broken hearts. That wasn't reality. *Reality is having someone mean everything to you . . . more than life itself.* The words of Martine from the dream came to him in a rush and he stopped toweling himself. What if he could never have her?

He tossed the towel on the vanity, reached for the jeans Martine had given him and didn't look in the mirror over the vanity once. He didn't need to see how his body reacted to just the thought of Jill.

* * *

Jill came out of the bathroom, with the robe on, to look for a brush or comb. Her hair had curled crazily from the steamy heat of the long bath, and she needed something to tug it back into some semblance of order. But she had only taken one step out of the bathroom when she stopped. Carson was there, on the bed, stretched out on top of the pale blue spread dressed in fresh blue jeans and nothing else.

His glasses lay on the turned-leg table by the bed. His eyes were closed and his bare chest rose and fell with each regular, shallow breath he took. She made herself move, to go toward the long dresser on the far wall past the bed, but found herself stopping at the foot.

In sleep Carson looked more than vulnerable, he looked content and peaceful, not driven by his work or his need to prove himself. She felt tears burn the back of her eyes. Damn him. Why did he have to be here, like this, now?

She turned to go to the dresser, but Carson moaned softly, drawing her attention back to him. He shifted, one hand swiping through the air to fall heavily on the bed by his side. The moan came again, louder, more distinct. He moved restlessly, then turned on his side, drawing his knees up to his stomach.

"No," he mumbled. "No, no."

Jill stood very still, watching, praying the nightmare would stop on its own, that it would go away and leave him asleep. But it wasn't to be. The next thing she knew, Carson's scream echoed through the room, and he sat bolt upright in bed, his eyes wide, unseeing. "No! No! Not her, not her!"

Chapter 10

Jill ran around the bed, scrambled up onto it and reached out for Carson. "Carson," she whispered, drawing him to her, holding him.

"Shh, it's a dream," she whispered. "A dream. It's not real. It's not real, at all."

He broke free of her, pressing back against the headboard, his eyes on her, yet she knew he wasn't seeing her. He was still lost in the horror of the dream. She got to her knees, going closer, touching his thigh, feeling the tightness in his muscles. "Carson, it's me, Jill. It's a dream, a dream."

He looked at her and blinked rapidly, then recognition came, and he reached out for her. Before she could do anything, he had her in a smothering hug, her face pressed into the hollow of his shoulder, his heart pounding against hers. "Jill," he murmured against her hair, his voice muffled and unsteady. "I dreamed...I..." He stopped and she could feel him taking a shuddering breath.

He drew back, his face so close she could feel each ragged breath he took. She loved him. She loved with a passion that only grew with each passing minute. She hated herself for it, yet knew there was no getting out of it. When he touched her, framing her face with both his hands and she felt the unsteadiness there, she admitted defeat.

What if there was no tomorrow? What if this was the last day she'd ever have on earth? Tomorrow and the next tomorrow and the next tomorrow seemed so far away, so unreachable, but Carson was real. And her need for him was real right now.

With a heartfelt sigh, Jill covered his hands with hers. She looked into the blueness of his eyes, then slowly, inevitably, went to him. She offered her lips to him, and she felt a shudder go through him before he moaned and took what she was giving.

Even as she tasted him and felt his tongue touching hers and entering her mouth, she knew she would never love another man as she did Carson. She loved him, she was going to be with him, and she would leave him when they were safe—if they were ever safe again.

Carson surrounded her with his arms and pulled her back into the bed with him. She could feel his heart against her heart, his body stretching out alongside hers, and she felt choked by her love for him. And choked by the hopelessness of it all. Now, today, that's all she had. That's all she could count on. And if this was her last day on earth, she was going to spend it with Carson, like this, sharing, touching and loving.

If she said *I love you*, if she spoke her heart, there would be no leaving, no way she could ever walk away from Carson. So she kept the words in her heart, knowing her body would say it without words. They would take a long time loving, so she could savor and remember every detail.

He tasted her, his mouth moving slowly, sensuously on hers, each movement bringing new sensations to her. His hands found her robe, the knot that bit into her stomach between their bodies, and it was undone. The soft velour was pushed back, but the leisurely loving she had envisioned never came to pass.

As his hand touched her skin, passion came with white-hot urgency and each touch, each movement, drove Jill into a frenzy. Her need to be one with Carson was suffocating her, overwhelming her. She tugged at the snap on his jeans, hearing the click of the fastener giving, then she pushed at the rough material. Carson reached down, helping her strip the denim from his body, then the jeans and robe were tossed off the bed.

His mouth was on hers again, smothering her moans as his hands found her and pleasured her, roughly, urgently and passionately. Then his mouth moved to taste what his hands had caressed and she cried out softly. Her nipples throbbed under his mouth, her breasts swelled and she was filled with sensations that flooded through her entire body before centering deep in her belly. A knot coiled there, a knot that begged to be released.

"Yes, yes," she gasped, and she circled his neck with her arms, trying to tug Carson over her.

Then he was above her, his body poised over hers, but even though she lifted her hips, he didn't enter her. The hard length of his arousal caressed her intimately, provocatively, yet didn't give her the final satisfaction. The gentle torment of the touch drove Jill onward and she tugged at him, wanting to taste him, to feel his lips over hers, to be filled and complete, but he held back.

She opened her eyes, looked at him, at his eyes that were dark with passion, and she pleaded, "Please, Carson, please."

As she whispered her needs to him, he came lower and lower until he took her mouth in a devastating kiss that seemed to draw her soul from her. His tongue caressed hers, invaded her moist warmth, and she found herself imitating his movements, tasting him, drawing him into her mouth, then running her tongue over his smooth teeth.

The kiss that should have been a prelude to the ecstasy to come left her trembling, as if he had ravished her already. But when she felt him move and felt his strength testing her, hard and firm and as wonderful as she remembered, he still didn't enter her. She arched to him, wanting, demanding the contact, begging him in gasping whispers to come to her. And he did. He touched her and filled her, slowly, leisurely and completely.

When she felt him draw back, she wrapped her legs around his hips, anything to keep him from breaking the contact. "No, don't leave me," she gasped.

He held himself over her with his elbows on the pillow on either side of her head and looked down at her. "Do you want me?" he whispered in a voice rough with intensity.

"Yes, yes, please," she gasped. "Please."

He dropped a hard, demanding kiss on her lips, then with one thrust, he was deep inside her. Over and over again, he filled her, lifting her higher and higher until she knew she would surely die from the exquisite sensations that were becoming the center of the universe for her.

With one more thrust, she felt as if she exploded, and was hurled into a place where all she knew was love and fulfillment, and all she heard was Carson cry out her name as his body arched against hers. Her being fused with his until there was just one person, one heart and one soul. And neither one of them moved as the pleasure of completion shimmered and scattered and they drifted softly down to earth.

Jill lay very still under Carson, and he didn't leave her. All the time, while her breathing and heartbeat slowed to a more normal rhythm, Jill found herself storing sensations—the weight of his body on hers, the sleek heat of his skin against hers, the way he could fill her and make her feel complete. Then he sighed, drew back and shifted onto his side, gathering her with him into the crook of his arm.

She rested her head in the hollow of his shoulder, and she felt the burning of tears as she acknowledged she could never be like this with Carson again.

He stroked her shoulder, then her ribcage and rested his hand on her breast. The nipple, still sensitive and swollen from his touch, reacted instantly, puckering with sensations and drawing up some invisible string that went directly to the core of her being.

She bit her lip to keep from sighing and lay very still thinking that if tomorrow did come, there would be a payback that she didn't know she could deal with, at all. If tomorrow came? She never dreamed in her life that she would be in a position to doubt the sun coming up tomorrow, or life going on.

Carson stirred and turned until his lips touched the top of her head and he nuzzled her hair. If life could be stopped at the best part, she would stop it now. While she still had the freshness of her recent oneness with Carson, the mutual pleasuring, the immense joy and this peace and quiet. She would freeze it before any consequences reared their ugly heads. And she wouldn't ever face a life of regret.

"Are you going to run away again?" Carson asked, as if he could read her mind, and it jarred her into reality.

She closed her eyes so tightly she could see colors exploding behind her lids. No, she wouldn't run away again. If this was ever over, she would have to face him and tell him the truth. "No," she whispered, "not again."

She twisted to look up at Carson and found him watching her intently. Each breath he took flared his nostrils, and his hair was disheveled, a stray lock on his forehead giving him a young look. "I won't let you run away, Jill, not again, and not to Boyd."

When she heard Boyd's name, she realized then that "tomorrow" was now, not the next day, not even the next minute. It had come the second after the lovemaking stopped. She moved back, disentangling her arms and legs from Carson's, and sat up, scooting back until her bare back was against the cold headboard. She reached for the rumpled bedsheet and pulled it to her breasts as some sort of protection.

"You need to know that I . . . I did this because you had the dream. You were screaming, and . . ." The lie sounded weak in her own ears, and her voice trailed off.

"Was this just to comfort me?" he asked as he raised himself on one elbow. His features were tight, with none of the easing that had been there moments before. "This was a mission of mercy?"

"No, of course not," she muttered. "It was because . . ." Why couldn't she just simply say she wanted him, that she had thrown caution to the wind and knew she would regret it later? Why couldn't she just tell him that she loved him with a deep ache that never went away, that she feared life with him would be impossible. It hadn't worked in Houston, no matter how hard she had tried, and she knew it wouldn't work any better now.

"Give me a reason, one good reason," he said, not moving, just watching her carefully. "Make me understand what's going on in your head. Make me see how we can make love with each other and after you can pull back from me the minute I start talking about 'us,' about anything beyond the moment." He sat up farther, not bothering to try and cover himself the way she did. "Don't you think it's time you made me understand why you walked out on me in Houston, why you walked away from our relationship?''

Not now, she wanted to scream, *not now, when nothing makes sense.* But she didn't. Instead she looked at him, into the intense blueness of his eyes and it shocked her when the words came, words that should have come two years ago. "We never had a relationship, Carson, it was a convenience for you.''

"Defining terms for me again?" he countered harshly, any closeness dispelled as if it had never been.

It was so clear to her now, so simple to put into words. "You wanted me there. You needed me there, but on your terms, at your times, when it was right for you. When you didn't have a business meeting, or a story wasn't breaking that had to get on the late news, or the ratings weren't going through the floor.

"You never shared with me, not your pain, not your doubts, not your fears. You never even told me about your nightmares, about you being in prison here. You wanted me there for you, but you were never there for me.'' The last statement left her shocked at its stark truthfulness. She had agonized over an encounter like this for so long, yet it was now, and the words were right.

He stood abruptly, getting out of the bed in one easy motion. For a second he stood before her, his image stark and real. The clear sun that streamed into the room exposed the muscles, the ridges of his chest, the sleekness that running had etched on his frame. The sight almost made her stop breathing before he reached for the discarded jeans and stepped into them. After long minutes of silence, he looked back at Jill.

Then he reached for his glasses and slipped them on. "I think I need to see clearly for this discussion." He looked at Jill and spoke softly. "You sound jealous of my work." The statement came from nowhere, but made perfect sense to Jill.

She clutched the sheet more tightly to her breasts. "You're right. I was jealous. Your work was competition for me, like another woman would have been, but not one of flesh-and-blood. It was one I couldn't compete with then, and I can't compete with now. It's a mistress I stand no chance against."

He looked shocked. "You actually feel that way?"

"Yes." She swallowed hard. "And even now, when we could die, I know you're thinking about what sort of story this makes, what kind of job the station is doing covering it on the news." He didn't protest at all. "You never stop. You never let go." She sucked in air, hating the tightness that ringed her chest. "You let go of me, but you couldn't let go of your work."

He raked his fingers through his hair. "You've got it all wrong. I needed you. I loved you more than I ever loved anyone in my life. And it wasn't enough for you."

"You would have been enough for me, but I never had you. I've had more of you in these past hours than I had in all the months we were together before, and I still haven't had all of you. You never even told me about your time here, about being in prison, and heaven knows what else.

"What more is there, Carson? How much of yourself have you shut up and kept to yourself? No, never mind." She choked back tears. "You haven't changed. That's why I left Houston, why I tried to make a new life for myself in San Diego, and you've even ruined that."

"With Boyd?" he bit out.

Boyd. He hadn't been in her thoughts, at all, in the past moments. But he was a reality. "I've done so much damage to him."

Carson hit the massive poster of the bed with the flat of his hand, and the whole bed shook from the force of the blow. "Why feel sorry for him? He's had you all this time."

Had her? She knew Boyd had never really had her. But before she could say that to Carson, the sound of a bell ringing over and over again echoed through the house.

The bell! Jill stared at Carson. "Martine said—"

"I know what he said." Carson moved quickly, up onto the bed, coming to her on his knees. In one motion he had her face framed by his hands, then he kissed her quickly and fiercely. "That's for now. Later, you're going to listen to me. We'll settle everything, even Boyd." He let her go. "Now get dressed, and I'll check and see what's going on."

A knock sounded on the door, and Carson quickly got off the bed. Jill watched him as he crossed to the door and opened it. His image blurred, and she had to blink rapidly to clear her vision.

Martine was in the hall speaking quickly. "More soldiers are nearing Santa Bella. They will be here soon."

"How much time do we have?" Carson asked.

"Half an hour at the most."

"Did you reach the man?"

"Yes, and he agreed to the deal."

"How much did he ask to get us out?"

"Five thousand American dollars."

Carson didn't hesitate. "I can get him that much as soon as we're out of here."

"Do not worry, I have money. It is the least I can do. You know I would not ask you to go, but things are so..." He paused. "It is like the last time. Everyone is changed. Things have changed. The rules do not count."

"Who's the man you contacted?" Carson asked.

"Jorge DeVega. He agreed to drive you to the Colombian border. Meet me in the room we were in before, as soon as you can. We need to talk before you leave."

Carson agreed, closed the door, then came back to the bed and took a dark T-shirt off the side table. He shook it out, then spoke to Jill. "Get dressed and come downstairs when you're ready." He pulled the T-shirt over his head, tugged it down and tucked it into the waistband of his jeans. Then he raked his fingers through his hair to comb it back from his face and adjusted his glasses. "We don't have much time."

Pulling the bedspread with her, Jill scrambled off the bed, tucked the soft linen around her, then hurried to the bathroom. She had a glimpse of Carson putting on his shoes just before she closed the door.

The flurry of getting dressed quickly stilled the need for much thought, but when Jill was stepping into her sandals, she realized that although everything had finally been said, she felt no better. If anything, she felt worse. Empty. A part of her was gone, and she knew she could never have it back.

Less than five minutes later, Jill stepped into the sun room and saw Carson with Martine standing by the windows. The men who had been at the gate were there, too; all of them with rifles and shoulder holsters. While Martine spoke to Carson, he was busy strapping his shoulder holster back on, then inspecting a black handgun.

Martine saw Jill first and turned, speaking as he pushed the gun into his holster. "Good. It is time to go." He motioned to the man who had struck Carson with the rifle outside the gates. "Sandor will take you to meet DeVega." He smiled, a fleeting expression that barely relieved the deeply etched lines in his face. "Sandor is a good man, and he is trustworthy."

Martine touched Carson's shoulder. "All you need now is the money." He crossed the room to an assortment of pictures on the wall, reached for a large one of an elderly man and pulled it back to expose a safe. He quickly opened it and Jill could see inside. It contained some boxes and stacks of papers. Martine took out a green metal box, opened the lid and counted out some money, then he put the box back in the safe and closed it with a click. With the picture back in place, no one would know the safe was there.

As he came back to Carson, he held out the money. "Five thousand dollars, and some extra . . . for the unexpected."

Carson took the offered money without really looking at it and pushed it into the back pocket of his jeans. Then he picked up a canvas duffel bag that sat on the floor by his feet. "I don't know how to thank you for everything," he said.

"Thank me by getting out of San Arman safely and forget you ever knew me." Martine motioned to Sandor. "Go with Sandor. And Godspeed."

When Sandor led the way out a side gate from Martine's compound, Jill stepped into a wild and uncleared jungle. Sandor led Carson and her through thick underbrush, where the heat mingled with the odors of soil, blossoms and the sea. He walked quickly, using a huge, curved knife to hack at any vines of plants that blocked the way. Finally they cut out of the dense jungle and onto a packed dirt trail no more than five-feet wide.

The glare of the late-afternoon sun was almost painful, and the heat had not been tempered by the coming night. Sandor looked both ways, listened, then turned and spoke softly, "Come."

They followed him along the baked earth trail to the right and up an incline. At the top, Sandor stopped and spoke in a normal voice. "DeVega."

Jill looked past Sandor and saw a man not more than fifty feet away, standing at the back of an oxidized-green pickup truck. He looked like hundreds of other San Armanians Jill had seen during the day, dark, medium-height, wearing an odd mixture of clothes—baggy black slacks, a plaid shirt with the sleeves cut out and heavy boots. It was his expression that stopped Jill cold. His eyes, dark under thick protruding brows, didn't blink at all. They seemed to pierce instead of stare.

When he spoke in a gravelly voice in heavily accented English, she knew she didn't like him. "It is not safe to be here. I was ready to leave without you."

"Without your money?" Sandor said, his voice with little inflection, but his words hit their mark.

DeVega scowled, his brows lowering across the bridge of his nose. As he stood straight, his loose shirt shifted, and Jill could see a gun in his waistband. "You brought the money, *si*?"

Carson stepped forward to stand shoulder-to-shoulder with Sandor. "I have it."

DeVega moved his hand to rest it on the butt of his gun at his waist. "You know the price."

"Five thousand."

"American dollars." DeVega took a step toward Carson, his free hand held out for the money. "Now."

Carson handed Jill the duffel bag, then took the money Martine had given him out of his pocket and counted out some bills. When he handed them to DeVega, the man counted them quickly, then looked up at Carson to demand, "Where is the rest?"

"You'll get it when you get us to the border."

DeVega's scowl deepened. "How do I know you have it?"

Carson counted out twenty-five hundred dollars from the rest, folded it over twice, then held it up for Martine to see. "The other half...when we are in Colombia," he said and took the duffel back. He put the money in a side pocket and regripped the handles.

DeVega stared hard at the duffel, then shrugged sharply. "We are wasting time. Get in the truck."

Carson held out his hand to Sandor. "Many thanks."

The man looked slightly embarrassed. "I am sorry for our meeting."

"It's forgotten. Take care of Martine . . . and yourself."

"Martine and I have survived worse than this," the man said, then turned and headed into the jungle.

Carson hooked the straps of the duffel over his arm and reached out to Jill. He took her by the arm, their first touch since the kiss on the bed, and Jill felt it in her soul. Words that should have cleansed her of this man seemed to have only deepened his effect on her. "You heard the man," Carson said. "Let's get in the truck."

Jill went to the truck with Carson, and while DeVega got in the other side, she tugged the passenger door open and climbed into the cab. The bench seat with ripped vinyl covering was as hard as a rock. She shifted near the middle, keeping her knee away from the gearshift in the floor, and inhaled the odor of age, gasoline and heat. Carson got in, slammed the door shut, put the duffel at his feet, then rested his elbow on the door.

When DeVega started the motor, the truck shook and vibrated, but it roared to life and sounded strong. Carson settled back in the seat, inches from Jill, and as the jeep lurched forward, he gripped the door. Jill held to the seat on both sides of her legs.

"We have to stay on the back trails," DeVega said. "It will be rough. This truck, it is not much to look at, but it has a strong motor. It can go anywhere it has to go."

Jill felt the first bone-jarring jolt as the truck bounced into and out of a huge pothole, and she barely cut off a gasp of shock. Her thigh jerked against Carson's and she tried to stiffen her leg, to keep it away from any contact with him.

But after a few more jarring movements, she gave up. Her body hit Carson, shoulder-to-shoulder, arm-against-arm, thigh-against-thigh, with every jolting movement of the truck. Finally, she just tried to give with the motion.

"I am DeVega," the driver said in an oddly formal way, without looking at his passengers.

"Carson and Jill," Carson said, neatly omitting their last names.

"You are friends of Arturo Martine?"

"No," Carson said quickly. "We broke into his place looking for help. He didn't want us there, so we paid him to contact you."

Jill couldn't tell if DeVega bought Carson's explanation or not. "I want you to understand one thing," the man said.

"What's that?"

"If we are stopped for any reason by anyone, I will tell them a story such as you told me about Martine." Jill could tell right then he hadn't believed Carson's explanation at all. "I will say you forced me to take you into the mountains. Is that understood?"

Carson didn't hesitate. "Yes." Unexpectedly he reached out and covered Jill's hand where it clutched the seat edge. Common sense told her to pull away, but she admitted that common sense wasn't something she had a great deal of at this moment.

"This will be a long trip," DeVega said, swerving to miss a huge pothole.

"How long?" Jill asked.

"One day, maybe two." He shrugged. "It is not easy getting to the border by the back route. If we could use the main road it would be less than a day. But this is the way we must go."

He gave the truck more gas and it lurched forward, its motor straining to make headway on the crude road. Carson didn't let go of Jill, and when she looked at him, she found he wasn't looking at her, but intently watching DeVega. She wondered what he thought of the man.

"This is a news flash from KHRT, Channel Three. There is still no word of the fate of station manager, Carson Davies, and Jillian Segar, the cohost of Dream Chasers. *There has been a confirmed report that the American consulate in the capital city of Puerto Luis was leveled by an explosion set by sympathizers of the Brothers of Liberty.*

"Two hours ago deposed president Javier Estrada was flown into Panama where he has been granted exile. Estrada declined any comment on the whereabouts of Davies and Segar."

During the long ride, Carson was relieved when Jill finally gave up her death grip on the front seat and allowed herself to lean against him. When he put his arm around her shoulders, he felt her hesitate, then rest her head against his shoulder. And despite their situation he found his focus was on her, and on the memory of the words she'd said back at Martine's.

Had she really perceived their life in Houston in those terms? Had she felt second, beaten out by his career? When she had spoken those words, they had been as much a blow to him as a physical hit in his midsection. James had said he was a workaholic, defining himself by his accomplishments. He swore he wasn't, yet now, when he really looked squarely at his life, he saw it all in blacks and whites.

His work as opposed to his personal life. His failed marriage. He'd always thought the blame of failure was fifty-fifty. Maybe it wasn't that cut and dried. His work was important to him. It let him do what he wanted to do, when he wanted to do it. Hadn't he told James that? But what if the things he got to do were without Jill? What if he could do anything in the world, yet not have her?

She shifted against him, gasping when the truck hit a nasty bump, and he looked down at her. The coming night shadowed her face, the fan of her lashes effectively hiding her eyes from him. What would his life be worth if Jill wasn't in it?

Hadn't he had a life like that since she left Houston? But he couldn't begin to remember his personal life during those months. He remembered the jobs he did, the work he completed. He closed his eyes for a minute. But the nights, the emptiness. He'd hidden from it for so long, until last night. Until he'd held Jill again.

It wasn't the sex, he admitted to himself, although he couldn't get enough of her physically. It was being close to someone, sharing himself with that person. Sharing? Wasn't that what Jill had said he never did? He opened his eyes to the long shadows of evening cutting through the land.

Sharing? He and Jill were running for their lives. That was sharing. It wasn't wrong for him to wonder how the station was covering the San Arman situation. He couldn't stop that side of his persona. He damn well hoped the station was playing up the angle of the two of them trapped here. That didn't mean he couldn't worry about here and now. Worry? He was damned scared.

He glanced at DeVega. The man hadn't spoken two words to them since telling them his conditions, and Carson remembered what Martine had said before Jill came down.

"Do not trust DeVega. Trust no one until you are out of San Arman." Then Martine had given him the duffel bag. "In there is what you might need—water, some food, and some protection."

Carson looked out at the untamed wilderness of intense greens and browns, an alien land that he had to break free from. He glanced back at DeVega. "How can you tell where we're going?"

DeVega shot Carson a dark look, then stared straight ahead. "I know this country like the back of my hand." He pointed to the trees that pressed in on the trail from either side. "Those trees, they are only found between us and the Colombian border."

"The direction—"

"Into the sun as it sets."

That seemed so elementary to Carson that he felt embarrassed. "I know, but—?"

"This trail goes to the border. It was cut for traders years ago, and has not been used for a very long time."

As they went higher into the mountains, DeVega fell silent and gave one-word answers to any questions. Carson wished the man would talk, so he could use the man's talking as a shield against thoughts.

"How can you tell when you get to the border?"

"I will know."

"How close are we now to the border?"

"A long distance."

When the trail became a steady uphill climb, Carson fell into silence and closed his eyes. But he immediately opened them. Each breath Jill took seemed to go through him, each sound she made, each movement. He took his arm from around her shoulders and sat straighter so he could reach for his duffel and pull it onto his lap.

DeVega braked to a stop at the side of a widening in the road, then got out of the idling truck and circled it at the front. When he came to the passenger door, he pulled it open. "This is as far as *you* go."

His hand moved to his waist, and the gun was out before Carson could do anything. "Now, get out," DeVega said and stood back from the truck.

Carson glanced at Jill, at the horror on her face, then spoke softly. "Do what he says." He slid to the ground and waited for Jill to get out and stand by the truck before he turned and spoke to DeVega. "You're just going to leave us here?"

"Walk to the west. You will either get to the border or not. It is up to you." The man held out his free hand. "And I will take the rest of the money."

Carson hesitated, then reached into the side pocket of the duffel bag. Thank goodness Martine had given him protection. He closed his hand around the coolness of metal, then as he jerked the handgun out of the bag, he swung the duffel at DeVega's head.

Chapter 11

Jill saw the scene as if the world was being seen in stop-action frames in front of her. Carson had a gun, then he swung the duffel bag in a wide arch toward DeVega and caught the surprised man squarely on the jaw. DeVega's head snapped back, and the gun fell out of his hand to skitter across the baked earth of the road. The man slowly crumpled, dropping to his knees, swaying, then falling face-first into the dirt.

"Grab the gun," Carson yelled at Jill, as he kicked at it, sending it across the ground to stop just inches from her feet.

When DeVega moaned and rolled to one side on the ground, Jill quickly stooped, picked up the gun and straightened. As she held the heavy firearm, she watched DeVega slowly move his head to the side, then look up at Carson. A thin trickle of blood showed at one nostril, and a red welt blotched his jawline. "I did not think..." He closed his eyes for a moment, then looked back at Carson. "Martine . . . I should have known."

"He didn't trust you, and neither did I," Carson said as he stooped, and without taking his eyes off DeVega felt for the duffel, then picked it up.

DeVega awkwardly pushed up with one hand, then rolled over until he was supporting himself on one elbow. Gingerly he fingered his jaw, then narrowed his eyes as he stared at Carson. "I will give you your money back. The trip this far is free."

"Keep the money as payment for your truck."

"What?"

"I doubt it's worth that much, but I need it . . . more than you do right now."

DeVega grunted harshly as he got to his feet. With quick jabs, he brushed at the clinging dust on his clothes, but his dark eyes never left Carson's face. "You cannot take my truck and leave me like this," he bit out.

"I can, just as easily as you were going to leave us here."

"And what do I do?"

Carson moved back a half pace from the man in the direction of the truck. "Either walk back the way we came, or follow us on foot." He spoke to Jill without taking his eyes off DeVega. "Get his things out of the back of the truck and put them on the road."

DeVega spoke quickly. "You will not make it. The soldiers of the Brothers of Liberty are all over. They are spreading out into the mountains looking for traitors. They will find you."

"Is that true?" Jill asked Carson.

"Who knows," he said. "Just get his things out so we can leave."

She went around to the back of the truck, laid the gun on the tailgate, put a bedroll, a jug of water and some canvas tarpaulins out on the dusty road. When she turned, Carson hadn't moved. "It's all out."

"Good, now take the bullets out of his gun."

She picked up the revolver and had to try twice to snap the chamber open, then tap the bullets out into her hand. "What do I do with them?"

"Throw them into the brush, then put the gun with the other things."

She tossed the six bullets into the thick ground cover by the road, then dropped the gun on top of the bedroll.

Carson glanced quickly at the stack on the road, then back to DeVega. "Unlike what you were going to do to us, I'm leaving you water and supplies. If you look hard, you might even be able to find a bullet or two."

Carson backed up more as he spoke to Jill and held the duffel out to her. "Take this and get in the truck."

She scrambled into the cab, closed her door, then looked out the open window. Carson motioned to DeVega with the gun. "Lay face down in the dirt, the way you were."

DeVega muttered in Spanish, but did as Carson told him. When the man was prone in the dirt, Carson backed up to the truck. "If you know what's good for you, you'll forget this ever happened." He got close to Jill's door. "Jill, take the gun and keep it on him. If he does anything he shouldn't, just squeeze the trigger."

He gave the gun to her, and she could feel heat in the handle where he had held it. It looked too small to be able to do anything, but its heaviness seemed to underscore the fact that it wasn't a toy. With vaguely unsteady hands, she pointed the gun at DeVega and curled her finger around the trigger.

Carson hurried around the front of the truck, got into the cab, and drove off in a squeal of tires and clashing gears. Screams from DeVega echoed after them.

"If Martine knew about that man, why did he send us out here with him?" Jill asked as they bounced over the rough road.

"What other choice was there?" Carson gripped the steering wheel tightly, navigating around the most gaping holes in the road. "No matter what DeVega is, we're heading for the border."

"Do you know where you're going?"

"West," he said, snapping on the headlights to cut an arch of light through the gathering dusk. "We'll go in this direction until we find Colombia."

She laid the gun on the seat between the two of them alongside the duffel bag. "Carson?"

He glanced at her, then back to the trail. "I know. This is madness. You hate violence. You hate guns. But we don't have any other choice."

She looked at him, the shadows hiding so much, yet making it easier to say what she felt. "I was going to thank you for what you did back there. You kept that man from abandoning us by the side of the road."

He shrugged, a sharp movement in the shadows. "I'm not going to let anything stop us from getting out of this place and back home." He cast her a sidelong glance. "It's too important to get back, to let someone like DeVega prevent it."

"I never knew you could do something like that." There was so much she had never known about him. "I mean, you just hit him."

"I did what I had to do." He took a deep breath. "Actually, when I was working out of the station in Chicago on the news desk, James and I were in the inner city and got into a tight situation with some gang members. The leader of the group had a gun on us, and I tackled him while James got the gun away from him." He shook his head. "James actually ended up getting the kid into some rehab program and making a model citizen out of him. I'm not inclined to do anything like that for DeVega, but I'll leave his truck near the border for him to find if he follows us."

She couldn't take her eyes off Carson. "I would never have imagined you doing something like that, fighting someone for a gun. Or doing what you did to DeVega."

"I owe that to Martine. He gave me fair warning, so I was ready for DeVega." He laughed harshly, a grating sound in the confines of the old truck. "It seems like scenes from another life. Actually, everything that happened before yesterday does. Or maybe like a dream. There's an old saying that everything before now has as much substance as dreams. That dreaming about something actually gives you a memory of the incident just as clearly as living through it does."

"But you don't have to pay consequences for dreams," she said without weighing her words.

He looked at her briefly, his eyes hidden by the shadows. "You're right. Physical cause-and-effect has no reality in dreams. But I can't help wondering how things would be if nothing counted that happened before yesterday?"

Dreams and reality. Consequences. Jill hugged her arms around herself. This moment was reality, not the past or the future. But she would be paying for the past for the rest of her life, in one way or another. "That would be a truly complete fresh start, wouldn't it?" she murmured.

"Yes," he said softly.

She looked away from Carson, out to the darkness on either side of the road and swiped at the sticky dampness on her arms from the lingering, oppressive heat. "I don't believe there is such a thing as a real fresh start." Coming to San Diego had only prolonged the inevitable, it had only put off the consequences. There had been no fresh start for her at Channel Three, and she should have realized that, the day she walked into the office and saw Carson behind the station manager's desk.

"You sound awfully cynical."

"I guess I am," she admitted, "even though my program is called *Dream Chasers*. I know you can't live your life chasing dreams." She had been chasing the dream that Carson meant nothing to her for the past two years. And for the past day, she had been chasing the idea that Carson had changed. Neither had worked. When the chasing had stopped the dreams had turned to dust, leaving only painful reality.

"A person has to have dreams, Jill."

"Do you have dreams, besides winning the ratings game?" The words sounded harsher than she had intended, but before she could say anything else, Carson answered her.

"Of course. I'm where I am because of dreams. Didn't you ever understand that?"

No, she hadn't, not at all. "What dreams?" she asked, hoping he'd answer her. Carson with dreams. The concept seemed contradictory to her.

She heard him inhale and felt the truck slow as the climb into the mountains grew steeper. "When I was six, in a foster home, I dreamed of a family. I dreamed of belonging, being with a person who wanted me there, who wasn't paid to be nice. As I got older, the dreams changed. I wanted to do something, to be someone, to make a success so I wouldn't have to depend on anyone again."

The words cut to Jill's heart and the tears burned her eyes, tears for a small boy whose innocence had died. The tears blurred the gathering night through the window. "Is that what you've done?"

"It's what I've tried to do—for better or worse."

"Any regrets?"

She held her breath until he said softly, "Of course, but probably not more than most people."

The tears slid silently down her cheeks, and she did nothing to wipe them away. Carson couldn't see them, and she couldn't stop them. She also couldn't talk past the tightness in her throat.

He was silent for several minutes as he kept driving, then he spoke without preamble. "I probably shouldn't say this, not now, but I want you to know that whatever has happened with us—or will happen—you aren't one of those regrets." He hesitated. "Am I a regret of yours?"

She thought about that and knew that he wasn't. She didn't regret being with him, holding him, and she didn't regret making love with him. She regretted needing more than he could give her, and not being everything he ever needed and wanted. She regretted not being able to compete with his ambitions and his obsessions. And she regretted the years ahead when she would have to get through life without him.

She wiped at her face with both hands, brushing at the dampness on her cheeks. "No, you're not a regret."

"Thank God," he whispered. "I would hate to be someone's worst time in their life."

The best and the worst, she thought, and braced herself when the truck hit a bone-jarring hole in the road.

A low rumbling could be heard over the motor, a distant sound that seemed to vibrate on the hot air. Jill felt dampness at her back from contact with the seat and realized the humidity had climbed drastically in the past few minutes. The air that had seemed heavy before now felt oppressive.

The rumbling came again, and she glanced at Carson, but before she could ask him what it was, brilliance shattered the night as lightning cut through the heavens. It flooded the land with white light before it faded away, giving the land back to the heavy darkness.

"Heat lightning?" Jill asked, but before it died away she saw the first huge raindrops splashing on the dusty windshield.

Within seconds, the heavens opened and the rain came down in an intense curtain of water, pouring onto the land and drumming on the oxidized exterior of the truck. Carson and Jill quickly rolled up their windows, then Carson flicked on the wipers. But only the driver's side worked, and even that ineffectively smeared the glass, making mud with the dust and water and blocking a good degree of visibility.

Carson leaned close to the wheel, straining to see through the windshield, and Jill didn't know how he could see more than a few feet in front of the truck. The headlights made little dent in the obscuring sheet of rain with the blackness beyond.

Lightning and thunder tore through the night, over and over again, and Jill found herself narrowing her eyes and bracing for the next rolling rumble or brilliant illumination. Storms had never been something she enjoyed, and with each roll of thunder she found herself bracing and counting—one thousand-one, one thousand-two. When she was very little, her grandma had told her that for each second she could count between the sound of the thunder and the flash of lightning, she was that many miles from where the lightning would strike.

Thunder rolled, and she counted. On thousand-one, one thousand-two, one thous— Lightning crackled through the night, washing the land in watery brilliance for a few seconds. Then the darkness came again.

"Damned storms," Carson muttered, fighting the wheel as the tires of the truck began to slip on a road that had become more mud than dirt. "I can hardly see a thing."

Another roll of thunder sounded, close enough to send a vibration through the truck, and Jill barely counted to one before the lightning struck. In a fiery burst that seemed incongruous in the heavy rain, the lightning hit to the left of the truck. A massive tree shuddered, then burst into flames as it literally split in two. One part of the tree fell into the jungle, but the other part fell like a flaming plume toward the road.

Carson jerked the truck away from it to the right, and Jill screamed. The flaming tree seemed to be coming directly at them, then the world began to spin. It took Jill a second to realize it was the truck going out of control on the slick mud. They whipped around and around, then stopped for a fraction of a second before the truck began to slide sideways as if on a sheet of ice.

Carson spun the wheel, cursed under his breath, and Jill grabbed the door handle. Just when she thought the truck was coming under control, they went sharply sideways and came to a thudding stop tilted at a precarious angle down to the right. The engine shuddered, then died.

The flaming tree was almost extinguished, its smoldering pieces mere feet in front of the shimmering glow from the headlights of the truck. And Jill had no idea why they had stopped until she saw the door on her side bowing inward, the window shattered, and the rough trunk of another tree pressing against the window opening.

Carson touched her hand, which was still gripping the edge of the seat. "Are you all right?"

She sank back on the hard vinyl. "I think so. Are you?"

"I'd be fine, if I knew where we were," he said, applying a fleeting pressure to her hand before letting her go. He stretched down to pick up the duffel that had been thrown off the seat and onto the floor against Jill's legs during the spin. He opened it, reached inside and took out a flashlight. After an attempt to open his window only to have the rain pour inside, he rolled it up tightly and tossed the flashlight back into the duffel bag.

He reached for the key in the ignition, turned it and Jill was surprised when the motor started right up. But when Carson pressed the accelerator, the wheels spun, the motor roared, and the truck did little more than shudder, then die.

"That was a short ride for twenty-five hundred dollars," Carson said as he sank back in the seat.

"We're really stuck, aren't we?" Jill asked, knowing the answer before Carson responded.

"Fatally stuck, I'm afraid," he murmured, and snapped off the headlights.

As they were plunged into darkness, Jill groaned and let her head rest against the back of the cab. "What can we do now?"

He shifted on the seat, and she looked over at him as a bolt of lightning illuminated the cab. In a wash of white light, Jill could see Carson rummaging around in the duffel bag again. "We'll stay here until the rain lets up. Martine said there's some food in here, and we're dry, at least for now."

"And when this stops, what then?"

He looked at her in the shadows. "It can't be far to the border. We'll walk." He paused, then used the flashlight to look into the duffel. Within minutes, he took out two sandwiches and some packages of apple juice.

Jill took a slightly mashed ham sandwich and nibbled on it between sips of the juice, but with every crack of thunder and bolt of lightning, she jumped. She couldn't forget the image of the tree being destroyed by the energy of the storm, and she finally gave up the pretense of eating. She rewrapped the hardly touched sandwich, tucked it into the duffel bag and sank back in the seat.

The air was heavy and humid, saturated with heat and dampness. In the flashes of lightning, the jungle looked frightening and alien. She wanted to get away from it, and away from everything.

As if he could read her mind, Carson said, "Getting out of here and getting home can't happen too soon for me."

Get out, go home, and make things right. No, she couldn't do that. She would talk with Boyd, get her life in order, but she didn't know how to make things right again. Her life had been irrevocably changed in these past hours. She just didn't know if it was for the best or not. Thunder rolled, she braced herself for the lightning, and began to count. She barely counted to two before the lightning came.

It was so close, so horribly close again. How was it possible that two days ago her most pressing problems had been camera angles, good location shots and Sam Rollins. Now those problems seemed unremarkable. She felt the seat move as Carson put the duffel bag on the floor, and she realized she had to consider approaching other stations for a show when she got back.

Carson had changed her life more than he could ever know. He'd made it impossible for her to stay at Channel Three, but not because she was running away this time. She would never do that again. She simply had to try to make a fresh start. She had to see if it was really possible. She had to see what there was for her without Carson in her life.

She shifted, aware of Carson putting away the rest of his food, and she found herself talking just to fill the spaces until the thunder came again.

"I wonder what everyone thinks happened to us?"

Carson cast her a slanting glance. "Anything they could think can't compare to the reality."

"That's the truth," she murmured.

"Actually I doubt that Sam even knows we're missing."

She found herself almost laughing. "I thought Sam was Mister Perfect in your eyes?"

"For the screen, he's damned-near perfect, but I have no illusions about his capacity for independent thought."

She chuckled, a tight sound, but it felt good to experience even that little burst of humor. "I didn't know you understood about Sam."

"I understand a lot, Jill. I wonder...?" His voice died off suddenly, then he asked, "Can you hear that?"

"What?" she asked, "the thunder?"

"No, something else beyond it. Listen."

She strained to hear something over the drumming of the rain. Then she knew what Carson was talking about. Booming. Some sort of gunfire, way off in the distance, but a heavier sound than the shooting had been in Puerto Luis. It was mildly surprising to her that she was beginning to distinguish something like the difference in gunfire. "Shooting. But it's heavier, more substantial." There was no popping sound in the echoing volleys.

"Heavy-duty hardware. We saw the tanks, and God knows what else they have been able to get from sympathizers." He sank back in the seat, and in the flash of lightning, she saw the tightness in his jaw and the tightness of his hands on the steering wheel. "We can only stay here for a while. If they're out there..." His voice trailed off, but he didn't have to finish the sentence.

Jill stared at the rain-smeared windows, wishing she could see through the downpour and the night. She hated not knowing who was out there, or what they were doing. But the night and storm were impenetrable. And the truck was actually beginning to feel like a sanctuary of sorts.

She cringed when a volley of gunfire sounded off in the distance, then a flashing thought came to her, an echo of one she had had at Martine's home. Would she have a chance for the fresh start? She wished she knew. The uncertainty of her life hit her full force. "Why... why would they be out there in this rain?" she asked, trying to keep the fear out of her voice.

"Maybe DeVega was right and sympathizers of Estrada are using the jungle for hiding. Who knows how the minds of these people work?" He looked out the side window. "I think we're safe enough for now, at least until this lets up, or dawn comes. And we can try and get some sleep."

"I don't think—"

"Rest if you can't sleep. We're going to have a walk when we leave here. Go ahead and settle back." He snapped on the flashlight, aiming it at the floor, then bent over and straightened with the gun in his hand. "I'll keep watch in case someone manages to find us."

She didn't argue. As he snapped off the flashlight, she leaned back into the corner by the door and closed her eyes. But as she shut out the sights of the world, every noise seemed magnified—the drumming of the rain, the distant gunfire, the rumbling thunder, and Carson shifting nearby. When the last roll of thunder hadn't even dissipated before the lightning flashed, making whiteness behind her eyelids, she opened her eyes.

She looked at Carson sitting behind the wheel, his profile a dark blur. "Carson?"

"What?" he asked without turning to her.

"Talk to me. Say something, anything."

His hand moved, skimming over his hair, then it went back to rest on the top of the steering wheel. "When I was in prison with Martine, we were in the darkness most of the time. Finally, I'd say, 'Talk to me, Martine, say anything, but let me hear your voice.' And he did. He told me about the San Arman he knew as a child, about his family. He talked and helped me hold on to my sanity."

Jill shifted to look more squarely at Carson. "Did you talk to him?"

"We took turns."

"What did you tell him?"

"Things. Whatever he asked."

"What things?" she prodded, ignoring the deep rumble of more thunder.

"He was interested in my work, about the way things were done on television. Why I was there in San Arman."

"Did the two of you talk about yourselves, about your past, your present, your future?"

"Of course."

"What did you tell him?"

"So many things I forget." He sighed, a soft sound in the cab almost drowned out by the echoes of the storm outside. "I told him about when I was ten and broke my arm. About the foster home I was in. One that I liked because the man and woman were pretty nice."

"What happened to those people?"

"Who knows? I was there six months when I was in the fifth grade, then the man got sick and they put me in a different home." She could hear the tinge of bitterness in his voice. "I stopped counting the homes after number seven."

When they had talked in Houston, Carson had always passed off her questions of his childhood with the simple answer, "It wasn't good, it wasn't bad." Or the evasive response, "I don't think about it much anymore." But now, the night gave her courage she wouldn't have had otherwise. "What happened to your parents?" she asked.

He shifted on the seat, leaning back and resting his head against the wall of the truck cab. "I told you."

"No, you never did. You said you were too young to really remember."

He took off his glasses and rubbed his eyes with his knuckles. "They were killed when I was three," he finally murmured. "I don't remember them, not really. Just images, impressions. The scent of lemons. I don't have any idea why I associate that with my mother." He stopped abruptly and fell into silence while he put his glasses back on. "This seems odd telling you all this."

"Why? I've told you about my family lots of times. They never got to meet you . . ." She bit her lip, remembering her mother's questions about Carson, when the two of them could fly out to Colorado. "But you know a lot about them."

He took a deep breath. "Absolutely. Ted and Judy Segar. Pillars of the community in Far Ends, Colorado. Your dad's the town pharmacist, your mother teaches piano and makes the best carrot cake you ever tasted. Your brothers were brats when you were growing up, and now they're best friends."

"You make my family sound like Ozzie and Harriet," she said with a chuckle, but the sound was unsteady. She felt strangely touched that he remembered things she could barely recall telling him. "Did I really tell you Jack and Joey were brats?"

"Absolutely. And that they were fraternal twins."

She nibbled on her bottom lip. "You remember so much." She hesitated. "I wish I had known as much about you."

"Why?"

"I guess it's because I always felt the past shaped the present, that where a person comes from makes a difference in what he becomes."

"And you could never figure out why I am like I am, could you?"

"No, I couldn't."

He was silent, while a rumble of thunder vibrated through the truck, when the crashing lightning lit up the interior. She had a flashing image of Carson with his eyes closed, his jaw set and his fingers worrying the smoothness of the steering wheel.

When he spoke, he said something that took her off guard. "Maybe you're right. Maybe I can't share enough of myself to create a real relationship with another person. I had years of practicing self-protection by not exposing too much emotionally to others."

"You've shared things with James and have a good friendship with him. You're closer than most men ever get."

"But a relationship—"

"It's like a friendship, just on a different level. How can two people be close if they aren't friends, man or woman?"

He looked at her and his voice sounded vaguely amused. "I didn't know you were that wise."

"It's got nothing to do with wisdom."

"What does it have to do with?"

"Sharing. Giving." She felt a tightness invading her throat and she muttered, "I don't know."

"All right. Do you share everything? Aren't there some things you hold back, maybe out of self-protection or out of necessity?"

"I guess most people do, but when you're building a relationship, you—"

"I know, you share." He exhaled harshly. "And you feel that I didn't share with you. That's what seems so strange to me."

"What does?"

He cast her a slanting glance. "I thought I shared more with you than with anyone I'd ever known in my life. I thought it was sharing, to love you, to need you, to make love with you."

Jill bit her lip hard. "Maybe it is for some people. But it wasn't enough for me."

"I think the next question is, what is enough for you? Is it being with someone twenty-four hours a day, living in their hip pockets?"

"Of course not." She looked out the front window at the sheeting rain. "It's about priorities, not hours spent with someone. It's caring about someone more than yourself. It's letting that person get closer to you than anyone else in the world. It's being your own person, yet knowing no matter what, the other person will be there for you."

"Ozzie and Harriet?" he asked.

She hated the touch of sarcasm in his comment. "No one can live a fairy-tale life," she said. "I just meant each person gives the other person what he needs. They complement each other, not distract or take away from each other."

"Where does love come into this picture of yours?"

"I thought I *was* describing love."

Thunder rumbled all around, a long continuous sound and when it stilled, Carson asked without warning, "Did you love me?"

Chapter 12

The bolt of lightning following the thunder seemed to echo in Jill. "Yes, I loved you," she said.

"And I loved you."

She closed her eyes for a moment before she breathed, "I know."

"I think we've had a breakthrough," he said.

"What do you mean by that?" she asked, looking at him again.

He cast her a slanting look. "You aren't arguing that I couldn't have loved you because I didn't come home that night, or because I didn't bare my soul to you."

She didn't want to think back to the past, the present was giving her enough problems. "That's over and done. I know you didn't deliberately hurt me. You didn't mean to stay in the production meeting until dawn." She knew that was true. As far as she knew, Carson never intentionally hurt anyone. "You didn't mean to put your success at the station ahead of everything in your life, ahead of everyone."

There wasn't the instant anger, or the instant denial she expected. Instead he a ran a hand around his neck under the collar of the clinging shirt. "I really didn't. That's why it hurt so much to find you gone."

"And after I was gone, you filled your time with work," she said, her voice sounding terribly flat in her own ears.

"There weren't many choices left to me after I talked to your mother. She certainly didn't give me any information."

That brought her up short. "You talked to my mother?"

"The next day. She said you were moving for a new career opportunity, but that was all. She certainly didn't offer to tell me where you ran to."

For two weeks she had stayed by herself at a hotel outside of Houston, contacting stations about a position. She had told her mother not to tell anyone where she was until she'd settled where she was going. But her mother had never mentioned that Carson had called her.

Lightning from another roll of thunder came, and Jill saw Carson in the crackling flash of light. His profile, etched by the whiteness, was all sharp lines and contours, with the normal color washed away. Yet she felt she was seeing Carson more clearly than she ever had before. He'd tried to find her. She had never suspected he would, after the note she left.

She felt a stinging in her hand and swiped at what was causing it. A bug. She couldn't see it, but she felt the pain go away as soon as she had hit it off her skin. She rubbed at the tingling. "My mother—"

"—was protecting you from the big, bad wolf," Carson finished abruptly. The personnel manager at the station in Houston had told him employee information was confidential, and he didn't want to think much more about the conversation with Mrs. Segar.

"No, Jillian isn't here. I'm sorry. She's making a career move and she's very busy. I'm sure she'll be in touch with her friends when everything is settled. Nice of you to call. Take care." Then the click, as final as he had known her leaving would be when he read her note. "I can understand a parent protecting a child from someone she thinks will hurt the child."

"No, that wasn't—" she began to protest.

He stared out the window, watching the patterns made by the rain smear and run. "It was. I didn't have to ask what you had told her about me. I hung up. I wanted the truth, but not that much truth."

"And you went on with your life," she said softly.

She shifted on the seat, and he could feel the action stir the heavy air. Perspiration trickled down his temple, and he swiped at it, then made himself look at Jill, at her shadowy form in the corner of the seat. He could never tell her how hard it had been to "go on with his life." Or how much of a shock it had been when he had seen promo tapes from the San Diego Station and she was on them.

He wasn't about to talk about his feelings during those days and nights. Once they were put into words they would have more strength and staying power. "What choice did I have but to go on with my life?"

"You're right," she murmured, "we don't have a choice, not really."

He looked at her, wondering how they could have been together at Martine's and shared each other and still they talked as if they were just acquaintances.

Sharing. The word stood by itself, and for a few seconds he thought about the concept. He'd never been good at it. Not in the foster homes, not later. James had been about the only person he'd ever met whom he could open up to. Even then there were barriers.

But with Jill . . . Didn't she know how close she came to his core, to whatever it was that made him the man he was? Just the concept was a bit intimidating for him. Vulnerability wasn't something he was secure with, at all. He took a deep breath and turned from her image to stare out at the night.

The rain was easing into a steady drizzle, but the heat never lessened. He wished he could open a window, do something to dispel the provocative mingling of the heat, dampness and the sweetness that clung to Jill. He heard her sigh, and he instinctively moved closer to his door, hating the way his body could respond to her without him even thinking about it.

Out of self-protection, he spoke through the stillness. "The rain's beginning to let up."

"A bit," the soft reply came, followed by long minutes of unbroken silence.

"Are you asleep, Jill?"

"No. I can't sleep."

"What are you thinking about?" he found himself asking.

She didn't respond for a full heartbeat, then she said, "Life and death. How close everything is. How intense it's all been these past hours."

He marveled that she could say something like that. It wasn't polite chitchat even with what had happened between them. He found himself envying her openness, her ability to say the truth without worrying about what it showed about her or how it exposed her.

"Big subjects," he murmured, an offhand response just for something to say, something that wouldn't give away what he really thought.

Thunder rumbled, but way off in the distance, then her voice came to him through the shadows, "No, lightning and thunder are big subjects. They make me feel very small, very insignificant, and very alone."

He took an uneasy breath. Did she know that he felt the same way during electric storms? No, how could she? He would have never told her that.

"Maybe lonely is a better word," she amended softly.

"Alone. Lonely. Not quite the same things, are they? You can be alone but not lonely, yet you can be lonely in a crowd," he said.

"Yes, you can," she whispered.

He could sense pain in her voice, yet he didn't know why it was there. "Are you lonely?"

"Are you?" she asked, not missing a beat.

He would have said no, if she had asked him that twenty-four hours ago. He wouldn't have even hesitated. He had never been a person who had to have people to be content, that's why he loved running so much. Hours alone running had been a blessing, a relief from the pressures of everyday life.

But now he faced the fact that he *was* lonely, except when he was with Jill, when he held her and touched her and loved her. He felt disconnected and cast adrift the rest of the time. "Yes, I am . . . sometimes. Are you?" he repeated.

"Of course."

He held the steering wheel tightly, needing to touch Jill, to have that link with her, yet almost afraid to act on his feelings. "How about now?"

Gunfire sounded off in the distance, and Carson could feel Jill tremble even without touching her. "Especially now," she said softly.

Before he let reason intrude, he did act on his feelings and reached for Jill, awkwardly gathering her to him. As he held her close to his side, he heard her muffled "Thank you," and he whispered "You're welcome." Let her think it was an attempt to comfort her, that it was an altruistic action on his part. She didn't have to know he needed the comfort just as much as she did.

"Tell you what," he said. "The rain has to stop sooner or later. Let's take this moment by moment, get through the night, then get to the border."

His gently smoothed back her fine, damp hair where it clung to her temple and cheek, then pressed a kiss to the top of her head. When a soft sigh escaped from her lips, Carson closed his eyes tightly and spoke on impulse. "This feels right, doesn't it," he asked, "despite what's going on out there?"

When she didn't answer, he touched her chin with one finger and tipped her face up. "Don't answer that," he said, then allowed himself one taste of her softly parted lips. The contact was no more substantial than the caress of a feather, yet it reached him on a level he felt certain he had never experienced before. He felt no need to demand a response, and he realized he actually intended the kiss to say, "I'm here for you."

He drew back, stunned at what had just happened, and let his head rest against the truck wall. He wanted to be here for Jill, but not just now, forever, to be everything she needed or wanted in her life. And he didn't know what to do about it. The sensation was entirely new and unique for him.

As he felt her shift to settle in his hold, he took off his glasses, leaned forward to set them on the dash, then settled back. He stared straight ahead, the world a blur without his glasses. He didn't need to look at Jill or be able to clearly remember her face, he knew it intimately, each gentle line and curve. With a vaguely unsteady hand, he touched her hair, then trailed a finger along the line of her cheek to a pulse that beat just under her ear. His fingertip lingered there before moving down to rest on her shoulder.

"Talk to me, Carson," she said.

After a few moments of silence, he began to talk in a low voice. Words seemed to come on their own, from someplace deep inside him he either hadn't known was there or had forgotten. He told her about himself, about his past, about his failures and about his triumphs. About those days and nights in the prison, the interrogation where his shoulder was dislocated, and his final release. As he spoke and the dam he'd kept his thoughts and feelings hidden behind for so long, burst, he felt closer to Jill than he ever had to any human being in his life.

Carson hadn't meant to doze off, and when he was jarred from a dreamless sleep he didn't even know why he had awoken. Jill felt heavy against his side, her head lolled over onto his chest. She hadn't moved. Then he opened his eyes to the pale light of dawn, to the hush that only came after a rain, and caught a hint of movement to his left. Then he realized the door to the truck was open and a blurred shadow partially blocked the first rays of sunlight.

Then something jabbed Carson in his shoulder, and a man spoke quickly in Spanish at the same time Carson heard the hammer of a gun cock.

"We should kill you here and let you rot in the jungle for what you have done."

Carson squinted up at the man, and his heart sank. They'd tried so hard and made it this far. It wasn't fair to be stopped now. He had to figure out how to get them out of this, how to protect Jill and get her to safety. The gun. He pointed to his glasses on the dash and murmured in Spanish, "My glasses." He slowly reached for them and slipped them on, hoping to catch a glimpse of his gun before he looked back at the man.

But as he turned without being able to see his gun anywhere, he glanced at a man he could clearly focus on now. He saw a rifle in the man's hands, and the gun Martine had sent with him, tucked into the waistband of the man's military uniform.

Carson felt Jill stir, and wished she would keep sleeping, that she would never have to wake to face this. But he knew how foolish that idea was. Gently he patted her shoulder, trying to wake her up without scaring her. But it didn't work. She mumbled something, struggling to sit up and as she turned, he felt her jerk with shock and heard her gasp.

"Don't move," he whispered.

He never took his eyes off the man standing above him in the mud by the truck. The man was stocky with a bushy mustache and dark, leathery skin. As he moved back half a pace, Carson saw three or four more soldiers with him, all of them with their rifles cocked and aimed. But there were no arm bands, and their uniforms looked professional—pressed khaki, calf-high boots caked with mud and formal insignias.

The one nearest, who seemed to be the leader, spoke again. "Death is too good for pigs like you!"

Slowly, Carson let go of Jill and twisted toward the door, holding both hands, palms out while he tried to think what to say. It had to be neutral, but it had to work, or this man would kill them. He didn't doubt that for a minute.

"Wait a minute," he said in Spanish. "I do not know who you think we are, but we did not do anything. We are lost. We have been here for hours. With the storm—" he motioned to the charred tree not more than ten feet in front of the truck "—we were forced off the road."

The man scowled at him. "That is your bad luck and our fortune. You are part of the scum who have invaded our borders, setting fires, looting and killing our people."

"No," Carson said quickly. "I swear. We had nothing to do with anything like that."

The leader jerked his rifle up. "Get out so I can get a good look at the two of you."

Carson glanced back at Jill, hoping she understood enough to keep quiet and not give the soldiers any clue to who they were. She sat on the seat, her face pale, but she didn't say anything. Carson nodded to her, then twisted around to swing his legs out of the truck. He tested his cramped muscles, then gripped the door on both sides and slowly pulled himself out of the truck onto the muddy slope by the road.

His feet sank in the soft muck, his shoes slid, then he got his balance and looked up at the soldier in front of him. "What do you want with us?" he asked.

"Both of you out of the truck," the man snapped.

He kept his balance with one hand on the door frame as he turned and held out his free hand to Jill. She hesitated, then put her hand in his and he gently eased her out into the rain-fresh air. She stumbled for an instant, grabbed at his forearm with her other hand to keep her balance, then looked up at the soldiers. Carson felt her fingers bite into his arm, but Jill didn't say a thing.

One of the soldiers up on the road spoke quickly to the leader. "The general said to bring anyone back that we found. We have to take them in."

The leader scowled, but slowly released the hammer tension on the rifle, then motioned sharply in Carson's direction. "Both of you. Your hands in the air."

Carson let go of Jill and hoped she understood what the man wanted. As he raised his hands in the air, Jill followed suit. "Who are you?" Carson asked.

"No questions. Come."

He reached for Carson, catching him by the upper arm, and jerking him forward, making him stumble and fall to his knees. Rain soaked into the denim of his jeans, and his hands pressed into the grass, forcing mud to ooze up between his fingers. Before he could get to his feet, two other soldiers had him by each arm, jerking him to his feet and pulling his arms behind his back. He felt pain sear through his bad shoulder, the cold metal at his wrists followed by the snap of handcuffs.

As the two men half dragged him up the slight incline to the road, Carson twisted, trying to see Jill. He struggled to get free when he saw the other two soldiers grab her roughly and handcuff her. "Stop it," he shouted at them, but they didn't even look at him.

They all but lifted her off her feet as they dragged her up the incline to the muddy road rutted by the skid marks the truck had made last night. Three jeeps were parked in the middle of the road, their heavy, lugged tires caked with mud and dirt.

"You do not need to take her in," Carson gasped as the two of them pushed him face-first against the side of the nearest jeep. Without his hands free to break the impact, he hit the metal hard and felt a knee in his back. The barrel of the rifle was shoved into the hollow under his chin, forcing his head up sharply.

"Silence!" the leader snapped. "You will come with us without trouble, or it will not go well for either one of you." He jabbed the rifle barrel sharply into Carson's throat. "Is that understood?"

Carson managed to move his head in a jerky nod, and he felt the one man let go of his arm. He started to sag against the jeep, but another soldier pulled him back squarely onto his feet. He tasted blood in his mouth, then turned and saw Jill just feet away from him.

Mud was smeared across one cheek, and her clothes had clinging mud and grass at the knees and around the ankles. Her face seemed incredibly pale in the cool light, and he could see her biting her lip hard, but she never once cried out or said a thing. He wondered why he had never suspected she had such courage. Then again, he thought, he'd never been in a situation like this with her before.

The leader moved over to her, putting himself between her and Carson, and he spoke to her in Spanish.

"You look too tiny to give us trouble," he said. "You are not going to make this harder, are you?"

Carson didn't know what to do except to cough twice, hoping she remembered the signal he'd given her with their hands in Puerto Luis.

"No," she said tentatively.

"Good. Good." The man turned and spoke quickly to his men. "Enough. They will get answers out of them when we get them back to the general."

Carson felt the world suddenly begin to recede from him, then he took a deep breath and brought everything back into focus. The last time he'd been taken for questioning, it had only been him. He couldn't let Jill go through that. "What do you want from us? Tell me," he said, his voice edged with hoarseness.

"Silence!" the leader said as he turned and struck Carson sharply in the shoulder with the butt of the rifle. Pain shot down his arm and up into his neck. "Get in there," the man said, motioning with the rifle to the front jeep.

Carson stared at Jill, then one of the soldiers grabbed him by the arm and pulled him toward the door. He stumbled sideways, then managed to negotiate the step up and hook his elbow on the roll bar for leverage. The soldier pushed the front seat forward, then nudged Carson into the back.

Carson went forward and landed hard on the ungiving backseat. As he looked up, he felt giddy with relief when he saw one of the other soldiers putting Jill in after him. She stumbled sideways, falling against him, and he heard her gasp softly before she twisted and managed to sit on the seat next to him.

He looked down at her, at her hair with the clinging leaves and dirt, then looked at the leader as he got in the passenger seat and rested the rifle across his lap and spoke quickly to the driver. "Get going. We do not have time to waste."

As the jeep took off, skidding slightly in the mud until it got its traction, Jill leaned into Carson's side. He couldn't hold her or touch her or reassure her. Then again, he knew he didn't have any real reassurances for her, but something had to be done. He moved slightly to press his thigh against hers, and when she moved closer, letting her head rest against his shoulder, he wished he could will them back to San Diego. He wished he could wipe the past few days out of existence.

Then he looked down at her and her fear-widened eyes met his. In that instant, he faced the fact she was his life. And she had been since the first moment they had met at the production meeting at the Houston station, since the first time he had glimpsed her face and felt startled by the deep violet of her eyes and the tiny perfection of her body, since the first time he had heard her voice and felt his stomach tighten with awareness. Even when they had been separated after she left, she had never ceased to be his life.

He just hadn't been able to admit that to himself until this moment, when death seemed to be so close. He'd always heard about a person's life flashing before him when he faced death. Yet it wasn't his whole life he remembered. It was his life since Jill had been in it. Nothing before mattered. Nothing without her had any value.

He looked ahead as they drove under a massive canopy of tangled branches and vines. His life. He closed his eyes for a moment and realized he would give that life to save hers. Corny, he thought, a bit uncomfortable with the magnitude of the idea. Yet he knew with a certainty it was the absolute truth.

No, he wouldn't let this happen, not to her. He'd tell them anything they wanted. He'd do anything they wanted. He'd sign anything they wanted. He's say anything they told him to say—if they left Jill alone. He didn't have any pride where her safety was concerned.

Jill felt Carson's thigh press against hers, she took comfort from it and tried to move closer to him. She hadn't understood a thing the men had been saying, but their actions had spoken louder than words. The anger, the aggression, the impatience to get on with whatever they intended to do with them.

She twisted to look at Carson, to make eye contact and she wished they could talk. She didn't know what to expect, what the men wanted, but Carson knew. She could tell by the tension at his mouth, and the way his jaw worked.

She looked back at the man who seemed to be in charge. He stared straight ahead, then as they began to go down instead of climbing, he stood up, gripping the top of the window frame.

Then she saw what he was doing. They were approaching a town, or what was left of a town. As they got closer and the road widened, she could see shells of burned-out houses, structures that had been leveled and reduced to piles of rubble. The people along the sides of the road were a dissolute-looking array and stopped what they were doing to turn and look at the jeep speeding past.

Others were walking through the mud with backpacks on, some simply carried brown-paper bags and what looked like pillowcases heavy with their contents. And their faces were what caught at Jill. They looked blank, as if the world was too much for them, and they had been stunned by life. The jeep kept going, slowing as more vehicles appeared ahead of them. Gravel and pavement replaced the mud, and the houses and businesses here were larger and less touched by poverty. But there were signs of fires and destruction everywhere. The man standing in the jeep began to shout in Spanish, waving the rifle and motioning for the traffic to let them through.

She wanted to ask Carson what was going on, but she didn't dare speak English. She had understood his signals when the soldiers had found them, but if they were separated, she had no idea what she would do.

She looked at Carson beside her, his hair ruffling in the breeze and the sun showing his expression with painful clarity. She didn't want to die, not like this. But if it happened, if the nightmare reached its most horrible conclusion, she knew one thing would never change. She loved Carson.

She had listened to him during the night, heard things about him she had never suspected, seen vulnerability in him that she doubted he had even known existed. She felt a part of him, even more than when they had made love, and that part seemed permanent, indelible. She loved that part, and the rest of him that made him the man he was. And suddenly all the roadblocks, all the obstacles she had been so aware of, began to dissolve. And she realized they had been dissolving since the day they had argued about her coming to San Arman.

Wasn't love enough? Wasn't wanting to be with someone and loving him enough? Wasn't knowing she would never be happy without him enough? He turned to her, his eyes meeting hers again, and her heart answered for her. More than enough. If death came in the next minute, the love she had with Carson was more than most people found if they lived to be a hundred.

Carson wasn't the same man she'd known before, or maybe she just saw him differently. Maybe she was a bit more realistic than she had been. Or maybe she just wished it. The single-minded involvement with work had been to fill the voids in his life, to push away loneliness. And she grieved for those voids, and it only made her love him more.

How she wished she could tell him, let him know, but she couldn't say a thing. Instead she turned and touched her forehead to his shoulder and silently prayed she would have time to tell him exactly what she felt. She shifted on the seat, her right hand aching horribly from the constriction of the handcuffs.

The jeep lurched and Jill looked ahead as they drove into a central plaza that seemed packed with army jeeps and trucks. Soldiers were everywhere, guns on their shoulders, and civilians weren't in sight. Businesses nearby were closed and boarded up. The jeep slowed, wended its way through the crowds, then came out the other side and sped up. In a few seconds, it screeched to a stop in front of a straight-walled building that looked larger than the others.

The soldiers jumped out, reached in to pull Carson and Jill out with them, then with a soldier on each arm, Jill and Carson were taken toward the building. They were hurried up the tiled stairs, through green-painted doors and into cool, musty dimness. It took a few seconds for her eyes to adjust, then Jill could see whitewashed walls and what looked like a reception area with one desk and a very severe-looking woman in a uniform behind it talking on the telephone.

She glanced up and motioned with one hand to the other side of the room. The soldiers all but pulled Carson and Jill in that direction, through an open door and into a much larger room with straight-backed wooden chairs facing a huge desk, pale brown adobe walls, and high, narrow windows that let in very little light.

Behind the desk sat a totally bald man wearing a full-dress uniform. When he stood as they entered, he was well over six-feet tall. He looked at Jill and Carson, then spoke quickly to the soldiers. The words meant nothing to Jill, but she supposed he was being told about the soldiers finding them by the road.

Jill stared at the man behind the desk, and when the others stopped talking he looked back at Carson and her. He came around the desk, going to Carson and stopping within a foot of him. He spoke quickly in a sharp voice. Carson shook his head no.

He stared unblinkingly at Carson, then turned abruptly on Jill. His size scared her, and she tasted sickness in her throat. Suddenly the room that had seemed so warm moments ago, made her shiver. It was all she could manage to keep her eyes up and not back away. He spoke quickly to her, then waited. She looked at Carson, but all she could read in his face was concern. He started to clear his throat, but the soldier behind him, struck him between the shoulder blades.

Jill swallowed more sickness, looked at the bald man, and took a chance by shaking her head no.

He cocked his head to one side, then reached out a hand toward her. When she flinched as he touched her cheek, he smiled, oddly pleased that she was afraid of him. "No?"

She nodded, hoping she was doing the right thing. His hand fell from her, then the man spun on his heels and went back behind the desk. He sank down in the chair, sat back and looked across the polished top of the desk.

His dark eyes were unblinking, and the overhead light glistened off his bald head. She heard him clear his throat and the room began to spin slowly for Jill. She felt as if her balance was deserting her, but the soldiers held her tightly. As the room settled, she focused on the man behind the desk, and she was shocked when he spoke in remarkably unaccented English.

"I will not waste my time by speaking Spanish to both of you. You are not San Armanians. But we will find out who you are and why you are here." He narrowed his eyes. "I am General Ramon Blanco, and you are in the custody of the Colombian Army."

Chapter 13

"...this update on the news from San Arman. A number of refugees have made it out of the country, but Carson Davies and Jillian Segar are still unaccounted for. A reward for information about their fate has been offered by the station, and all the surrounding countries to San Arman have been contacted. Until the government is more stable, it is impossible to get any accurate account of what has happened to foreigners in the country. None of the refugees remembers seeing Davies or Segar..."

The room began to slip again for Jill and she swallowed hard, trying to focus on the man across the desk from her. Had he said what she thought. He was with the Colombian Army? She thought for a second she had imagined it, wanted it so badly she hadn't heard him right. But when she looked at Carson, she could tell he felt as shocked as she did.

"Carson?" she said, her voice unsteady.

Carson moved a step closer to the desk, the soldiers right behind him. "Are we in Colombia?" he asked the general.

The man stared at Carson. "This is Colombia. You did not know that?"

"I can't believe it. We must have crossed the border without knowing it," Carson murmured.

Jill felt her legs go weak and was actually glad of the support of the two soldiers still holding her arms. "We…we made it," she whispered, but her relief faltered when she looked into the general's face.

His expression looked grim, almost angry. "So, you *are* American," he said. "My men did not sense it, but there is something about your kind. As soon as you walked in here, I knew."

His tone didn't indicate he thought much of Americans. "Yes, and are we glad to be here," Carson said. "We can explain."

"You can explain the truck you were in?"

"Of course." Carson twisted his hands to show the cuffs on his wrists. "Can you take these off?"

When the general waved that request aside, Jill bit her lip hard. Her right hand throbbed painfully. But the bald-headed man sat back in his seat and nodded to the soldiers. They all left except the leader who went behind Carson and stood very still. "Now," the general said, "What are your explanations? What is your part in the atrocities committed against the people of Colombia?"

"What atrocities?" Carson asked.

"The border raids. In the little time since Estrada was deposed, there have been several raids on our border towns. There has been burning and looting and killings. We will not tolerate it. Not from San Arman and not from Americans involved in the San Arman strife."

"We aren't involved in anything except getting out of the country ourselves."

"Then how do you explain being in possession of the truck?"

"We paid a man to give us a ride to the border."

Jill blinked as her eyes began to blur and she watched the general sit forward. "Where is DeVega?"

She heard Carson inhale, but when he spoke his confusion sounded real enough. "Who?"

The general pounded a fist on the desk, the cracking sound echoing in the office, and Jill jumped. "DeVega, a man who would sell his soul and the soul of his brothers, if the price is right! Why were you with him? What part do you two play in the tragedies inflicted on our nation? And where is he now?"

Carson shrugged sharply. "DeVega is back on the trail somewhere on foot."

The general's mouth twisted in a travesty of a smile. "A falling out among thieves?"

"No, we aren't—"

"I do not know why you were the ones to stay with the truck, but it proved to be a mistake." He sat back in the chair. "My men have been looking for the invaders, and we suspected DeVega might be involved. We were right."

"We don't know anything about DeVega, except the fact that he was willing to take us out of San Arman."

"I find it hard to believe the man has developed a charitable streak."

"He wanted five thousand dollars to do it. We've been trying to get out of San Arman since yesterday, when Estrada fell."

"Why?"

"I didn't want to stick around and see how kindly the new government would look on Americans."

He held out his hand. "Where are your papers?"

"We don't have them. They were confiscated yesterday morning by the Brothers of Liberty."

The man sat forward again and rested his elbows on the desktop. Making a tent of his fingers, he peered at Jill, then at Carson before he spoke. "These are troubled times in San Arman, and those troubles have invaded our country. A village was destroyed last night. Someone has to answer for it. Americans have been down here. Americans have taken money to be down here. DeVega works with anyone."

Jill thought about Rexel. He had obviously been offered enough money to choose sides. "We aren't mercenaries," Carson said. "I'm Carson Davies, and she's Jillian Segar. We're Americans who were in the wrong place at the wrong time. DeVega is nothing to us. He was simply a way to get to the Colombian border."

"Prove it," the general said evenly.

"How?"

"That is your problem."

"If you let us use your phone, we could call—"

"Who would you call—your cohorts to warn them?"

"No, friends in San Diego."

A knock on the door drew the general's attention. The heavy woman who had been behind the desk in the outer room, came in. She glanced at Carson and Jill, frowned, then shook her head and crossed quickly to the general, leaning down to speak to him in a low, indistinguishable voice. The man nodded twice, then the lady left, sparing only a quick look for Jill and Carson before she closed the door.

The general sank back in the chair. His face seemed pinched, almost pale now. "The death count has risen to five townspeople and three soldiers." He slapped the desk with the flat of his hand. "And you tell me you know nothing of it!"

Jill knew what had happened. She had seen a hint of it when the soldiers had been roaming the streets of Puerto Luis. People out to do harm, to flex their supposed new power. They must have spread over the borders, thinking they were chasing Estrada supporters and accidentally involved the Colombian town. Or maybe they just wanted to get what they could and this town had been there.

"Just a phone call," Carson was saying, "a phone call can take care of everything. One call."

The lady who had just left came back without knocking and went straight to the desk. She set some papers in front of the general, then stood back. He studied them, glancing up a few times, then rested one hand on them. The lady stood back, but didn't make a move to leave.

"Carson Davies?" the general asked.

"Yes."

"You work in television?"

Jill could feel Carson weighing the consequences of admitting the truth to the man. Then he took another step toward the desk. "Yes, we both do. In San Diego, on Channel Three."

"So it seems." The general motioned to the soldier and spoke in Spanish, just a few clipped words, but enough to make the man silently take the handcuffs off Jill, then Carson, and step back. As Jill rubbed her numbed wrists and felt swelling in her right hand, Carson moved to the desk and looked down at the papers.

"I'll be damned," he muttered.

Jill crossed to him and looked down at the papers. The top page held two grainy black-and-white copies of photos, one of Carson, a snapshot someone had taken in the bright sunlight. The other photo was of her, a publicity shot she

had had taken last year when the station had been publiciz-
ing her show.

"Well done," Carson said, pointing to the caption below the wire-service pictures.

*"Americans Jillian Segar and Carson Davies on location
for shooting the Channel Three Television show* Dream
Chasers *have disappeared in San Arman. During the overthrow of President Estrada, Davies and Segar dropped out
of sight. All avenues of investigation are being pursued. A
reward of twenty thousand dollars has been offered for information."*

Carson looked up at the general. "I think you're twenty
thousand dollars richer, sir."

The man looked up at Carson. "And I regret the incon-
venience. This apparently came over the wire in Cartagena
last night and was brought here just moments ago. How can
I make it up to you?"

Carson didn't hesitate. "Get me transportation to Cartagena and show me to a telephone."

"I will take care of the transportation." He looked up at
the woman and spoke briefly to her. Then he spoke to Carson again. "Isobel will take you to a telephone where you
can be private."

The woman started out of the room and Carson hurried
after her. Jill hesitated, holding her sore hand with the other,
then went after Carson. She went back out into the outer
room. The lady pointed to a phone on a table near an open
window, then silently slipped out of the room closing the
door behind her.

Without missing a beat, Carson crossed to the phone,
picked it up and dialed long-distance. Jill watched him and
waited. She didn't know what she expected right now. She
heard Carson give the number of the station to the opera-

tor, then he looked over at her. "What luck to have crossed the border."

"What luck to be in a place where the picture had been distributed," she murmured.

"Damn right." Then he spoke into the phone. "I'll hold."

He looked back at Jill and held out his hand. When she went to him, he took her left hand in his and shocked her by kissing it. Then he looked at her. "We have a lot to talk about, love," he said softly, then into the receiver he said, "I'm here. Just make the connection."

They did have a lot to talk about, but before Jill could say anything, Carson was talking into the phone. "Yes, Carson Davies, calling collect." He kept looking at Jill, but spoke into the receiver. "Anyone who'll accept the charges will do."

He sank down on the edge of the table, his thumb making soft patterns on the back of Jill's hand. He started to say something to her, then spoke into the receiver. "Hey, James, you heard right. It's me. Yes, Jill's with me. We're a little worse for the wear, but we made it out and we're in Colombia. God knows where, in Colombia, but it's somewhere near the border."

He squeezed Jill's hand, but kept talking to James. "As soon as we can. What have you been doing? Have you been using the story as a leadoff. Great. I knew I could depend on the news staff. Tell them to break into regular programming for the announcement we've escaped. But keep it quiet. Don't let anyone know until it's on the air."

Jill watched silently, and swallowed hard. In a matter of minutes, the man she thought had changed reverted back to type. When she slid her hand out of his he barely noticed, but kept speaking into the receiver. "Tease them, James. Blurbs. Just enough to get them to tune in to the regular

news. By the time you get on the air, I'll try to be someplace where we can do a clear phone hookup."

He lifted the phone and began to pace, intent on his plans.
"Two minutes' leadoff. Do a section on the overthrow.
What happened to Estrada? What country took him in?
Figures."

Jill went to the window and looked out at the ruined
town. But she saw little of what was outside. All she was
aware of were Carson's words and the chill that made her
shiver. His focus was his work again, completely. Only he
could put together the news program. Only he could make
sure it had the impact it should have. Only he could do
it . . . no matter what "it" was.

"We'll get out of here as soon as we can, and I'll be in
contact as soon as we're near a telephone again—probably
in Cartagena. What time is it there? All right. No matter
what, don't let them break the story until just before noon
your time. Break in on the soap near the end and give a
teaser. Sure, sure. That's it. Tell Rob in production to make
sure the six o'clock news is slick tonight. And I want coverage on everything. Any other people who escaped . . ."

Jill closed her eyes, feeling the hope and surety that she
had experienced only hours before fading into nothingness.
A wish. A dream. A fairy tale. No, a nightmare.

"Jill?"

She turned and looked at Carson. He stood by the table,
the receiver in his hand, his finger hovering over the dial.
"What's the hotel in Cartagena where Sam and the others
are staying?"

She simply looked at him, her mind shutting down more
rapidly with each word he said. Pain could be hidden from,
she knew that, and right now she wanted to hide forever.
"Wh-what?" she mumbled, unable to get the word out at
first.

"The hotel?" He looked at her and frowned. "What's wrong? Your hand, for heaven's sake. What's wrong with it?"

She looked down at her hand, at swollen fingers and a deep purple welt on the back, then she glanced up at Carson. Suddenly the room began to recede, the image of Carson blurred, then shot away from her into a soft grayness. Her throbbing hand went out, trying to stop the world from leaving her, but her hand closed on air. The next second she felt herself falling forward, but she never felt the impact, at all.

Jill had never been so hot and so cold at the same time in her life. She tried to get away from it, to turn and run, but she couldn't move. The heat seemed to come from the inside out, from her hand, up her shoulder and into her brain. Then cold followed it in smothering waves, and all the while she felt an insurmountable grief that threatened to choke her.

Was she dead? She didn't know. She had no concept of time or place. Only blackness and the sensations that coursed through her. A voice was there, someone talking, soft, persistent, yet she had no idea whose voice it was. She only knew she had to hold onto it to keep from slipping farther away than she already was.

As the heat increased, the images came, drifting through her mind, flitting in and out, blurred and unformed, sailing on the waves of heat. And her grief deepened. It ran into her soul, producing a sorrow that was unspeakable.

Yes, she had to be dead. She couldn't feel like this without death producing it. Yet there were snatches of reality. A cold hand, a brush across her cheek, a whisper, a hint of comfort, then the grief and pain again.

Images deepened, and she knew what they were. Carson holding her and dancing. Carson bending over her. Carson pulling her to him. Carson on the beach coming to her in the morning. Then the city, the explosion, the fires, the people, the agony of a country, and her own agony. Martine coming through the gates. The house over the ocean. The bedroom.

She was almost able to hold onto that memory, but then it flashed out of her grip as easily as quicksilver. She was in the jungle, with its rutted roads. DeVega with a gun. Carson with a gun. The rain, the truck skidding. The night of shadows, when Carson talked to her until she felt saturated with him, filled with him, despite the fact that their only contact was him holding her, letting her rest against him and sleep.

The heat grew, searing through her, flames licking along her veins. She cried out from the pain, and she cried out when the images were of Carson leaving her. He was walking away—away from her and toward the station. No! she wanted to scream, but no sounds came from her and he kept going.

No! No! The heat roared in her ears and her heart pounded frantically. She reached out, but she knew she couldn't touch Carson. She wondered if she ever had.

"No," she whispered. "no."

Suddenly the heat was gone. It dissipated into a mist so gentle and cool that she cried from the relief. A hand was on her, stroking her cheek, brushing at her hair, and soft words drifted in the darkness.

For now, she could rest. Later she would figure out why she felt so tired and so very sad.

Carson stood by the hospital bed and looked down at Jill in the halo of light from the bedside lamp. The midnight hour when her fever had broken had come and gone, yet still she hadn't wakened. He ran a hand over his jaw, the stubble of three days' growth of beard rough against his fingers. The scent of flowers that crowded the room—flowers from fans, well-wishers, workers at the station—made him nauseous.

He swallowed hard and knew he shouldn't stay. He didn't want to face Boyd again. His times with Jill had been snatched when Boyd had left to take care of things, but Carson was thankful he'd been the one with her when the fever broke. The one to hear her sob softly, the one to brush away her tears, and the one to hold her and feel the blessed cool clamminess of her skin.

Carson moved to the window and twisted the cord at the side until the blinds were open to the night. He knew Boyd should have been the one to hold her hand during the fever. Boyd should have been the one to comfort her when she cried out, when the tears started. But Boyd had just barely made it back to his apartment when the doctor had called him to come back.

He knew Boyd was trying to figure out what was going on. Why Carson took every chance he could to be with Jill. And why Carson hadn't left the hospital since the airlift had landed in San Diego and Jill had been brought here.

"Carson?" His name was said softly from the doorway.

He turned and looked across the shadowy room to see James stepping inside. Still wearing the blue Channel Three blazer from the eleven o'clock newscast, James moved silently across to Carson. His voice was low, almost a whisper.

"I knew I'd find you in here. I saw Boyd down at the nurses' station talking to the doctor. They said her fever broke."

"An hour ago, but she's still unconscious. The doctor doesn't know when she'll come out of it."

James touched his shoulder, his fingers tightening in a reassuring squeeze. "She'll be fine. She's just worn out from everything that's happened, then this fever..." He looked at Jill. "It's been a pretty intense time for both of you. You're exhausted."

Carson shrugged and turned to the window. He stared out at San Diego at night, at the lights haloed by the bay, and the downtown section bathed in a gentle yellow glow. A huge moon hung in the dark sky and stars dotted the horizon. Everything looked so normal, so sane, yet his life had been altered so drastically in the past few days he hardly recognized himself.

"You need to get some rest, Carson."

"I'll rest when I know Jill's going to be all right."

"If you don't rest now, you're going to fall over and you won't be any good to anyone, least of all Jill."

Carson knew James was right, but he didn't seem to have the energy to walk out. "I think I'll sleep in the lounge for a while."

"That's all you've done since you came back. You need to get a good night's sleep. You need to go back to your place, take a hot shower and sleep for twenty-four hours. Boyd's here now. Let him take over."

And that puts it all in perspective, Carson thought.

The door opened again and Boyd walked in. He looked remarkably fresh, his blue suit neat as a pin, a stark contrast to Carson's rumpled clothes, which James had brought by hours ago. Boyd glanced at Carson, and didn't say a thing as he crossed to the bed. He bent over Jill, taking her bandaged hand in his, and he spoke without looking away from her.

"Why are you still here?"

Carson ran a hand over his face and exhaled. "Just waiting."

"I'll do the waiting now," Boyd said. "You can leave whenever you want to."

He never wanted to leave Jill, but there was nothing he could do about it, not now. "I'll be in the lounge."

Boyd let go of Jill's hand, carefully putting it back on the sheet. Then he came to Carson. "Go home. Go back to the station and do what you do best. You aren't needed here."

Carson felt his nerves bunch painfully at the back of his neck. "And you weren't here when Jill needed you."

"I'm here now." Boyd narrowed his eyes. "I appreciate you getting her out of that hellhole, but I can take care of her now."

"Sure," Carson said, his jaw tightening.

"Are you leaving now?"

"Where I go is none of your damned business."

"It damn well is my business. The fact is, Jill and I are going to be married. She's tried to get over you for a long time, and you've caused her nothing but pain. God, man, you almost got her killed this time." He took a hissing breath. "Why was she the one bitten by that bug and not you? Where's the justice in this world?"

Carson absorbed the verbal blow, the words as powerful as any punch in his middle could have been, and pushed his hands in his pockets. Without saying another thing, he moved past Boyd to the bed and looked down at Jill. It literally hurt him to see the translucent pallor to her skin, the darkness of her lashes fanned against that paleness and her hand, still bandaged but almost back to its normal size.

He had no right to be here. Boyd was right.

He looked back at Boyd. "I've never meant to hurt her. I've always loved her."

The man seemed to tighten from the inside out, then he spoke in a low voice. "If you love her, leave her alone. Let her get on with her life and get on with her healing. Just leave her alone and go back to your damned station. They need you more than Jill does."

Carson felt his hands curl into fists in his pocket, but he didn't do what he wanted to. He didn't strike out at Boyd. He simply looked at Jill one more time, letting her image imprint itself on his mind, then silently left the room.

In the hallway, James came up behind him. "What are you going to do?" he asked.

Carson stopped and leaned back against the coolness of the wall. "About what?"

"About Jill. About you still loving her."

He closed his eyes tightly and rested his head back against the wall. "I'll let her go. I have to." He swallowed hard and whispered, "But I just don't know how to do it."

Jill knew she wasn't dead when the grayness began to go away. She could actually feel things and know what they were. The coolness of a sheet against her arms and legs. The solidness supporting her. She laid very still, then began to remember. And with each passing second, she knew more and more.

When she opened her eyes, she already knew she was in a hospital and it had something to do with her hand. The odors were there, all overlaid with a sweet pungency. Her hand throbbed, but not painfully—just with a vague tingle. And she was thankful. She was alive.

She opened her eyes just a bit, the glare around her almost irritating at first and everything was blurred. Dots of bright, pure color were everywhere. Flowers?

"Jill?"

She turned slowly to her right, and saw a blur of someone by the bed. A man, large and out of focus for her. Carson. She felt relief flood through her. He hadn't died either. They'd made it. But as her eyes adjusted slowly, Boyd came into focus. Instant disappointment was replaced by raw fear.

Was Carson dead? No, she thought quickly. Wouldn't she have known he wasn't in the world with her? Surely she would have felt the loss, felt the void in the world. Then she remembered the horrible grief in her dreams, the choking sorrow.

She touched her tongue to her dry lips, and when she spoke her voice was hoarse. "What . . . what happened . . . to Carson?"

Boyd moved closer and bent over her, touching her hand with his warmth, but the contact had no comfort in it for her. "Shh. Take it easy. I'm just glad to have you awake again. You've been sick for a long time."

"What . . . ?"

"A fever. You were bitten by something in the jungle, on the back of your hand. You had a reaction to it, maybe an allergy. That combined with the jungle, the running, the lack of sleep and food, it all did you in." He smiled and patted her hand. "But you're going to be fine, Jill, just fine. All you need is rest."

She licked her lips and closed her eyes for a moment. Her mind was crystal-clear, yet she didn't seem to be able to make her lips form simple words. The weakness in her was insidious, and it grew worse with the simple effort to talk. "C-Carson? Where . . ." she croaked.

Boyd squeezed her good hand, then let it go and stood back. He took his time filling a glass with ice water, then held it for her to take a sip through a straw. When she swallowed once and felt the coolness slip down her tight throat, she sank back in the pillows.

Boyd put the glass down, then looked at her. "Carson is fine. He got off without a scratch. He's at the station, I suppose."

She closed her eyes tightly, feeling as if the world had just been yanked out from under her feet. The station. Work. Carson hadn't taken very long to focus on it again.

"You've been unconscious for three days," Boyd was saying. "They airlifted you into San Diego from Colombia, and brought you here. Your fever broke last night." As she opened her eyes she saw Boyd sit down on the side chair and lean closer to her, his voice lowering. "Just concentrate on healing, sweetheart, concentrate on getting better."

Jill knew then what the grief in her dreams had been all about. She'd lost Carson again. And this time she didn't know if she was going to survive. She felt the heat of tears trickle down her cheeks, and she was too weak to even try to stop them.

"Oh, no, don't cry," Boyd said quickly, reaching for her hand again, holding tightly to her. "Please. You made it. You're back. We can get on with our lives."

She blinked, felt the coolness of moisture on her cheeks, and saw Boyd clearly—the real Boyd. A good man, a kind man, a man who wouldn't hurt her, who wouldn't make her furious or sad, a man who wouldn't ever make her second to ambition or success. A man who was there for her when she needed him.

She wished it was enough, that there was enough substance there to build a life on. But the truth was finally clear to her. She didn't love Boyd the way she'd have to love him to make a marriage work. Her feelings for him were safe, stable, but not even close to real love.

She closed her eyes and wished for the gray nothingness again. If she could fall back into that softness, a place where she wouldn't have to think or deal with reality, she could get rid of this pain. But she didn't drift off. Sleep eluded her completely, and she finally knew what she had to do. She wouldn't ever have Carson, but she couldn't ruin Boyd's life, no matter how appealing the safety of his love was to her. She wouldn't use him as a shield, as a buffer. He deserved so much more than that. And she had to tell him.

His hand moved from hers, and his touch on her cheek was warm, gentle. "Jill? Jill?"

She opened her eyes, and felt real pain at the look of concern on his face. "Boyd. We . . . need to talk."

"Not now. Rest. Take some time to get your strength back." He stroked her hair back from her forehead. "There's time later to talk, lots of time."

"No. There isn't any time."

"There's the rest of our lives," he said.

"No, there isn't." She could feel the tears coming again, trickling down her cheeks. "Things have changed. I've changed."

"No, you've gone through hell. I know Carson managed to tear you apart again. But things haven't changed with us. I still love you."

"I'm sorry . . . so sorry," she managed in a choked whisper.

His image shimmered before her eyes, and she heard him take a deep, unsteady breath. "It's Carson, isn't it? It's always been Carson."

"Yes," she managed.

He stared at her, his face almost blank. "And he's going to make you happy?"

"No," she said. "He's got his own life, and I have mine. I just have to figure out what that life is for me."

"Can't it be with me?"

"No. You deserve so much more than I could ever give you."

"What if I told you you're all I want? I'll take what you can give?"

She closed her eyes tightly for a moment, and wondered if she was making the worst mistake of her life. Then she made herself look at Boyd again, at the pain beginning to tighten his expression, and she knew she had to say the words now. "I'm sorry, s-so sorry."

He ran a hand over his face, then slumped back in the chair. "I'm sorry, too," he whispered.

Chapter 14

Carson ran along the stretch of beach near the city of Del Mar, the late-spring night slightly chilled by a cool breeze drifting in off the Pacific. Nylon running shorts and a red tank top stuck damply to his skin, and each breath he took echoed in his ears.

The weather had been perfect for the past three days, yet he took little notice of it. He spared only a passing glance at the rolling waves shimmering with the dancing light from a partial moon in the clear sky. His bare feet made faint slapping sounds on the sand, occasionally splashing when he ran across the foaming front of the receding tide.

When he heard the distant sound of music drifting on the night air, he looked ahead at the hotel. Its lights shone through the darkness, silhouetting a scattering of people walking on the beach or sitting on the dining terrace overlooking the ocean. The music came from the band in the lounge, which opened onto terraces.

His suite in the ten-story glass-and-brick structure was on the top floor—a bedroom, sitting room and kitchenette. But he spent most of his time on the balcony. No phones, no contact with anyone, time to think, time to come to terms with the mess he had made of his life, and time to wonder what he was going to do with the rest of it.

When he couldn't sleep and the long hours of night loomed ahead of him, he dressed in his running clothes, then headed down to the beach and ran along the deserted sands. But the euphoria he'd come to expect with the intense exercise eluded him now. He ran longer and harder than he ever had, yet his exhaustion wasn't complete enough to let him sleep for more than a few hours at a time.

Maybe I should have gone to Houston, he thought as he stopped. When he'd called in to tell the station he was taking a few days off to recuperate from the ordeal in San Arman, he'd almost gone to the airport and flown back to Houston. He turned to the dark water and stared out at the horizon. Houston wouldn't be a haven, not with memories of Jill everywhere, memories he knew better than to believe he could leave behind.

So he drove twenty miles north to Del Mar, found this place and burrowed into it like a wounded animal hiding until it either lived or died. Twenty miles, but it could have been a thousand. Separation was separation. He hadn't gotten in his car since he'd arrived. He didn't trust himself to, not until he knew he wouldn't swing south on the freeway and turn off at the hospital off-ramp.

He looked back at the hotel. He didn't want to go inside and past the guests right now. And the silence in his room was beginning to be deafening. Maybe it was getting near the time for him to leave, to face the world and get on with his life.

What life? his soul taunted. Without Jill, he couldn't think of anything that was worth doing. And when she married Boyd... He sank down on the sand, pulled his knees to his chest and wrapped his arms around his legs. He'd give anything to go two minutes without thinking of Jill, just two minutes of peace. He craved relief from regret and pain.

He rested his forehead on his knees. He knew from the news she was all right, that she was getting better, that she was going to get out of the hospital any day now. After the blanket coverage those first few days with his picture flashing side-by-side with hers, the pieces had become few and far between.

He'd watched some of the coverage in the lounge at the hospital. He knew nothing could be as dramatic as the footage of the plane landing at Lindberg Field and the ambulance waiting. He watched himself hurrying after the stretcher carrying Jill, then climbing into the back of the ambulance and the doors closing.

He could almost feel her hand in his now, so hot and dry from the fever. He could remember his prayers, and the eternity it had taken to get to the hospital. Then the waiting. More praying, then her fever breaking. The giddy relief, then the confrontation with Boyd.

He'd seen just a few items on the news since he'd been here, updates, then nothing. More news took over and Jill was effectively forgotten for now. But not by him. Never by him.

He exhaled harshly, then stood, looked to the right, at the hotel, then turned left and took off at a jog into the night. Just another mile or so, then he might be tired enough to sleep for a few hours.

Jill stood by the window of her office and stared out at the clear morning. Things hadn't changed too much here. The

Channel Three vans were lined up in the parking lot, the satellite dishes stood to one side, employees moved from the offices to the studio area in the back buildings. She could hear people walking down the hallway outside her door. No, things hadn't changed. It was she who had changed.

It had been over three days since she'd awakened to find Boyd by her side, three days since he'd left, and the next day she had checked herself out of the hospital and gone back to her home. Today was her first day at work. She had walked in, been inundated with questions and good wishes from her coworkers, then taken refuge in her office.

Carson was conspicuously absent. He hadn't tried to contact her at the hospital. He hadn't called her at home, and he was about the only person who hadn't dropped in to welcome her back. She had begun to rationalize what had happened between them as the heat of the moment, overreaction from the danger they had been in, a need to hold onto someone. She loved him, but she had allowed illusions to take the place of reality. She had allowed her feelings to warp her thinking.

Now she wished he'd come in so she could end it, once and for all. She had done her best to explain things to Boyd, and her need to confront Carson was almost a physical ache, as necessary as it was frightening. Never again would she walk away leaving loose ends that could come back to haunt her.

She tugged at the cuffs of the white silk shirt she wore with beige linen slacks, then stepped out of her low-heeled pumps. She wiggled her toes in the soft carpet and realized she felt exhausted already. The fever had left her with little energy, but she was going to take things slow and get back into the routine of work. *If* she stayed here. She would only know if she could still work around Carson after she had faced him again. And she didn't have much hope it would turn out that she could.

When the phone rang, she turned and reached for the receiver. "Jillian Segar."

"Jill." She recognized Boyd's voice and sank down in the swivel chair behind the desk.

"Hello, Boyd."

"Just checking to see how you're doing."

"Fine, just fine," she murmured, wondering if she would ever be anything as mediocre as "fine" again. "How about you?"

"I'm doing all right." He hesitated. "I was just wondering how it's going now that you're back to work."

"I'm here. I'm not setting the world on fire, but I'm here."

She could hear him take a breath before he asked, "I was wondering if you've thought about us, if you could give us a chance again?"

Boyd had called her every day, checking on her, and wishing her well. He'd never mentioned their talk before, and she hadn't expected it today. His patience only made her feel more guilty about what had happened. She knew now that her relationship with him had been used as protection from her unresolved feelings for Carson. With Boyd she never had to face intensity, or questions, or pain. She had given him pain. He had never given her any pain.

"No, I'm sorry. It wouldn't be fair to you."

"I'm not asking for fair."

She closed her eyes. "Boyd, I...I'm barely back to work. I explained—"

"Sure. Just asking. I'll be in touch," he said, then hung up.

As she set the receiver back in place, a soft knock sounded on her door. She braced herself the way she had all morning when someone knocked, and called, "Come in." But when the door opened, it wasn't Carson. James peeked inside the office. "Busy?"

"No, not at all," she said, waving her hand across her desk, empty except for the telephone. "Come on in."

He walked in, closing the door behind him, then crossed to the desk and sat in one of the two wooden chairs that faced the desk. "So, you came back to the salt mines, eh?"

"Yes, and I'm glad to be here."

"Even this place is better than a prison in San Arman."

She knew she must have paled at the mention of what could have been, and she tried to pass off her reaction at the reminder. "Yes, even this place."

James wore the Channel Three T-shirt, with the logo emblazoned across the front of it, with jeans and running shoes. He looked at Jill for a long moment before asking, "They let you out of the hospital pretty fast, didn't they?"

"I checked myself out. I'm just weak." She rubbed the barely visible spot on the back of her hand. "The fever takes a while to get over. What's been going on with you?"

"I've been taping a few segments so Bree and I can take a vacation in a week or so. Maybe you could use a real vacation. You look awfully pale." His face was serious. "Should you be here? I thought you would be making marriage plans, getting everything settled with Boyd."

When he looked at her with honest concern in his eyes, she almost blurted out everything. Almost. But he was too close to Carson, too involved to be brought into this and be put in the middle. "That's all settled," she murmured, "and work is the great cure for everything." She swallowed hard. "I think that's one of Carson's rules, isn't it?"

"You've been talking to Carson?"

"No, not yet."

"Do you have any idea where he is?"

She looked at him. "He's in his office, I guess."

James shook his head. "No. He's not. He's only been here once since he got back with you."

She stared at James. Why had she felt Carson's presence so strongly? Why had she been holding her breath certain he would come through the door at any minute? "No, you have to be mistaken."

"He came in three or four days ago, told his secretary he was going off to rest up for a few days, and that he'd be in touch. He hasn't been touch, and no one knows where he went."

Jill couldn't believe what he was saying. Carson would have never walked away when he was in the middle of the biggest story the station had ever handled, a story he was personally involved in. "Are you sure she understood what he said?"

"Damn sure. Things do go on without Carson, but he's got to get back for the next production meeting in two days. We'll be flying blind without him." He looked at her intently. "I thought he might have been in touch with you."

It made no sense to her, at all. "No, I haven't seen him since I collapsed in that jail in Colombia. And he wasn't at the hospital."

James leaned forward. "Sure he was."

"No. He never came by."

"You don't remember because you were out like a light. But he sat by your bed, at least when Boyd would let him, and he didn't leave until your fever broke." He touched the edge of the desk with both hands. "Jill, he didn't leave the hospital for all that time. He slept on the couch in the lounge, what little sleeping he did. He paced outside your door like a caged animal, or sat in the chair by your bed staring at you and holding your hand." He sat back and narrowed his eyes. "He wouldn't even have left when he did if Boyd hadn't told him he'd take care of you and that Carson didn't belong there.''

She touched her tongue to her lips. No, James had to have this all wrong. She would have known he was at the hospital, or sensed it. No, she'd been wrong about so many things, why did she expect she would be that astute? One thing she did know for sure. ''He wouldn't stay away from the station, not like that.'' She'd been there when all Carson had thought about was making contact with the station and setting up the news breaks to announce their escape from San Arman. ''This is his life, his obsession.''

''It's *part* of his life, and maybe obsessions change with time. I know this place didn't exist for him when he got off the plane with you. I wonder if it ever will in the same way again.'' He ran both hands back through his graying hair. ''He's certainly not off on some breaking story.''

That brought Jill upright, her hands pressed flat on the desktop. ''James, he…he wouldn't go back down there, to San Arman, would he?''

He shook his head sharply. ''No. He hates that place and everything about it.''

''That's what he said before, but he came down when we were there just to control the program shoots, to make sure it was what he wanted.''

''No, he didn't. He told me when he got back here with you that he went down because he was terrified you were in danger. He'd heard things about Estrada's government when he was in New York, rumors, and he flew directly down there from the conference.'' He shook his head. ''Believe me, Jill, nothing could have dragged him into that hellhole except fear for what could happen to you…and to the others.''

She wanted desperately to believe that Carson hadn't come to San Arman out of the need to control but because of her. But how could she allow herself to even think that? How could she start that cycle all over again? "He could have called to find out how we were."

"He told me he tried, and you were never in your room. He said something about a dream he had in New York, but I didn't understand."

The nightmares. She finally understood so many things, except why he stayed away from her at the hospital. "You said Boyd told him to leave the hospital?"

"Boyd was worried about you, and since you're going to get married, he took precedence over anyone else there." He raked his fingers through his hair again. "I thought Carson was going to hit him, but he didn't. Instead, he walked out on everything. Damn it, he's gone off the deep end. You know better than anyone else that he wouldn't normally walk away like this. He *is* obsessed with the quality of the station."

"Yes, he is," she said softly, her life beginning to twist back into balance, and the sadness she had harbored for days began to dissolve. It was replaced by a nudging ray of hope. "What . . . what do you think is going on?"

James shrugged. "He was talking about how he . . ." His voice trailed off and he stood, then reached out to touch her hands laying on the desk. "I really don't know what's going on with him. You'd have to ask him that, if you can find him. I have to get back to work. If he calls, if he gets in touch, tell him I need to talk to him."

So did she, as soon as she could. Either there was hope or there wasn't. But she had to know one way or the other. "There has to be some way to find out where he is."

"I've tried everything," James said.

"Did you look in his office to see if he left any messages or hints?"

"No, I never thought about it after I talked to his secretary."

She stood and came around the desk. "Come on. Let's go and see what we can find."

"We?" he asked as he stood. "You really want to find him?"

She didn't hesitate. "I *have* to find him."

Carson saw the station from a distance, as he drove down the eucalyptus-lined street. At two o'clock in the morning at the hotel, he had realized there was no place for him to run. He'd accused Jill of running away before. That was something he wasn't going to do. He had to come back here and face his life. He had to face Jill, wish her well with her marriage to Boyd and mean it. Strangely, he knew he would when he said the words. He wanted her to be happy, no matter what the cost to him.

He chuckled softly as he turned his car into the station parking lot. Damned noble, he thought, then swallowed hard. No, just the most honest thing he had ever experienced, and it all came from loving her. Love was supposed to make people happy, to make them complete. All it had done was tear him apart and leave him empty.

He slipped his security card into the slot by the gate, watched the metal barriers swing open, and drove through. Knowing what he was going to do didn't make it any easier to do. It just gave him direction. He swung into his parking slot, got out into the clear noontime air and turned toward the employee door.

For a split second he thought of getting into the car and driving away. How could he manage to face Jill and see her with Boyd? How could he endure the knowledge that Boyd would hold her and love her and make her happy? He shook his head sharply. If he could just get through today, the to-morrows would take care of themselves, he hoped.

He swung the door shut on his car, and strode up the walkway to the door. Pushing it open, he stepped into the familiar surroundings of red, white and blue. He saw the logo on the wall, the splash of a red heart with *The Station with a Heart* cutting through it like an arrow. With a frown, he made a mental note to change the station's logo. He didn't want to think about hearts—not the station's and definitely not his own.

He nodded to the guard behind the security desk just inside the doors, then strode down the hall toward his office. The halls were deserted while the noon-hour programming was in progress, so he didn't see anyone before he got to his office door and pushed it open.

Jill heard the door click open and thought James had come back. But when she turned, the world stopped. Carson stood in the entrance, the shock in his face echoing the shock she knew must be mirrored on hers.

She stood motionless behind his desk, her hand on the open page of his personal phone book. The room shifted in front of her, and she found herself pressing her hand flat on the book to keep herself standing. Then Carson came clearly into focus. His face seemed a bit thinner, and the tan from San Arman was beginning to fade. His hair was slightly mussed, as if he had run his fingers through it in frustration, and the gray suit he wore with a blue shirt seemed pale.

The glasses were in place and the glare from the windows reflected on the lenses, hiding his eyes. But she knew he was staring at her as openly as she was staring at him. He made no move to come farther into the office. "Jill. I didn't expect you to be in here," he finally said.

She stood back from the desk, rubbing her hands together nervously. "I didn't expect to see you, either." She took a breath, in an effort to ease the tightness in her chest. How could she love a man this much? "I'm . . . I'm surprised."

Then he did move, striding into the office and swinging the door shut behind him. "It's my office. I don't see why it would be unusual to see me here."

As he came around the side of the desk, she backed up in the other direction until they had reversed positions, she in front of the desk, he behind it. "I meant, you've been gone."

"So have you," he murmured. He sank down in his chair, then looked up at her. "So, how are things going for you?"

"I'm here. I'll be fine."

"Good." He sat back and took off his glasses, casually tossing them onto the open book on the desk. "Is this where I ask how you like the weather?"

She shrugged. "What does that mean?"

"We're making small talk, aren't we?"

Yes, they were, and it was making her nerves raw. She wanted to talk about the two of them, about what there was, about what she hoped there could be. "You're right."

He sat forward and motioned her to one of the chairs facing the desk. "Then sit down and we'll talk."

She sank down slowly but couldn't relax. She perched on the edge of the seat, her hands clasped tightly on her lap. "Where have you been?" she asked, needing to know.

"Del Mar, at some hotel near the ocean."

She exhaled. "I . . . I thought you might have gone back to San Arman to get the rest of the story."

He stared at her, the blueness of his eyes unprotected by his lenses. "If I never see that place again, I'll die happy."

"Then why did you go down there?" she asked, needing to hear the reason from his own lips.

He sat back and ran a hand over his face. Then he looked down at his hands as he rested them on his thighs. "I'd heard rumors about the Estrada government, and with my crew down there..." He looked up at her. "I was worried about all of you."

"Why did you stay at the hospital with me?"

"You remember me being there?"

She avoided the question with one of her own. "Why were you there?"

He stood abruptly and shrugged out of his jacket. He laid the jacket over the back of the chair, then turned to the window. One by one he undid the cuffs of the blue shirt and slowly rolled back the sleeves to expose his forearms. She could see his hands clench before he pushed them into his pockets. "If I answer that, it can't stop there." He turned back to her. "Can you deal with that?"

She didn't have to think about it for more than a single heartbeat. "Yes, I can. Can you?"

"I think I have to. But I want to preface this with a statement. I want you to know that I wish you well with Boyd. I hope he's everything you ever wanted and will ever need." He narrowed his eyes. "I really mean that, Jill."

"Carson, I'm not—" she started, but he stopped her with one hand held up palm out.

"No, listen to me, listen to everything, or I won't be able to get it out rationally."

She sank back in the chair and didn't take her eyes off him.

"I'm not being noble," he said. "I'm not that much of a saint, but I want you to be happy. I mean that." He closed his eyes for a moment. "And I regret what happened in San Arman between us, but only if it caused you pain."

"Do you regret making love with me?" she asked softly.

"I regret only one thing, that it only happened twice." He dropped down in his chair again and sat forward, burying his head in his hands for a minute before he looked back at Jill. "You've been right about me all along. I want to control things and people. I want to prove my worth by what I can do. And I'm selfish. I'm damned selfish. In Houston I wanted you there for me when I wanted you there. I wanted you to take away the emptiness. And you did.

"I didn't even know I was lonely until you left me. And I didn't know just *how* lonely until I saw you here again with Boyd." He took a deep, ragged breath. "I sound like some lovesick kid." He chuckled, a rough unsteady sound, but it was like music to Jill's ears. "The fact of the matter is, I'm out of control where you're concerned. I feel that there's a hole in my self-worth if you aren't with me, and I never want to be without you. It's my fault. I know that. I accept that. And I'll live with it."

Jill watched Carson, her love for him increasing tenfold as he spoke. She didn't know where to begin, what to say. Words came she didn't even consider before they were uttered. "You were at the hospital because you love me?"

He looked at her, his eyes stricken. "Love you? I was there because when you collapsed in that miserable jail, and when I thought you were going to die, I knew you were everything to me. I couldn't conceive of a life without you." He sat back. "And that's what I'm facing."

She stood and came around the desk but stopped before reaching out to touch Carson. She had to say something, and if she touched him none of the words would be said. "Will you listen to me for a minute?"

He looked up at her. "You know that taking off my glasses is a form of self-protection. If they're off, you're this blur—a soft image without edges or clarity. I thought it would make this easier. It doesn't.''

She picked up his glasses and stared at them. How often had she cursed them because she couldn't see his eyes? She fingered the cool metal earpiece. They were a part of Carson, the man she had fallen in love with over two years ago, just as much a part of him as his personality, his essence, his touch.

She handed them to him and he took them, then slipped them on. "I guess it's time to face the truth, isn't it?" he asked as he looked back at her.

"Yes," she murmured. "Finally."

His expression tightened, deepening the brackets at his mouth. "It's come down to this, hasn't it? A last talk, a confrontation where all the questions are settled." He sat back and rested his head against the folded suit coat on the high back of his chair. "I hate it. I really hate it."

"Carson, you like to control, you're obsessed with quality work, you're selfish sometimes, but you're a loving person. You're gentle, intelligent, exciting, and you're the man I fell in love with in Houston. In San Arman I saw a part of you I didn't know existed. But it does. It always has."

"Survival makes people do strange things," he muttered and swiveled his chair until he faced the windows.

"Sometimes it brings things into perspective." She touched his shoulder and felt him flinch from the contact. Drawing her hand back, she stared down at him. "Carson, I'm not marrying Boyd. I couldn't."

He turned and looked at her. "What?"

She crouched down by his chair, steadying herself with both hands on the arm. "I'm not getting married to Boyd."

He stood abruptly and moved to the window. With his back to her, he cursed, a single word that vibrated in the office. "I even ruined that for you, didn't I?"

"No, you didn't." She stood slowly. "There wasn't anything to ruin. I cared for Boyd, I still do, but I never loved him. I realized that in San Arman. I realized that was why I had told him I had to think about his proposal, and why I had never... why we had never made love. Because I didn't love him."

He spun around. "You and Boyd..."

She shook her head. "No. How... how could I, when I loved you all the time? I told him that, when I was in the hospital. He doesn't understand. Neither do I, but I know that I've never stopped loving you."

He stared at her, not moving. "Is this because of what happened in San Arman, the violence, the struggle to survive?"

"In a way, but those things only clarified my feelings for you. When you found me on the beach, I'd decided not to marry Boyd, but I thought you... you were the same person I left two years ago. I didn't think we could make a go of it, and you never mentioned loving me still. I thought..." She exhaled shakily. "It doesn't matter. What matters is the fact that I realize I love what you were, what you are, what you will be."

Before she could say anything else, Carson reached out for her and drew her to him. They stood absolutely still, neither person moving. Jill closed her eyes, absorbing the feel of the man, the sensation of being surrounded by him, and she felt the burn of tears in her eyes. She'd come so close to never knowing this again. So very close.

"I'm actually glad of what happened in San Arman," she whispered, her voice muffled against the beat of Carson's heart.

His hold tightened on her. "Couldn't we have done this an easier way?"

"Do you love me?" she asked.

"Love you? I finally figured out what love is, and I love you more than life itself," he breathed roughly.

Jill's world became perfect in that moment, and she lifted her face to Carson. "We aren't ever going to be like Ozzie and Harriet, are we?"

He smiled, an unsteady smile that faltered even more when she slowly began to unbutton his shirt. "I think the only way we'll be like them is that we'll be happy together."

She opened his shirt, pushed her hands under the crisp cotton and felt the sleek heat of his skin under her palms. "Oh, we will be happy. We've gone through the worst, seen the worst, and it only brought us together."

He stooped and kissed her fiercely, the same kind of kiss he'd given her in the bedroom at Martine's just before they'd had to leave. "Are you sure?" he asked as he drew back.

She reached up and took his glasses off. After carefully putting them on the desk, she began to undo the buttons on her blouse. "Does the lock on your door work?"

He smiled at her, a brilliant smile. "It's a dead bolt," he said as he let her go to cross the room and slide it into place. Then he turned, took the phone off the hook and held out his arms to her.

She went to him, stepping into the circle of his embrace, and it seemed as natural as breathing to her and just as necessary.

A knock sounded on the door, and Jill and Carson both held their breath. "Yes?" Carson called.

"Carson, is that you?" James called back.

"Yes, it is," he said and pulled Jill more tightly against him.

"What's going on?"

"James, I'm going to be in conference for at least an hour. Come back then. No, make it two hours."

Jill could have sworn she heard a soft laugh from James before he called out, "I'll see you tomorrow."

Carson smiled down at Jill. "Smart man. I knew there was a reason we were such good friends."

She touched his face, felt the heat under her fingertips and pressed a kiss to his chest. "I love you."

He trembled. "When I was in the prison with Martine he told me he had experienced real love once, in his soul, that love was the true reality of life." He took an unsteady breath and held her to him in a smothering hold. "I never knew what he meant until you."

She tasted his skin, absorbing his unique taste the way she wanted to absorb the man himself. "We owe a lot to Martine," she whispered against his chest.

"He said there would be a time when I wanted more than I had." Carson moaned when her tongue found his nipple and teased it. "He was right again. I want more, and I want it now."

She lifted her face to him, her breathing rapid and unsteady. "I want you," she whispered and together they found the dreams they had both been chasing all their lives.

Epilogue

Arturo Martine sat in the garden room and stared out at twilight bathing the ocean in rich pinks and purples. In the past two months things had settled back into a familiar pattern, even though the government had changed. Things had actually returned to what could pass for normal to the casual observer. The new regime wasn't that much different from Estrada's government. None of them was.

He fingered the wicker of the chair arm. Fresh food could be had without having to pay exorbitant prices, Santa Bella was relatively peaceful, and he had gone on with his life. Every once in a while he thought about Carson, and today he couldn't seem to get the man out of his mind.

When DeVega had not been seen again after he drove off with Carson and Jill, Arturo had sent out feelers to find what had happened. He had never felt right about sending them off with that man, yet he had had no choice in the matter. Then the truck had been found halfway off the road, just over the Colombian border—abandoned.

DeVega had not been a loss. He had not been mourned. But Arturo had not breathed easy until one of his contacts found that Carson and Jill had made it into Colombia and back to America.

Some things in this life work out, Arturo thought, as he reached for a newspaper clipping from the table by his elbow. It was a week-old item from a San Diego newspaper, and it had come in the mail pack from the city just today. The postmark had been from San Diego, but there had been no return address and not even a note with the clipping, only five one thousand dollar bills.

He looked down at the grainy black-and-white photo at the top of the single-column article. Taken in bright sunlight, it showed Carson holding Jill to him, and both of them were smiling, but not into the camera. They were smiling at each other, their expressions those secret looks that only people who loved each other had.

The headline under the photo read, *San Diego Television Personalities Wed*. The article told about the wedding, a very traditional ceremony, and it briefly recounted the couple's harrowing escape from San Arman.

Near the end, two sentences had been underlined. *Davies and Segar are taking a leave of absence from their work for a month, while they honeymoon at Nassau in the Bahamas. When asked for a comment after the ceremony, all Davies would say was, "It took me a long time, but I finally found the real thing."*

Arturo read and reread the final two sentences, then laid the clipping back on the table. He settled back in the chair, for a fleeting moment considering taking a trip himself, maybe to the Bahamas. Then he knew how foolish that would be.

No, his life would not touch Carson's and Jill's again, but it made him feel satisfied that Carson Davies was one of the lucky people in the world. He had found the one person who could make his life complete.

*   *   *   *   *

®. *Silhouette Intimate Moments* ®

COMING
NEXT MONTH

#337 RUNAWAY—Emilie Richards
With the help of journalist Jess Cantrell, Kristin Jensen posed as a prostitute to find her missing sister. Despite the constant danger, she found herself attracted to Jess. Was it purely physical . . . or could Kristin's hazardous search be leading to a safe haven of love?

#338 NOT WITHOUT HONOR—
Marilyn Pappano
Held hostage as a political pawn in a steamy South American rebel camp, Brenna Mathis, daughter of a military advisor, discovered that Andrés Montano, leader of the rebel forces and her former lover, had masterminded her abduction! Could the man she'd once loved still be the captor of her heart?

#339 IGUANA BAY—Theresa Weir
Elise Ramsey had been kidnapped—twice in one week! The first man wanted to use her as an alibi at his murder trial. The second, ruggedly handsome bounty hunter Dylan Davis, wanted to prevent her from testifying. To make matters even worse, Elise realized she was falling in love with this madman!

#340 FOREVER MY LOVE—
Heather Graham Pozzessere
Brent McQueen and his ex-wife Kathy were thrown together unexpectedly when smugglers mistakenly believed he had information they needed. Chased by killers and racing to uncover the truth before it was too late, they found passion flaring anew as they discovered that a love like theirs was, indeed, meant to last forever.

AVAILABLE THIS MONTH:

Take 4 bestselling love stories FREE

Plus get a FREE surprise gift!

Silhouette Intimate Moments ®

**Beginning next month,
Intimate Moments will bring you
two gripping stories by Emilie Richards**

Coming in June
Runaway
by EMILIE RICHARDS
Intimate Moments #337

Coming in July
The Way Back Home
by EMILIE RICHARDS
Intimate Moments #341

Krista and Rosie Jensen were two sisters who had it all—
until a painful secret tore them apart.

They were two special women who met two very special men
who made life a little easier—and love a whole lot better—
until the day when Krista and Rosie could be sisters once
again.

You'll laugh, you'll cry and you'll never, ever forget. Don't
miss the first book, RUNAWAY, available next month at your
favorite retail outlet.

Silhouette Books ®

A collector's edition hardcover romance FREE!

—————— S I L H O U E T T E ' S ——————

Diamond Jubilee Collection

Annette Broadrick
Ann Major
Dixie Browning

To celebrate its 10th Anniversary, Silhouette Romance is offering a limited edition, hardcover anthology of three early Silhouette Romance titles written by three of your favorite authors!

These titles—CIRCUMSTANTIAL EVIDENCE by Annette Broadrick, WILD LADY by Ann Major and ISLAND ON THE HILL by Dixie Browning—were first published in the early 1980s. This special collection will not be sold in retail stores and is only available through this exclusive offer:

Look for details in all Silhouette series published in June, July and August.